MW01412591

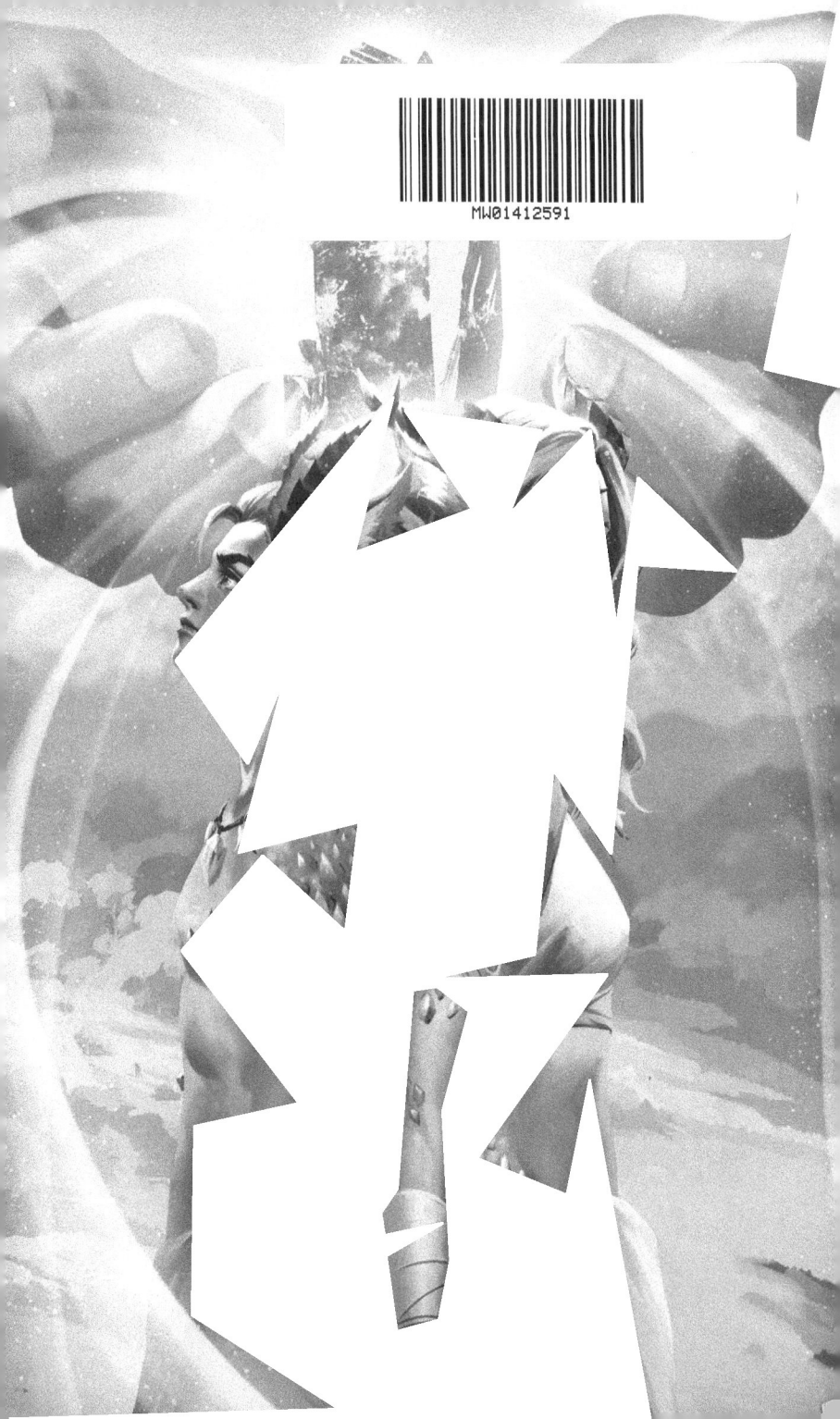

The Wilds
Valkys Lands

NEVOLD

- Mountains
- Orahai
- Forever Deep

NEVERTOLD
-The Son-

Nevertold Series - Book One

Copyright © 2022 - M. R. Moraine
All rights reserved.

No part of this publication may be reproduced, distributed, or transmitted in any form or by any means, including photocopying, recording, or other electronic or mechanical methods, without the prior written permission of the publisher, except in the case of brief quotations embodied in critical reviews and certain other noncommercial uses permitted by copyright law.

To request permission, contact the publisher at
info@lovelywoods.co

ISBN-13: 978-1-943619-99-3
First U. S. Edition: August 2022

Editor - Amanda Meuwissen
Cover Artwork - Hoangtejieng (Fiverr)

Printed in the United States of America.

Lovely Woods Publishing
7287 153RD ST W, #240806
Saint Paul MN, 55124

LOVELY WOODS
PUBLISHING
lovelywoods.co

WELCOME TO THE
WORLD OF NEVOLO!

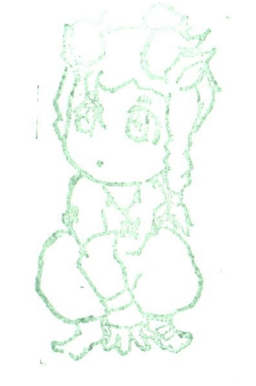

ALL THE BEST,

To my mother.

These are the words I could never find
to say who you were
and what you meant to me.

NEVERTOLD

BOOK ONE

- The Son -

- Table of Contents -

Prologue	1
Chapter 1 - *New*	8
Chapter 2 - *Innocence*	20
Chapter 3 - *Found*	33
Chapter 4 - *Return*	47
Chapter 5 - *Guardians*	69
Chapter 6 - *Sisters*	81
Chapter 7 - *Relief*	87
Chapter 8 - *Freedom*	100
Chapter 9 - *Seeing*	115
Chapter 10 - *Escape*	131
Chapter 11 - *Together*	142
Chapter 12 - *Fight*	150
Chapter 13 - *Reality*	160
Chapter 14 - *Love*	170
Chapter 15 - *Blind*	182
Chapter 16 - *Awake*	196
Chapter 17 - *Change*	203
Epilogue	215

PROLOGUE

And now I know... I was wrong.

The girl's hazel eyes were unwilling to let tears fall, holding on with pained regret. The droplets that did emerge glowed brightly, overflowing from deep within her body, and puddled on the floor in pools of worldly energies as reminders of her recent mistakes.

"Everything is breaking. I can feel it," she said in a half-whispered cry.

The words did nothing to heal her wounds, only serving to pass the time as her face glistened.

A band of crimson moonlight slowly danced across her cheek, as if dripping from the moon itself. The color reflected from the crystal sea that ran its meridian, appearing as if made of shifting, colored glass that almost seemed alive. Her long strands of auburn hair, styled to impress, grabbed the light and glittered its own color in response. The simple dress she had scavenged from her mother's limited wardrobe was worn with her best effort and had taken the better part of an hour to fit the way she wanted, but the excitement of wearing it had disappeared hours ago, as she hid in the shadows of her workshop.

When the rest of her tears uncontrollably erupted, they carved lines down her face, branching burning streams that she barely felt. The worst of her pain was reserved for what she clasped tightly in her hands. Something she dared not let go, despite how it stung from the pressure. Not even when it cut into the soft skin between her fingers did she relent, with blood emerging as if secretly set free.

Her hands finally slackened, flowering open to the shine of a radiant crystal. It stretched the length of her palm—long, slender, and carved into a perfectly symmetrical shape. Flawless by any definition, energy swirled inside its walls in a misty cloud, charged with a piece of her soul.

She knew little of what she had done, if any of it could be reversed, or the consequences if she tried. She scoffed at herself for not being skilled enough to navigate through these new feelings and sensations, but she suddenly realized that the beautiful object she held was completely worthless, and finally let go.

The crystal tumbled, spun once in what felt like an eternity, before hitting the wood flooring directly on its tip. The impact sent a lightning snap that left a fissure up the entire length of the jewel. Like an open wound, it spread a lattice of many other tiny cracks until it was almost completely marred. It bounced and danced across the floor then, spinning on its own axis different from what would be normal. It took its final resting place just out of reach, then crushed down into the wood plank flooring with its own gravity.

The light that had called the crystal home lifted away in a ghostly wisp. The girl paid it no mind. The light waited, as if to give her the chance to reconsider. At any moment it was ready to rush lovingly back to her, shining a bit brighter when she finally opened her eyes, though she did not look to the wisp. She knew it was there, she could feel it, but her focus was on the marks in her hands from holding onto the jewel so tightly.

The wisp fought to remain as long as it could outside the safety of a proper vessel. When no salvation came and having nothing binding it to the world, it dissipated without flash or fanfare, silently disappearing forever.

The girl immediately stopped crying and became motionless. The last bit of tears dripped from her chin to the floor, and a soft breath of air escaped her lips. There she sat silently dead inside, ready for the gods' undertakers to ferry her away.

When the sounds of happily approaching footsteps shuffling down the road broke through the eerie quiet, she did not react. When three rhythmic knocks on the door hit her ear, she did nothing.

"Hey, Tam," a young man, about her age, announced as he entered the house with a basket overflowing with food.

He looked to have come straight from laboring in front of a fire, wearing modest attire, fitting of a man who spends days apprenticing as a blacksmith. Spots of ash and dust spotted his clothing with his hair a perfect mess that looked good on him.

"I brought you something to eat." He smiled, still trying to find his breath. "Well, more like my *mother* sent you some food."

In the low light of the room, his cobalt eyes had to adjust. He hadn't immediately seen her, but eventually spotted her sitting quietly and thought nothing of it, continuing to the workbench.

"I swear she loves you more than me some days." He feigned arm pain placing the basket down, "I'm sure she'd trade me for you, if she had the chance. She has enough boys, I'm sure she would love a girl in the family," he started to ramble, "I mean who wouldn't want you—," he looked up from the basket frozen for a second, trying to recover. "For a *daughter*. I mean, I wouldn't...not for a daughter, or a sister, cause that would be weird. I mean not for my mom! I know she wants a daughter like you. For me. Not *for* me! I mean she would trade. Funny right?! Right..."

He laughed nervously and scolded himself while the room fell silent.

"Umm, your mom told my mom that I'm supposed to tell you to make sure you stop for a while and eat something, so if you're hungry...," he said, embarrassed breath making his already lack of it worse.

He concentrated on emptying the basket, knowing the food delivery was his mother's way of trying to help him. He didn't mind, because he knew he could use the assist.

"I also made that part you needed," he composed his next words and spoke slower, pulling the item from his pocket and setting it on the workbench.

Grasping at the darkness, he found the lantern he'd previously modified, per Tam's instruction. A small ring around the base, set at a slope, rotated freely when he tested it. Inside the lantern's glass housing was a series of metal tubes and wires that ran to a stand. He held up the lantern in the moonlight and put in the new part he'd made. It fit perfectly.

Searching the pile of parts on the table nearby, beneath the clutter he found an ordinary looking rock with a stony grey texture and small breaks in it to reveal a crystal structure beneath. There were three shallow chiseled lines etched in distinct patterns that he checked for accuracy. Once satisfied, he placed the stone within the lantern onto a holder designed for it.

Next, he gingerly placed the lantern on the bench and ran his finger across the stone's surface as if to wipe it clean. He then hit a switch on the lantern's base and it began to make a barely audible hum. After a few rotations of the stone, a single spark jumped off and ignited it, as if it was made of tinder. It stayed lit, independent of any fuel source.

As light slowly built in the room, it revealed the machinery and contraptions that lined the walls; edge to edge, top to bottom. An amateur Altician's workshop, all built custom by him and Tam. The machines looked less than refined, thrown together with mismatched parts, but it was a working setup that would rival the efficiency of some of the best city-state facilities. A sanctuary where they could practice freely.

The boy finally caught his breath. "Sorry I came over so late, but I ran into scouts of the Grand Army at Last Town's Crossing. Of course they stopped me, concerned for my safety and all. Didn't want to let me pass when there obviously wasn't anything going on," he said with joking annoyance. "Supposedly there were some Valkys in the area making trouble, but I didn't believe it. There hasn't been Valkys sighting in years...so naturally, I wasn't about to let that stop me," he boasted and looked back at Tam, noticing the dress she wore.

It made him stare and immediately feel his face flush warmly. He swore it felt hotter than the fires of the furnaces he toiled in front of daily.

"You're wearing a dress? You normally don't...I like it." He paused for breath again, wishing he'd taken more time to be presentable, but shook the idea since he'd never been cleaned-up around her before. Working as they did, neither one of them was hardly ever clean. "It looks...you look pretty," he finished, at which he was surprised she said nothing.

The awkward silence became too much, and he changed the subject as quickly as he could.

"Uh, hey. So...your idea, the one that you told me about yesterday?" He placed the empty basket on the floor. "And I don't want to know where or how you came up with it, but I was thinking... it could work. Maybe. I think you'd have to be crazy to try it, 'cause I still don't think you can define it so easily, like the other elements. But if what you say is right, you'd only need a large enough stone. Not even a stone, it would have to be all crystal really. And it would have to be perfect, and I mean *perfect*," he urged, waiting for an expectantly happy response at having her ideas validated, but again he received nothing.

"Tam?" his voice rose with concern. "You're not mad at me for saying you were wrong before, are you? Or are you mad 'cause I went through the woods by myself? I'm fine, just look." He patted his chest lightly. He'd gladly accept her lack of response as either anger or concern, but as he moved a few steps towards her, he realized she still wasn't moving at all. It didn't look as if she was even breathing.

All his selfish concerns disappeared. Not realizing her condition as soon as he'd entered tore at him harshly and sent a twinge crawling up the back of his neck. His legs couldn't move fast enough, and he almost fell as he knelt near her. His knee hit the broken jewel, and it made a hollow, unsettling ringing as it rolled away. He caught a glimpse of it, the crystal with a long crack along its surface, and his eyes widened, trying to work out what he was looking at.

"Tam, what did you do?" he asked hastily.

"It's gone, Keagan," her softly spoken words escaped, barely including a glance from her lifeless eyes.

"What do you mean gone? What's wrong?"

She grabbed her chest. "Empty...it's empty...and he...I want him...to feel this..."

It was hard for Keagan to understand her as each word seemed to be harder and harder for her to speak, as if she couldn't hold in air. She looked to the crystal, and her body swayed in its direction—drawn to it.

Keagan held her back and followed her eyes to the jewel on the floor. "No! You did it, didn't you? Why?!"

"He was supposed to...I thought we were...," she paused and took in enough air to say, "I want to make him suffer." Those words came out effortlessly with a justified strength to curse the one she hadn't named. It had a haunting sound that scared Keagan.

"Stay here, I'm going to get help," he said and made sure Tam was sitting comfortably, but before he could fully stand, she grabbed him by the wrist.

"...help me," she pleaded.

"I'm trying to, but I can't fix what's wrong with you. I need to find someone to—."

Her hand rose to meet his face and she lovingly caressed his cheek. Keagan froze at the sudden and unexpected show of affection, and it admittedly made him swim with enjoyment. He'd waited a lifetime for her to show him an affectionate touch, and it felt better than he could have imagined.

The feeling lasted for a few beats of his fluttering heart, when suddenly it was stolen away by a sharp, piercing pain.

Tam had somehow summoned the crystal from the floor, to her hand, and lodged it in his chest.

Nothing in Keagan's short life had prepared for such an immobilizing mixture of sensations. His only recourse was to look down to the point of pain, concreting the fact that it was the crystal that had been stabbed into him.

He became light-headed, and his vision blurred from the pain and inability to comprehend the situation. When he made an attempt to speak, his voice was absent, lost behind the surges of agony. He spoke with his eyes instead, giving Tam a terrified stare and silently pleading for mercy.

"You will help me," she demanded with a growing intensity in her voice.

I'd do anything for you, he thought, in a moment of clarity.

Alterence, in all its complexity, was made simple by Tam, who used the crystal unaided by any machinery. With a thought and a light press of her finger, lines of energy snaked across the crystal's surface, multiplying and configuring connections between hidden points.

In any other situation, it would have been beautiful the way she conducted the pulsating energy—like living art. The jewel flowered with renewed life and energy, and in that moment, Keagan's friend, colleague, and unrequited love gave and took everything.

Affection and pain. Trust and betrayal. A battle forged in the tormented soul of one girl, and he would be the one to bear witness to her transformation. His soul was hers, forcibly torn from his body as he screamed with a previously unknowable pain, a sound that carried briskly throughout the night and echoed in the silence of the sleeping village.

CHAPTER 1
NEW

"The world only knows how to give."
- Great Mother Veacha

Third quarter of the Indigo Moon, Year 362 AA (After Alterence), 12th summer of the Orahai

Seven Steps Forest

With a slow, inaudible breath, she felt her lungs fill and held it while she moved, the young girl who was far beyond her seventh step. Far beyond what it took anyone unfamiliar with the aptly named forest to get lost in its dense and repeating foliage. But lost, she was not. Her controlled and eased exhale provided her comfort enough to settle herself for her next movement.

Relax, she told her body, most especially her racing heart. She shifted her entire weight to balance on her palms as she brought her feet forward. She looked far too young to be venturing out on her own, as she had been told countless times, but she didn't like to listen. She wouldn't let age be the factor that determined when she could become a hunter or a useful tribeswoman, not when she knew she was beyond capable.

She would not wait for someone to label her something that was instinctual and came naturally. Things like that indescribable feeling that made someone want to prey, made them want to capture their own dinner, and by their own means. It was satisfying. Exhilarating. And even when hunger wasn't the drive, she could always find sport in the chase.

In the world of Nevold, she was Manyari, and that meant only her talent and skill mattered. For her people living in the wilds, it was simple. Live today so you might fight tomorrow, and so yesterday's fights allow others to live today.

It was a deeply ingrained mantra not actively practiced by the child huntress. She let the others worry about the grander concerns of the tribe like revitalizing their lacking numbers. She simply wanted to *hunt*.

Barely into her eighth summer of life, she was already quite convinced that she'd never care about raising a child. Infants weren't particularly appealing, slightly ugly if she'd had to say, and she was far too independent to have to be tied down to one. There was too much effort and care that went into raising one from what she saw.

She forgot about her people for the time being and focused her mind on listening for the slow footsteps of woodland prey and keeping herself concealed. Her full stalking posture had her nearly flat against the ground with arms and legs tight to her body. She mimicked the swaying brush when wind passed through, blending into the environment. It was a skill she liked to flaunt.

She adjusted her head ornament, the bone skull of a scaled Valkys, as it was too large for her without strapping through the eye cavities. Running parallel to the curve of the skull, where something would have normally sprouted if the creature was still alive, protruded her actual living horns, long and spiraling. They pivoted independently of the mask and moved in segments like tendrils, and were a muddied brown color. They billowed in the wind as she slowly shifted the skull again to fit tighter.

Her ears, long and with black fur covering them, twitched as they slowly crept out from hiding in the concave cavities built into the underside of her horns. They flicked in every direction, making no noise, and bounced eagerly as she moved. They took in all the sounds and vibrations from meters around as a reward, painting a view of her surroundings better than her orange, hazel-flecked eyes could see at times, impressive as they had the clarity and range that could rival most birds of prey.

She thoroughly enjoyed all the sensory gifts passed down by the Valkys side of her ancestry. They made her feel invincible. Proud, though arrogant, to be so fearless when alone in a forest that even the most seasoned hunters would be cautious in. She grinned large enough for her cheeks to pop out the side of the helmet.

Before moving on, she smeared more moss and dirt across the whole of the white bone helmet. She wanted to match that section of the forest, which had many small budding flowers everywhere. One larger flower in particular caught her eye and she placed it between her two horns. She would claim it was for camouflage, never admitting she'd put it there because she thought it was pretty.

She snaked her way through the forest undetected, not only because of her disguise or meticulous movements, but by how she seemed to effortlessly slip past objects. Her reddish-tan skin, with its occasional stripes and dots of darker discoloration, held the secret of her free movement. With almost unnoticeable scales that completely covered her there was little friction from her surroundings as everything seemed to bend away from her, like a creature moving through water. At the more vital parts of her body, scales had begun to grow bigger and more raised. Places like her shoulders, the sides of her neck, knees and elbows, her outer thighs, forearms, and on her right-side chest over her heart, all showed signs of change. And when the light broke through the branches, it made her skin shine a radiant, iridescent shimmer of reds and oranges.

Like her horns, her scales were another all-important trait passed down the long lineage that was usually forgotten. A lineage that existed long before Manyari were brought into the world, when Man and Valkys were not enemies and were able to form a bond that bridged two different peoples. So long ago it seemed like a fairy tale, no more real than the gods that slept and supposedly watched over all from above.

Her ears swiveled back and forth, suddenly facing forward as they honed in. A large buck-toothed rodent, with its uselessly small front paws and abnormally large back ones, hopped into her view, scavenging for food. A rahtani. An all too common, skittish creature that had the ability to replace their numbers as easily as they were diminished by predators. It cautiously pushed up onto its hind paws, which gave it several extra centimeters of height, to reach a branch with fruit.

The girl crept closer and unsheathed a dagger slung across her chest. Without moving, a spectrum of color swept across her as she instinctually changed the direction of her scales to make sure light wouldn't reflect toward the unsuspecting animal. A slow straightening out of her limbs kept her perfectly balanced as she clawed fingers into the ground. Her muscles tightened visibly and it further redefined her outline.

I am a MIGHTY Valkys and I'm going to eat you, she thought gleefully.

On the brink of her attack, she relaxed suddenly, and one of her ears swiveled back. She knew without looking who had found her.

"Tahdwi," she grumbled quietly, preceding the arrival of another Manyari child.

Tahdwi, her self-appointed *best friend*, had an uncanny ability to track and find her, with what she supposed was some sort of dark, *yarik* power. Tahdwi had appeared out of nowhere, dressed far more casually with a simple dress. Her hair, a nice earthy brunette, was artfully braided around the top of her head and horns. Compared to the single flower on the girl's bone helmet, Tahdwi had a garden of different flowers woven into her hair and clothes. Her scales glistened with a more blueish-green accent to her naturally tan skin color.

"Ashava," Tahdwi named her friend, skillful enough to not alert the rahtani.

"Not now," Ashava urged, and retracted her ears back below her horns in a menacing way.

Still not looking at Tahdwi, she tried to stay the effective hunter and maintain her lock on her target.

Tahdwi's ears wiggled happily enough that Ashava could hear them. She shifted back to stop her friend's ears and push them back under her horns.

When Ashava returned to her lower position, Tahdwi followed and took a short breath.

"Ashava, you'll never guess—" but Tahdwi was quickly silenced. Her eyes crossed as she looked down at Ashava's hand covering her mouth. She smiled and joyfully pushed it away. "You'll never guess what happened? There were more babies today," the girl squeaked, as if the words were forced out.

"You didn't even give me a chance to answer," Ashava whispered as she shook her head. "So what?"

The rahtani stopped reaching for the fruit for a second and looked around. Ashava panicked and dug her feet immediately into the soft ground a little more, believing she'd lost her element of surprise.

"There was a boy!" Tahdwi practically howled.

Ashava flinched and watched her prey scurry away, along with a dozen other animals that were startled by Tahdwi.

"Tahdwi!" Ashava pulled her helmet off, and released the tangle of black hair that matched her ears. She turned to Tahdwi, visibly angry, but was taken aback by the big, happy-eared grin of the girl. It wasn't until Ashava really processed the information that her scowl transformed into shock and amazement.

And secretly, excitement.

"A boy?! Nuh-uh."

"YES!"

"Who was the mother?"

"*Great* Mother Saleal," Tahdwi corrected.

"Right, right. And was there any like me?" Ashava curiously hoped.

"I don't think so. No second-mother births. They all had the same father, remember?"

Ashava tensed the side of her face, but quickly cleared herself of the feeling of disappointment.

"Did you tell anyone else?"

"No..." Tahwdi sounded a bit offended. "You're my *First* friend, most important! I wanted to tell you first."

"No one?"

"NO!"

"Good!" Ashava pivoted masterfully on her heel, twirling like a dancer that she would never agree to be called. In the same motion she secured the helmet and dagger to her sling and aimed herself straight in the direction of their village.

Tahdwi admired the grace of the spin, until Ashava planted both feet and shot away with one powerful burst, starting their unfair race.

"Hey!" Tahdwi complained.

"Better hurry up, or I'm gonna see him first!" Ashava yelled over her shoulder, while vaulting over deadfall.

"What? Wait! That's not fair!" Tahdwi said, now in full pursuit. "I'm the one who found out!"

"Come on, Tahdwi!" Ashava called back to her. "You're gonna miss it!"

Tahdwi had no chance to keep up but tried her hardest. Through sheer will and burning muscles, she managed to catch up and locked angry eyes with Ashava, who laughed at the ugly face Tahdwi was making. Tahdwi didn't stay mad long and eventually laughed.

Ashava slowed to a pace they both could maintain so they would see the boy together.

At the speed they ran, it would only take a quarter of the time to get back to the village. They followed the unmarked paths, past the boundaries between the forest and the clearing that opened up to rows and rows of crops reaching high for the midday sun. They were painted with colors from filtered sunlight through the canopy of huge petals that were tall enough that an adult Manyari could stand fully and still be shaded.

Ashava and Tahdwi each selected one of the cultivated paths between tall stalks as their racing lanes. Each time they would look at one another, they laughed, seeing different colors wash over them, and they soon forgot about the competition all together.

Out of nowhere, water rained from the clear sky, dousing the girls with increasingly heavy drops. They didn't stop running, but did exchange a concerned look. There wasn't a cloud to be seen, so they knew this wasn't a surprise rain shower. They immediately peered through the thick canopy to the center of the field, where they saw the large boulder, the size of a small hut. Its decorations of paint and twisted rope designated it as the East watering stone, which functioned as a waymarker back home. Its glow was bright enough to be seen in the daylight as it spewed water haphazardly in random directions.

The large boulder had been set there before the field was even a crop, and took twenty Manyari to move. Outwardly, it was as normal as any other large stone, except it had crystalline properties that made it useful as a storing vessel for yarik—the world's energy.

Being caught in the fields during watering times was a good way to get in trouble as yarik could be dangerous, regardless of the element. A stone of that size required near constant attention and focusing of its power, and turning it on or off was never a simple affair.

Ashava frantically looked for the fieldworker, but she failed to see one. There were also consequences for abandoning a yarik stone, but it was evident that someone had left in a hurry.

The moment the village could be seen through the end of the field, a riled cheer erupted. News had traveled fast and Tahdwi's *secret* wasn't much of one anymore.

Ashava looked disappointedly at her friend, "Tahdwi!?"

"I don't know how they could have found out!"

"Well, they know!"

"I didn't tell anyone…" Tahdwi apologized.

Ashava grabbed Tahdwi's hand and hurried to the center of the village. Absent of traffic, they furiously careened around corners and down the dirt paths that separated the rows of small, similar looking homes of their sister Manyari. The clamoring of voices billowed from just beyond what they could see, and grew louder as they reached their last turn. A stylish drift around the final corner and they found themselves at the outward edge of a crowd of Manyari, twenty deep and all women.

Before them stood the Chieftess's hut with its forecourt where the announcement would most likely be made. A wall of women much taller than the two still growing girls screened anything from view. They decided to split and look for breaks in the crowd, but each time one would appear, it would be filled by a curious Manyari trying to see. Ashava grumbled loudly enough that it surprised those near her, who looked down, thinking they'd be faced with some sort of animal.

She became increasingly aggravated, not only with her inability to see, but how her lacking height did her no benefit. Being young meant she was shorter, but compared to other girls her age, she was also the runt. A fact only whispered about in close-knit circles as no one would dare insult her or her family. Most girls took victory in that they had already hit growth spurts, and would probably always be taller than her. More importantly, other girls already had their first experiences with yarik, where Ashava had not.

Ashava watched the people eye her oddly, but ignored them as she scurried away along the outside of the crowd in an increasingly futile attempt.

"I can't even see the front," she huffed under her breath. "Where did Tahdwi go?"

"I think she's up there," a girl of equal height, with plain dark features and horns that looked small for her age, informed Ashava. "Her mama came and got her."

Ashava huffed again.

"I'll stay with you," the girl offered. "It's nice here. Less people."

"No, Deuna, I got to find a way to the front."

"You sure?" Deuna asked bashfully.

"Yeah," Ashava mildly answered.

"Ashava, this way!" Tahdwi's hand appeared from within the crowd, grabbed Ashava, and pulled her in.

"Okay. Bye," Deuna pouted.

Tahdwi navigated Ashava and herself through the towering forest of people, retracing her path. They squeezed in and out, between, and under, to quickly make it to the front, but not without angering a few along the way. Once there, they waited. Waited longer than they were ready for, considering how hard they fought to get there on time. It slowly wore on Ashava's nonexistent patience.

"So, does it have a name?" Ashava asked.

"Yes."

"What is it?"

Tahdwi hesitated and responded timidly, "I don't know..."

"What do you mean you don't know?"

"I didn't have a chance to find out. I came to get you as soon as I heard."

Ashava scoffed, listening to others who might know. The people around her began to clamor and discuss wildly about the rumors floating about, but nothing was answered. Most didn't see when the two female Manyari *Wind Riders* exited the hut. Their armor, aerodynamic layered leather with finely carved bone helmets and intricate spears, made them look like a pair of Valkys waking from a den.

They looked around for a moment and then turned back to part the door. The Chieftess of Orahai finally emerged in a grand exit donning her most formal of head dresses, similar in structure to the skull that Ashava was frantically trying to hide. The Chieftess's hair was beautiful highlighted brown, kept in a tight weave that fell over her right shoulder. It rested beautifully beside the patch of green scales, over her worn and slightly frayed shawl that had been passed down for generations. Its colors were muted, but against the drab browns and yellows of most everything around, she stood out as a woman of importance.

Her horns stood tall, bound together and held upright with a golden plate, exposing her ears which flared outward. When she spread her free hand to welcome her people, her outfit chimed with the sound of adorned stones hitting against each other. In her other arm was her own recent addition to her tribe. A baby girl, who she hushed as she began to fuss. The crowd took the direction as if for them and quieted themselves.

The Chieftess basked in the loving smiles of those who had gathered and took the moment to admire each of them. During her sweeping gaze, she spotted her daughter and summoned her to join her side. When Ashava didn't immediately move, Tahdwi pushed her into the open area of the assembly. She stumbled and flushed with embarrassment, scrambling to hide the skull behind her. She strode to her mother, acting as if nothing was wrong in a painfully obvious attempt but eventually gave up and presented the skull to her mother as if it was a gift and bowed courteously.

"You're in trouble," the Chieftess said with a raised eyebrow and took the mask gently.

"I know," Ashava accepted.

"Hold your sister," she directed and placed the baby in her arms.

They both turned to face the crowd, one with a joyous smile, the other with a half-worried one. The Chieftess placed both hands firmly on her daughter's shoulders and presented her family proudly. Ashava looked up as her mother squeezed her reassuringly.

"I didn't expect something this important to stay secret for long, so I'm sure you know why I called you here." The Chieftess smiled, which started a wave of smiles in response. "Yes, our family is a little bit bigger today!"

The crowd cheered, and she waited patiently until they calmed themselves.

"And what you have heard is true. Mother Saleal has given birth," she paused for greater effect, "to a boy!"

Immediately, she was drowned out by the sounds of uncontained joy, letting it last for as long as their lungs could project their happiness. The voices eventually hushed to murmurs and she continued.

"Without question, we are all in her debt. You have all made this village a sanctuary, a place where we can survive, and that has not always been easy. But we stand here as proof that Manyari did not give up. That we few will continue to fight, for we are still here, and always will be. Today, we give thanks to her, for she is now and forever, *Great Mother Saleal of the Orahai*."

For a third time, the crowd burst into uncontrollable cheers, the likes of which made the forest around them rumble. The two guards parted the doors again and the Great Mother walked out with the face of exhaustion and pride. The midwife had done her best to make her presentable, but sweat still covered her face and dampened her robes.

Her dark blonde mane of disheveled hair was a mess held in wraps and stood out as the only different color amongst the shifting dark haired heads of the rest of the tribe. She scanned the happy faces, trying to give everyone a deserved 'thank you' before turning to her Chieftess.

"Thank you, Ejah," Saleal smiled.

Ejah helped the Great Mother present her son to the world. Saleal gently cradled him in her arms, pulling the blanket from his face to allow him to see the sunlight for the first time. His small horns barely covered his small ears, getting lost in the already full head of short red hair. He hardly made a noise as he focused on her. The oceans of his blue eyes connected to the fields of her green and they spoke to each other before they would ever speak real words.

Ejah cozied up to the new mother and brushed the head of the child lovingly. She palmed his head and smiled gratefully as the child cooed.

"You made a beautiful child. And that hair," Ejah said almost enviously. "You sure he's yours?"

"Funny," Saleal cracked an appreciative smile.

While they admired him, a small wisp of energy floated past, which only he saw. He grasped for it as it gingerly moved out of reach.

An older woman emerged as if secretly summoned. The Wisewoman of Orahai, with her silvery hair the odd tinge of red that suggested it was once a vibrant color. Her gray scales ran the curve of her chin, small but noticeable. She was adorned like Ejah, but with a wardrobe far less faded and more decorated. Each trinket and piece of jewelry described a lifetime of work serving her people, though some would simply consider her to be a hoarder. She never argued the point, but did always find a use for everything she carried. It was her task to be prepared.

She calmly watched the newborn reach out for the wisp that she also saw, "This child is blessed by spirits," she suddenly proclaimed.

The congregation took that as a cue to let out another resounding cheer, but Saleal didn't let it enter her mind. All she could feel was love and pride for her boy, dreaming of all the greatness his future would bring.

You are my world now, was her truth from that moment, and it would be more real and meaningful than any breath she'd ever take again. Her life would be for him—with him. Now and for always.

The cheers continued and embraces were traded, not subsiding until someone from the crowd asked, "What's his name?!"

Saleal, admiring the tiny life in her hands, almost missed the question, but responded a curiously happy, "His name...?"

"Yeah?!" someone else confirmed the question, and then the audience forcefully hushed themselves and held completely still.

"His name," she thought, looking to the sky. "His name is..."

CHAPTER 2
INNOCENCE

"You are more yourself today, than you were or will be."
- Blessing of the Seasons

First quarter of the Blue Moon, Year 367 AA
5 years later, 17th spring of the Orahai

"Ke-mah-ni," the young Manyari girl sang his name, crossing her arms and staring victoriously with piercing cyan eyes. "You lost again. You better not be letting me win."

Kemahni, the sole son of Orahai, made an unappreciative thud against the ground when being pinned by the Chieftess' youngest daughter, Kiyadeh, of his same age.

"That's three times, Ke!"

"I'm not *letting* you," Kemahni huffed in resigned defeat.

"Let's play again then!"

"You always pick games you win. It's no fun."

"I won't try as hard," she lied.

She used Kemahni's chest to push off, but stopped when she felt an abnormal bump.

"What's in your shirt?"

"Nothing."

"What are you hiding? I wanna see it!"

"No, Yaya. Stop!"

She fought him against his will and pulled down his shirt to reveal his secret. Underneath was the formation of thicker, larger scales, above his sternum.

"You got your first hard scales? You got it before me? How? That's not fair. How long have you had this?" she bombarded him.

"What's going on?" Ashava suddenly broke into the conversation.

Ashava, Kiyadeh's older sister, stood watching curiously as the two tussled. Kiyadeh stood quickly and pointed excitedly at Kemahni.

"Kemahni's got—"

"Yaya, don't tell her!"

Ashava looked sternly at her sister. "Kiyadeh, Mother's looking for you."

"But guess what Ke—"

"Go, you know she doesn't like waiting."

"Fine. Don't go anywhere," Kiyadeh finished at Kemahni, "and don't tell her without me! I'll be right back!"

Kiyadeh rushed away as fast as her tiny legs could carry her, to the annoyed head shake of her sister.

"What is she going on about?" Ashava asked to the nothing behind her.

Kemahni had bolted away, but she glimpsed him entering his family hut. She cracked an interested smile and slowly followed.

Inside, Kemahni flew past his mother, who almost mistook him for a rush of air as he zoomed into the back room.

"Kemahni?" his mother called.

Her voice scared him into frantically looking for something to drape over himself, since Kiyadeh's roughness had stretched his shirt and left his scales visible.

Saleal came into the room with the faintest scowl of worry. "Kemahni, are you in here?"

The commotion near a chest in the back alerted her to his presence. She moved curiously around a partition of banded branches and found Kemahni struggling to find the hole of three different shirts, none of which fit properly.

"What are you doing?" Saleal asked in laughter as he fought the clothing. "Would you like some help?"

"No. I'm okay."

"You don't look okay," she said, pulling at all the shirts.

"No. I can do it."

She felt him resist, holding onto the last shirt as she pulled it away.

"I'm trying to help you."

Once freed of the shirts, Kemahni crossed his arms trying to hide his chest.

"What's wrong?" she asked sweetly.

"Nothing." He shook his head. "I'm cold."

"You're cold?" she said doubtfully, feeling the warm morning through the doorway.

He nodded quickly.

"Then you should put one of these other shirts back on, but not all three." She smiled.

He shook his head again.

"Okay, Mahi, what's wrong?" her careful mothering tone asked.

Kemahni's arms loosened and slowly dropped to his side.

Saleal beamed. "Your first hard scale. Seems like it came in overnight."

"I don't like it," he grumbled.

"It's a perfectly normal and wonderful thing."

Saleal helped him dress in one of the other shirts but lost her smile for the second he was obscured. Once the shirt no longer covered his face, she held his chin gingerly.

"You're growing, Mahi. We all do, and when we do, we have a chance to be better and stronger. Don't you want to be strong?" His head rose and his ears perked up from beneath his horns. "Like Ashava. She has big scales, and she is tough, right?"

"Yeah…" he agreed.

"Just think, someday soon, you'll be able to beat her in a race. Maybe even today."

"You think so?"

"I know so," she said confidently. "Because you are Manyari, and Manyari do not fear…"

"We fight!" he cheered.

"Who we fighting?" Ashava added gleefully to the conversation as she walked through the door, feigning an attack posture.

Ashava, now into her thirteenth summer, strode confidently to meet mother and son. Her armored leather made her equally ready to fight anything real or dreamt up by Kemhani. The pair of yarik-less axes solidified her battle-readiness.

Saleal gave her a welcoming smile. "Good morning, Ashava."

"Gooood Morning, Great Mother," she returned with enthusiasm.

"You're looking well."

She bowed her head. "Thank you. Feeling well!"

"You might need that today. Kemahni is full of energy and might give you a workout."

"Thanks for the warning."

They exchanged a hearty smile. Then Ashava felt an unexpected tug on her belt as Kemahni had snuck around without either noticing.

"Hey Ashava!"

"Hey Ke. You're getting good. Didn't even see you."

"Look, look. I got my first hard scale today!" Kemahni boasted without acknowledging Ashava's compliment.

"Oh yeah?"

Kemahni pulled down the collar of his shirt and presented his scale proudly.

"Well look at that." She tapped it twice. "Very nice. Guessing that was what Kiyadeh was all excited about?"

"Yeah." He paused, but then grew a shockingly large grin. "But she's not gonna beat me anymore, because I'm gonna be strong like you."

"You think so?"

"Yup. Probably stronger," he said, "but don't be mad. We can still play together."

"We'll see about that," she happily contested. Ashava rose to meet his mother. "I'll take him now." She ended with a bow and held out her hand for him to grab. "We'll be back before sunfall."

"Great." Saleal returned a grateful bow and bent down to Kemahni. "Be good to your Guardian, and do as she says."

"Yes, Mama."

Saleal hugged him quickly, and let go with another solemn smile that Kemahni missed. She waved once, but neither noticed as they were already preoccupied planning their activities for the day. Saleal held the worry inside where no one could see, and let the joyfully bounding steps of the two leaving children be enough for her to return to her daily tasks and forget about her deep thoughts.

Meanwhile, Kiyadeh exited her home and turned to head deeper into the village. As she reached Kemahni's hut, Saleal was exiting. Her eyes grew wide and she came to an abrupt stop when faced with the Great Mother.

"Where's Ke?"

"He's with Ashava."

"No! They're gonna leave without me!"

Without another word, she sprinted for the outskirts of town with the same panic as before.

"Be careful!" Saleal cried out, knowing the words probably wouldn't reach her.

"Was that my daughter?" Ejah asked from down the road.

"Might have been, or some kind of runaway Valkys."

Ejah held her straight face, unappreciative of the joke. "I'm gonna have to give that child direction soon if she doesn't start taking responsibility and stop thinking everyday is for play."

"She is a child. Let her stay that way for as long as she can."

"We don't have that luxury."

"I suppose not," Saleal barely spoke, as she looked far into the distance, toward the escaping Kiyadeh and her son far away.

On their way out of the village, Kemahni and Ashava took a route through the fields. They looked around before sneaking under the high canopies of flowering stalks. Kemahni tugged at Ashava's belt.

"I want to fly," Kemahni requested.

Ashava swayed her head. "This might be the last time, Ke. You're getting too big."

"No, you're strong, you can always do it."

"Probably," she flexed childishly, "but when is it my turn?"

"When I get bigger?" He shrugged.

"Until then, I'll show you how to do it right!"

Ashava surprised him and suddenly hoisted him into the air. He erupted in gleeful laughter and immediately extended his arms and legs to mimic a bird. They soared down the lane between the stalks, jutting from one lane to the next as they made their way through. While held aloft, Kemahni let his hands tap the stalks, making a rhythmic tempo. He nabbed one and it broke free.

He held his mock weapon and declared, "Look, Ashava, I'm a Wind Rider."

"Then this is the longest jump anyone has ever done!" she said.

They both laughed and broke through the last line of the field. Immediately on the other side, Tahdwi was crouched, tending to newly tilled crops. She was looking in their direction, having heard their not so quiet playing.

Tahdwi had already begun to grow into a young woman with delicate curves, looking as she eventually always would—adult but forever youthful. She retained fair skin and a roundish face, and was skinny without much muscle definition. Her horns were close together back along the curve of her head, with her ears out and at attention. She let them sway in the gentle breeze that seemed to always follow her. The life nearby unnoticeably bent towards her, like how grass would brush gratefully at her ankles, or how a soft rain would hover above only to cool her on a warm day.

Ashava slowed, "Time to land, Ke," and placed him down, where he dropped the stalk in his hand.

"Tawi!" Kemahni exuberantly shouted, still having trouble saying her name.

He ran over to her and leapt into her waiting arms. She embraced him with a long and tight hug, the kind he always expected from her. Kemahni pushed away long enough to squish Tahdwi's cheeks together and kiss her appreciatively on the lips.

"Good morning, Kemahni," she thanked him.

He hugged her again as she rose to greet Ashava with Kemahni cradled in her arms.

"Should I be jealous?" Ashava asked.

Tahdwi kissed Ashava on the cheek. "How about now?"

"Nope, not anymore."

"Are you going to have a baby?" Kemahni asked the two.

Ashava and Tahdwi glanced embarrassedly at each other, but held their gaze for a lingering moment.

Ashava laughed, "Not anytime soon, but maybe one day. Maybe Tahdwi can with your help."

"Why not you?"

Ashava paused and exchanged another look with Tahdwi.

"Because we all know she'll be a better mother." Ashava winked, and Tahdwi appropriately blushed.

Kemahni looked up at Tahdwi and nodded with a big smile, "Mama says that someday I get to help everyone!"

"Yes, and we all look forward to that someday." Tahdwi nuzzled Kemahni affectionately before placing him down.

He hopped and skipped around with a newfound joy in his bounce. They watched him briefly, admiring the innocence.

"You know you would have made a good mother," Tahdwi said.

"Maybe, but I think it's best we focus on you fulfilling that role, and I'll just be there to help." They both watched him carefully disappear in and out of the field. "Honestly, I sometimes think it's better that I can't. He's enough some days and can you imagine if I had a child?" Ashava shuddered.

"If they had your strength and fearlessness, I think they'd be okay. It's what I admire about you."

At that Ashava had to pivot to hide her beaming face. She looked back at the crops that had come through. "Fields are looking great."

Tahdwi knowingly smirked and caressed one of the flowers. "They are," she said but her face saddened when she noticed the broken stalk. "Oh, that is no good." She moved quickly to retrieve it.

"Yeah, sorry. We might have gotten a little carried away," Ashava said.

"You should take care with all life," Tahdwi softly scolded, but let her smile immediately return. "It's okay. This is how it is sometimes." She beckoned Kemahni to join her.

"I'm sorry Tawi," he said.

"It's okay. I will show you how you can make things better."

Tahdwi pulled the head of the flower through her hands to free the seeds. They tumbled into Kemahni's waiting hands, as he awed at the amount that was being deposited.

"Endings don't have to be endings," Tahdwi taught, while she removed a single seed from his hand. "With love," she carved a small hole for the seed, gently placed it, then covered it, "anything can grow."

She rubbed one of her two crystal earrings, activating the yarik inside. Ashava and Kemahni watched with anticipation as Tahdwi bent down closer to the seed. She closed her eyes and spoke softly as a wind carried her voice.

> *Grow with my help*
> *So I may too*
> *A little of me*
> *I give to you*

She barely vocalized the words, yet both Ashava and Kemahni heard her voice as if it was said directly in their ear. Slowly, the ground shifted and out pushed the leading bud of the seed. Kemahni dropped to his knees, wide eyed at the sudden germination. Ashava cracked a proud smile and joined the two to look at the sprout.

"You really are amazing." Ashava praised.

"Thank you." Tahdwi blushed.

"I didn't know you could do that!" Kemahni exclaimed.

"I didn't do anything that it wouldn't do on its own. I just gave it a little help."

"I want to learn!"

Ashava and Tahdwi gave each other an incredulous look, but amused him nonetheless.

"You don't need yarik to make the world move," Tahdwi lovingly said, "you just need to believe in the bonds between us all."

"Yeah, you're already strong," Ashava bolstered, then she winked with the eye he couldn't see, "and hey, I can't use yarik and that never stopped me!"

"Will you ever be able to use yarik?"

"No," she chuckled.

"Why not?"

"Some things are just the way they are, and you can't fix them, so you learn to be okay with them and not let them slow you down. Remember that: don't let anything stop you from being the best you can be."

"Nothing will stop me!" Kemahni sprang to his feet, saying, "I'm gonna be super strong!" and struck a powerful pose.

The girls laughed and watched him pick back up the stalk as a weapon, swing it around wildly, imitating how he thought weapon strikes looked. He lost himself in mock-battle, away from Ashava who thanked and hugged Tahdwi before leaving her to tend to the field.

"Alright, strong one, let's see if you can beat me to the wall," Ashava challenged.

Kemahni discarded the stalk again and hopped around Ashava ready to race, stopping to run in place as a means of intimidation. "If I win—"

"IF you win." Ashava teased.

"You scared I'm gonna win?!"

Ashava raised a bemused eyebrow. "Terrified."

"If I win, you have to carry me all the way back home."

"You're really trying to break me with that aren't you?" She grinned widely at the puzzled child, and turned him around. She patted him on the back and he jutted forward. "But first you have to win. First one to the wards?"

"Yup!" Kemahni gleefully agreed and planted his feet.

Ashava mimicked his posture, but only for show.

"Ready. Steady." She paused.

Kemahni false-started twice before angrily turning to her, "Are you gonna say—"

"Go!" Ashava said as she launched in a quick sprint.

"Hey!" Kemahni cried, having no trouble getting traction and coming to full speed.

The competition took them out of the village and deeper into the fields. Eventually, the gap between Kemahni and Ashava grew distant, kept that way by Ashava, who smirked everytime Kemahni pushed himself to maintain his lead. When he looked back, Ashava slowed and placed her hands on her knees, reaching for him with feigning fatigue. He smiled in preemptive victory, crested the small hill, and used the downward slope to increase his speed.

The last few races had taught him to never stop running, not until he reached the goal. Not until he was victorious.

The moment he crested the hill, she grinned with great intent and took a wide turn around the base of the hill, accelerating quickly.

Kemahni's steps and breath were heavy but his pace had not relented. He saw the top of the ward wall rise over the crest of the next short hill. The wards that comprised the wall were large wooden pillars spaced about twenty meters apart. Atop each carved and decorated pillar was a crudely shaped stone, brimming with yarik energies that stretched an invisible wall of blade-thin water between the wards. Distortions would intermittently appear to give the wall dimension, but only for a fraction of a second. From the other side, it reflected the trees to give the illusion of an everlasting forest that concealed their home.

Before the wall was the slow end of the Cascade River, a leapable river that ran down from the Shelf Mountains and swerved gently along the length of the ward wall. Lucky for him, there was no sign of Ashava, and his excitement swelled. He quickened as much as his already tired body could to race to the finish.

When the goal ward came into view, his face soured.

"No!" he said in disbelief.

All his joyous feelings promptly left when he saw Ashava leaning on the ward. She pushed off with one hand to greet his arrival.

"Took you long enough." Ashava said plainly.

"What?! How?"

"Yarik."

"You liar!"

"I was so worried about losing, it just came to me. Pure force of will!" Ashava said in an obviously fake boast.

"You cheated."

"I don't need to cheat, and I don't need yarik," she smiled secretly.

Kemahni furrowed his brow and huffed in disagreement while he crossed the river, kicking the water to make big splashes.

"The race isn't over till we both touch the ward."

Ashava stepped aside and waved Kemahni to pass. He shambled in defeat, and as he moved to place his hand on the wooden structure of the ward, he felt a spark of energy zip into him that he'd never felt before. The odd sensation surprised him, but he didn't pull away from it. It seemed to move back and forth in rhythmic intervals. It became slightly overwhelming, and he didn't let his hand linger, pulling it back slowly. The concealing wall between that ward and the next distorted, but not enough for either of them to notice.

Ashava hopped back across the river, beckoning Kemahni to follow. He did the same jump with a lot more effort in order to clear.

"You did good today. You were faster than I've ever seen you. I was worried for a moment," Ashava feigned.

Kemahni took a moment to respond, returning his focus to what she'd said.

"No you weren't," Kemahni asserted.

"You're right, I wasn't."

She laughed, and pulled him in close. She attacked his most ticklish spots, forcing him to let loose a roar of laughter. He squirmed until freed and tumbled away to catch his breath.

"One day, I'm gonna win," he said between breaths.

"I have no doubt." Ashava stood and looked briefly at the area. "Hey, let's play Grave Walkers. I'll hide first."

"You always make me be the Valkys first."

"I like hiding more."

"I like hiding too!"

"Okay, okay." She conceded happily. She turned him about, patting him on the shoulder. "Go hide."

Kemahni nodded over enthusiastically and sprinted away to find a hiding spot.

"Don't go too far and stay on this side of the river," she said with diminishing effort, doubting he had heard her before he vanished.

On a hill, just out of sight, the Wisewoman of Orahai was balancing on her staff, watching from afar as the two played. She leaned more into her staff to glimpse them until they disappeared from view.

Near her was a wisp of light that came into existence. It held the shape of an orb that was bigger than her head. It wavered listlessly in the air beside her, moving slowly toward the two in the distance.

The Wisewoman stepped to the side and waved an open hand. "Dearest spirit, would you be kind enough to watch over him. He is very important to us."

The orb dipped once in what looked like a bow, then danced in between the grass until it was gone.

"What a wonderfully interesting spirit," the Wisewoman spoke of the oddly energetic creature as it hurried away.

Back at the river, Ashava's genuine smile grew larger the more she got excited to play. She sat quietly and crossed her legs, but before covering her face, she saw something out of the corner of her eye. Something small and imperceivable that she almost immediately dismissed as a catch of light from one of her scales. It didn't distract her as she fully closed her eyes and twisted her ears forward to listen for Kemahni's escaping sounds.

She tapped her foot, and softly counted, taking time between numbers. "One. Two. Three. Four. You better run some more." Her ears twitched. "Five. Six. Seven. Eight. Better hide, before it's too late. Nine. Ten. Ten-one. Ten-two. You better do both, coz I'm coming for you!" She announced the last verse loudly to be sure he would hear.

Her voice was clear, even in the hole beneath the giant boulder where Kemahni hid. He had dug it out over the past few times they played in this area and it was finally ready. If he hadn't won the race, he'd at least win this game.

Confidence rolled over him, feeling protected in his hideaway that Ashava couldn't have known about. It felt as if there was an aura there that kept him secret. A sanctuary where nothing could touch him. He closed his eyes and wished his Guardian would never find him, having to stop himself from giggling.

Outside his hideaway, spirits began to gather, all seemingly curious of what he was doing. As if a beacon to Kemahni's location, the boulder began to glow along unseen lines, and the spirits did the same in harmony. They danced about and then suddenly held still as the glow faded from them and the large stone.

Then all was silent. All was still, until the spirits moved in a group on one side of the boulder, facing the wards. Far off in the distance a very faint hiss could be heard, if one was listening close enough. It caused great alarm in the spirits as they scattered, fleeing in the opposite direction from the danger they knew was coming.

CHAPTER 3
FOUND

"You cannot hide what I already know."
- Excerpt from The Righteous Warrior

Ashava had been eager to score her second win of the day, but her excitement to find Kemahni had worn from her face. She carelessly made noise, looking for clues as to his whereabouts as she had been looking for awhile.

"Okay I admit it, you're getting good," she said as if to coax him out.

She hunched down to inspect the ground when she was suddenly surprised by someone behind her.

"Found you!"

Ashava tensed as her scales flared, with her ears and horns extending fully.

"Kiyadeh!" Ashava growled. "Both you and Tahdwi are going to make my heart stop one of these days. Did you follow us all the way here?"

"Yes. You left without me."

"I never said I was going to wait for you. Now, go home before you make me lose."

"You guys never let me play."

"And you always want to include yourself in everything. He doesn't like you as much as you think he does."

"That's not true. We are friends!"

"Go home, Kiyadeh, before I tell mother that you ate the last bundle of berries she was saving," Ashava said.

Kiyadeh pursed her lips so intensely that it appeared as if she would strain a muscle if she held it any longer. "Fine," she huffed and stomped away.

After her third stomp, the ground shook and the trees in the distance swayed.

Ashava looked back at Kiyadeh, who had lifted her foot and was denying any responsibility for the tremor.

"Stay away!" Kemahni yelled fiercely in the distance.

They both heard the cry, immediately pinpointing the direction with synchronized ears that sprang up, swaying and pivoting in unison.

"What was that?" Kiyadeh asked.

"I don't know." Ashava said seriously.

"NO!" Kemahni cried out again far beyond their distance.

Ashava listened closer to his distress and ordered without looking at Kiyadeh, "Go home. Tell Mother to be prepared."

"For what? What's happening?"

"Do it, Kiyadeh," Ashava repeated her command with required compliance.

That time, Kiyadeh didn't protest and headed straight home, looking back a couple times to see if Ashava followed, never stopping her run.

Ashava headed toward the commotion until Kemahni emerged. He dashed at her desperately, running haphazardly, almost losing his footing twice along the way. Seeing he would not slow his speed on approach, she braced herself to receive his full force, as he leaped carelessly into her arms. He gripped hard to her waist, strong enough to hurt.

"Kemahni, Kemahni, it's okay. Tell me what's wrong," she asked with little response.

A dense fog crept in through the trees, ominously covering the ground unbeknownst to Asahva as she cared for Kemahni. She tried to unbury his face from her stomach but stopped after a few failed tries. She was finally able to pull his chin up to see the genuine terror that gripped him.

"What in Nevold has got you so scared?"

"Something BAD..." He had trouble breathing and talking at the same time.

"You did something bad?"

"NO! Something bad is coming!"

His tone was anything but playful. This was no trick, no game he was playing. His worry began to become hers.

"It's okay, there's nothing that's going to hurt you," Ashava said, petting him lightly on the head. "Me, on the other hand," she joked as she finally was able to loosen his hands. The moment he was less close to her, he resecured his hold. She surrendered and endured his clutch, convinced that he'd be unable to maintain it for long.

A chasing spirit, that only Kemahni could see, hovered close. Kemahni looked to the side, and the orb of light moved in response. It dipped up and down briefly, moved away, then came closer again. Kemahni shook his head slowly and retreated back to his Guardian.

"Ugh...Kemahni." Ashava exhaled sharply.

She looked skyward, asking some unknown gods for relief. Her gaze dropped to the spirit she could not perceive, looking past it, in the direction of low-pitched, guttural whistles. An announcing call far from cheerful.

Ashava's calm made an obvious outward change, as she forcefully made Kemahni relinquish his grip, and stepped past him. The water of the river pulled gently toward the ward, up onto the opposite shore.

The spirit swooped down to Kemahni, who carefully listened to its hidden voice. A flock of birds made a ruckus and escaped from their homes atop the trees. Low clouds began to roll toward them and the bellowing strange noise grew louder. The spirit rose and moved to

Ashava's side to wait with her for the reveal of things to come. After much internal debate, Kemahni joined them, but stayed to the side of his Guardian that would keep him away from the spirit.

Steam rolled forward stopping just short of the wards. From within the white clouds a herd of beasts emerged much like aquatic animals breaching water, moving out to see what lay on the other side. Most retreated into the mist, concealing their numbers, but one remained with half its body revealed.

"Valkys," Ashava said in disbelief.

The lead Valkys stumbled forward, shakey with its footing. Its once strong body weak from starvation, its bones visible through the skin. The shoulder and hip plates appeared ready to tear through its stretched skin of thick hide. Its quick shallow breaths sounded pained as its boxy torso barely expanded. Along the length of its spine were hollow stacks of bone, billowing out the mist that had hidden their arrival.

The Valkys blinked, cleared its eyes, and a portion of its vitality was suddenly reinvigorated the moment it spotted the Manyari. It pulled itself upright onto its hind legs with great effort and set forth a horrendous howl. It lurched forward back onto its front paws, like a toppling tree transforming into a battering ram. The ground shook, and the two Manyari gave their full attention.

Replying howls came from the steam and soon one beast became two. Two became four. And four quickly became too many to count. Each new beast looked as emaciated as the first, but still managed to repeat the rise up and fall to four legs. The more that appeared, the more aggressive they became, not only with Kemahni and Ashava, but between themselves, momentary squabbles in the form of hunched shoulders, inflated bodies, and concentrated puffs of steam from their nostrils. A quick decision was agreed upon, and they crossed the ward wall with little care.

The wards did not react.

"Why didn't the wards sound?" Ashava's frantic words spilled, as she reached an arm out to push Kemahni farther behind her.

"Ashava..." his voice peaked in fear.

The Valkys huffed and snarled as their march brought them into the river. The water rose upward from their feet, summoned by their yarik-charged bodies as they soaked in the liquid. They focused yarik inward, making fire and water coalesce inside them, rapidly creating steam and building pressure. The bone stacks on their backs sealed the flow of vapor, with water sweating out from small holes to regulate the contained forces. They spread wide, fanning to start a circle, steam still spewing forth in cascading waves around their bodies like a cloak of white, hiding their numbers once again.

A sudden burst of steam sputtered in a pop, and a hole bursted open in the clouds. One of the Valkys wasn't able to handle the pressure and died in an explosion of watery red liquid that ruptured a weak part of its hard, leathery skin. It gave a last whimper and slammed to the ground, ignored by the rest who continued pursuit of the two Manyari. Pressure built to a critical point, and in unison, they closed their nostrils to force the yarik-fueled steam through their gaping mouths.

The steam took the shape of vertical blades that flew toward Ashava and Kemahni. Ashava reacted quickly to the unexpected attack and leapt out of the way with a loose hold on Kemahni. They tumbled harshly, nearing the side-edge of the expanding cloud of steam. Ashava recovered effortlessly to her feet, where Kemahni did not. He crashed into the ground but stopped before disappearing into the white mist.

Kemahni complained upon recovery, unaware of the deep cut in the ground where they had once been.

"Are you okay?" Ashava shouted nervously.

Kemahni was about to respond when his footing was taken from beneath him. He was pulled into the air by his ankle, his head narrowly missing colliding with the ground as he swung inverted. He reached his arms out long to grasp anything, digging his fingers deep into the ground where he could. His strength was far from enough to keep him from being torn upward and left to dangle upside down. He strained against a massive paw holding him, his fear growing stronger as the rest of the Valkys slowly emerged from the dense cloud.

Kemahni squirmed to fight its grip, kicking and punching at the hand, only stopping when he felt the tightening grip on his ankle followed by a shooting pain that traveled all the way up his leg.

He reflexively wailed, but managed to call out, "Ashava, help me!"

"Kemahni!" she screamed.

Ashava dashed forth to save her kin, spectacularly dodging a barrage of incoming attacks, slipping in between yarik blades and rapidly closing the distance on the boy.

The initial shock waned from Kemahni, only to be replaced by a fear he'd never felt. A fear that children hardly think or know. A fear that comes at life's end.

A fear of death.

The Valkys opened its massive mouth, ready to receive its meal. Kemahni flailed harder, despite the pain that was mounting in his leg. He remembered the dirt still in his hands and flung handfuls of it in the mouth of the Valkys. It was enough to create an unfavorable taste for the beast, and it turned its head to spit. Kemahni took the opportunity to curl toward his ankle and bite down hard on the soft palm of the hand that held him. The Valkys yelped a high whistling sound and released him.

Kemahni fell but was able to roll in midair to orientate his feet downward. The moment he landed, his ankle reminded him of the damage, and he immediately crumpled to the ground. He cried out once more, trying to ignore the pain as he started to crawl away from the disoriented Valkys who was fast regaining its awareness.

"Ashava! Help!" Kemahni cried again.

Ashava raced faster than her body wanted, fueled by the fear of losing him to the Valkys as the mist closed around him. She burst through the cloud and was surprised by the slow swing of a massive, tree-sized arm of a hidden attacker. She narrowly missed being struck as she slid under, releasing her weapons from their holsters at the same time. Coming to a halt, she skillfully rolled away as a huge foot emerged to stomp down on her. It impacted with a force that shook her balance, but with a quick counter swing of her axe, she stabilized and planted her feet firmly.

The moment the shaking subsided, she sliced at the Valkys in her way. Her hit was precise and the wound noticeable, but she scoffed when it did nothing to deter the beast. She looked disappointedly at her axes and their lack of yarik that she wished they had. It took three more hits at the right angles to get the Valkys to fall to a knee. She launched feet first, and kicked the Valkys square in its face. It toppled over and hit the ground, releasing all the steam it had been holding in an almost harmonic sound.

The moment she landed and curved around the fallen Valkys, a second appeared out of the mist to block her. It hunched over and looked at Ashava with hungry eyes. She growled at its arrival and returned her axes to her hip. She watched and waited for the inevitable attack, and when it came, she leaped into the air.

The mighty fist of the Valkys collided with the ground, giving Ashava the back of its hand as a ramp to land on. She ran up its arm, flipped in the air to avoid its other hand that grasped at her, and threw it off balance. She landed on its back, spinning around one of the bone stacks, and tightened her legs in a crouch. She pushed with her taut legs in a snap of power, but the Valkys didn't give her a sturdy enough catapulting surface and failed to get the distance she wanted. She twisted in the air to orient herself to Kemahni, and once landed, she had to race to meet the still crawling child and pulled him to his feet.

"Can you walk?" she asked.

He hobbled and shook his head. "No..." he whimpered.

Ashava wasted no time cradling him into her arms, "Hold on to me tight."

He winced when unexpected pressure was applied to his leg as she pulled him tightly to her chest. She checked him once more, but when returning her view forward, she watched the steam cloud completely closed around them. Panic set in further, and she didn't know which way to run. More whistling calls came from before her, behind, and every which way. It echoed and rang all around, and it sounded as if she and Kemahni were surrounded by an impossible number.

The Valkys finally emerged, slow, and unceremoniously arrogant. After the seventh one appeared, Ashava stopped counting, and lowered Kemahni gently to the ground.

"Stay behind me," she deathly insisted.

With little choice, he did as she asked with a protecting push from Ashava. He held on to her waist as the Valkys advanced. She growled and yelled, wearing her voice raw, pushed up on her heels, and spread her arms wide with axes in hand. It did little to intimidate the ravenous beasts, and she quickly saw her ineffectiveness.

She tossed her axes to the side and turned back to Kemahni. "We'll be okay," she said with a false, yet comforting smile.

Kemahni attempted a return smile but barely let the corners of his lips curl. It pained Ashava that he had given up so easily. It hurt more that she had too. The Valkys behind her began to charge their powerful steam, eagerly moving in on the Manyari, almost as if they were being propelled by their steam. Kemahni heard the awful noise, but his Guardian wouldn't let him look past her to see.

"Don't worry about it. Look at me. Look at me. It's okay."

He nodded, his eyes catching glimpses of the Valkys through the gap between her arm and body.

"We're together. We'll get through it, as long as we are together."

He nodded again, a bit calmer.

Ashava scooped him into her arms once again and pulled his head close to her chest so he couldn't see. She turned to face the charging Valkys but was amazed to see they had all frozen in place, focused on a spot midway between them and Ashava and Kemahni. She loosened her grip, allowing Kemahni to peer out and see the same scene, save for the one thing Ashava didn't see.

In the field before them was the spirit zipping wildly back and forth. The entire herd of Valkys had turned to the spirit that presented itself as a bigger prize. They tracked it in unison, heads bobbing in full, sweeping motions.

"What's happening?" Ashava asked.

Kemahni wanted to explain but was transfixed by the spirit.

Two of the more eager Valkys charged their yarik. They hastily blew blades of the wind at the spirit, but it remained unafraid and faced them without moving. It seemed to immediately regret the action, as a section of its round structure was cut deeply, allowing light to pour in a fountain from its wound. The Valkys hungrily took heavy steps toward the spirit, fighting with each other for it. Without caution, they shot blasts of wind in concussive succession, though this time, the spirit evaded.

Kemahni watched intently at the spirit, nodding understandable at its sacrifice. He shook his Guardian, "Ashava, let's go!" pointing away.

The clouds lessened around the newly formed opening, revealing a path back to the village as the Valkys gave chase after the spirit that Ashava couldn't see. Kemahni quietly thanked it.

"Why are they leaving?" Ashava confusedly asked.

"Come on!" Kemahni pulled at her arm. "We have to go!"

Ashava shook from her bewilderment and listened, sweeping him back in her arms without further question, and made her way to their growing exit.

"What were those?" Kemahni asked.

"Valkys, obviously!" she said, holding him tight against her.

"But where did they come from?"

"That doesn't really matter right now. We have to tell the others."

He shifted himself to look over her shoulder and watch the Valkys disappear from sight, sinking into her with a bit of relief.

Of the stampeding horde of Valkys that fled, a dozen or so fell behind. They snorted angrily at their inability to keep pace and refocused their attention on the escaping Manyari, continuing their original pursuit.

Ashava's hands grew tired from Kemahni's weight. An old adage of *A child is not heavy until you carry them a while* jostled in her mind as they hurriedly found themselves back in their home fields. The whole of her muscles ached, but she began to feel relief the closer she got to the village, whether it be from numbness or the idea that she'd soon be able to place him down.

At the edge of town the tribe gathered, unsure if they should be concerned by the commotion they heard in the distance. In the middle of them all, Ejah had her hands raised in an attempt to calm her people.

"Let us not waste worry and panic on what we do not know," Ejah comforted. "If there was something of concern, or something had crossed our borders, the wards would have sounded."

"But Kemahni and Ashava are out there. They may be in trouble," Saleal said worriedly beside her Chieftess.

"As you said, Ashava is with him. She is well trained. They will be fine," Ejah said with secret worry.

"Ashava!" A keen-eyed tribeswoman cried out.

Everyone turned the second that Ashava hit the village perimeter, eager for information, though none wanted to ask. Ejah broke from the circle and moved to intercept, followed closely by Saleal wanting to retrieve her son.

"What's happening?" Ejah asked before Ashava came to a complete stop.

Saleal ran anxiously to Ashava, who transferred Kemahni into her arms. She hugged him tightly, crying as the worry lifted.

"Valkys..." Ashava said between breaths.

Everyone froze at the unthinkable.

"Here?" Ejah asked. "No..."

Ashava affirmed it with a worried nod.

"Why didn't the wards warn us?"

"I don't know... but they're here."

"Did they follow you?"

"No... I don't know. I don't think so." She shrugged nervously.

Saleal injected, "We need to find them before they find—"

The village.

Saleal's words cut short when she saw them. At first, it was the clouds that poured out of the fields like flood waters. Then the bone stacks that puffed steam as they swam through the tops of the flowering crops. The whistle of air changed in pitch and grew louder the closer they came.

"No…" Ejah denied and fought to not say.

The village they had worked lifetimes to hide was found, but that fear did little to stop Ejah's immediate rallying of her people. Those who couldn't fight secured the young ones and moved to the inner village. The girl of the morning horns fiercely trumpeted the songs of battle, and the Manyari organized with the efficiency of a routinely practiced drill. They formed lines, weapons in hand, and waited for more instructions.

Ashava, tired, retrieved a weapon from the village stores and stood at the front of the lines with her mother.

The Valkys finally revealed themselves from the fields, not slowing their pace. Ejah held her sword high into the air. The rest of the tribe understood the signal and readied a charge. Wind Riders, always in full gear, took positions at the rear and crouched in preparation. They rose their lances skyward and waited.

Ejah let the Valkys close the distance, and adjusted her grip on her sword. She brought a second hand to the yarik stone just above the hilt and swiped her hand across. The stone came to life and glowed responsively.

The Valkys cleared the fields, charging at their full speed through the open land before the village. As they were almost to the line, Ejah sliced her sword horizontally across the landscape and sent a blade of wind, not dissimilar to those of the Valkys. It cut through the air, widening as it traveled, and slashed deep into the square heads of the forward Valkys. Only one fell to the attack as the others continued relentlessly.

Ejah gave the first battle cry, followed by the other Manyari of Orahai who yelled in unified response. Ashava led the charge with her mother, their people following valiantly behind without reservations, into battle.

The last of the yarik ebbed away into nothing, and the shouts of battle finally lulled to low murmurs of sadness and questions. No one had woken up that morning expecting conflict and that reality was still settling in their minds.

Ashava retrieved her axe from the last downed Valkys and wiped it against the grass to clean it of blood. She had done her part, but wished she could have done more if she had more battle experience or access to yarik. She reassured herself she had done enough and was thrilled to be part of battle. Her first real battle that she quickly was finding a taste for. It was a rush she had never known, but she soon found out that she was the only one with those positive feelings.

No one said a word, and it was a surprise to see them all facing her as she returned to the village. Their attention gradually shifted to Ejah as she moved to intercept her daughter.

"How did this happen, Ashava?" Ejah needed to know.

"I don't know."

"You were there when they appeared. How did they get past our defenses?

"I don't know," her voice slightly rose. "Kemahni and I were playing games, and before I knew what was happening, Kemahni came to me. That's when this all happened. Ask him!"

"I'm asking you, Ashava."

The villagers had begun to emerge and survey the damage, Kemanhi and his mother as well. The whole of them gathered to welcome the returning warriors, treating the ones in need.

"We're okay, we won."

"I don't care about the Valkys, THAT we can handle," Ejah growled, and proceeded to point at the village and its people, "I want to know how *THIS* happened."

"Wait... *I* didn't do this. This isn't my fault!" Ashava saw Kemahni approaching and called to him. "Kemahni, tell them. Tell them what happened!"

He remained silent at his mother's side, averting his look.

"His fault falls on you, Ashava. You are the *Guardian*. You are responsible for him and his actions when he is in your care, that includes not putting him in danger." The group of people started to grow larger, and Ashava could feel the eyes on her as the Chieftess scolded her. "Most of all, you put all of us in danger. You were to keep this village secret. Keep it safe!"

"What was I supposed to do?!"

"You weren't supposed to lead them here! We keep ourselves hidden, deep in the forest to stop things like *this* from ever happening!"

"I'm confused. Have I missed something, because I protected him? Isn't that NOT the most important thing?"

"You are supposed to be smart enough not to have brought this death upon your people. We are so few," Ejah's voice cracked in pain, "this loss is too much to not go unatoned." Ejah daggered her view at her oldest daughter.

"You can't put this blame on me. If you haven't noticed, the world is dangerous and doesn't care about anyone. We pretend like nothing can hurt us here, but when something does come, we shouldn't be afraid to fight. It's horrible we had to fight at all, but we won..." Ashava's voice strained.

Ashava's focus jumped from person to person, narrowing in on the wounds and blood that covered them, until she locked eyes with the Manyari that held a fallen companion. Ashava knew that the girl probably couldn't see her through heavily watered eyes, but the look of distress was painful enough.

Another woman held her sister in her hands, struggling to carry the body. When others offered to help, crying by her side, she wouldn't accept, simply wanting to feel the weight and the dwindling heat of the body.

The responsibility of her actions was on everyone Ashava traded glances with, and the deep abyss of sorrow that overtook the day. She physically felt her worth in the tribe lessen, to a point where she understood why they looked at her as if they would trade her life for any of their fallen sisters.

"Our sisters ARE DEAD! That ultimately falls upon me, because I should have never let you think you could handle the responsibility of the outside world as you are!"

"Mother?!"

"Ejah!" Saleal said, attempting to calm the Chieftess.

Ejah turned stone faced to Saleal, who was sheltering Ejah's youngest daughter Kiyadeh with Kemahni. The side of Ejah's face quivered unnoticeably. "You can't even see what you've done and I can never let this happen again. Ashava… you are no longer the Guardian of this tribe or its son."

"No! You can't do this. I… I did the best I could!" Ashava urged. "I didn't mean for any of this to happen. I didn't…I didn't do anything wrong." Ashava's words disappeared from her throat.

Her eyes finally rested on Kemahni, who was putting his weight all on one leg, bracing against his mother. He hid his face from Ashava the moment she looked at him.

"Kemahni… I'm sorry. I didn't mean to have this happen. Not to you, not to anyone," she announced.

He buried his head further into his mother's stomach as he had with Ashava.

"Please, don't give up on me," she begged.

Ashava accepted disappointment from all around, without restraint, and finally let the death of her sisters weighed greatly on her. The Chieftess took a long breath and it made Ashava feel as if she couldn't breathe. The axe dropped from Ashava's hands and the tears came to answer her sudden flow of emotions. The guilt of those injured and the ones who lost their lives devoured what little innocence remained in her. She mourned the loss of carefree days that might never come again and the chaotic world that she learned lay outside their borders.

But mostly, she cried for how she would never be the same.

CHAPTER 4
RETURN

"You're supposed to get better with time, not worse."
- Fisher Allieghman

Waxing of the Violet Moon, Year 376 AA
Nine years later

Training Lodge, Wind Flow Crater

    The sun had already crested the high ledge of the crater walls outside Kiyadeh's room. It made her shift from beneath her covers. She rolled happily toward the light, allowing the spots like freckles on her face to show more prominently. An almost imperceptible shift in color beautifully followed the most illuminated parts of her tan, sun-touched skin, emphasizing the slashes of lines, and a slight peppering of spots on her cheeks and nose.
    The minor scales of her well-defined body flexed from her feet to her head, in a noticeable upward wave as she stretched, shining a vibrant greenish blue. She scratched at the larger scale plates at her shoulders and across her chest, reaching underneath to get more relief. Her dedication to her body had garnered her an array of defensive

scales along a majority of her vital parts. Sans clothing, she looked fully armored, like a skintight suit that moved in fluid tandem with her muscles, floating along the surface of her body.

Quietly, an unfamiliar voice entered her half-woken mind. "Do you think she is up for the task?"

"I wouldn't be much of a trainer if she wasn't," another responded.

Kiyadeh's eyes flicked open and within seconds she had flung herself out of bed. She scrambled to find each piece of her leather armor, fitting into the whole of it in less time than she ever had or thought possible. Even the armor of her spear arm, with its metal interlocking plates and multiple straps across her torso, was quickly fitted. She skipped putting her colorfully distressed tunic on over her head and grabbed her training spear resting against her barely adequate stick bedframe. She rushed out the door without further concern for much else.

The bright sun of the day blinded her as she forgot to squint before exiting. She dug her worn spear into the ground to support herself, while she waited for the momentary blindness to pass. During which her horns moved upwards, and she rotated her ears to listen for the two who were speaking. One of the voices was her trainer, Tassa, the other a cheerful feminine voice of someone who had just arrived.

Kiyadeh was quick to adjust to the light and restore her vision. She stood respectful at attention when they approached, head held high and not making eye contact.

Tassa was a specimen of a finely crafted warrior. Her body had every ounce of power needed, defined through muscle, and nothing more. Her posture told of assured skill, knowing she could strike with deadly precision from resting without warning. Scars lined her extremities along major hard scales, but nowhere else on her visible torso. One would think that if she could survive such battle wounds, that her foe would have suffered a much more dire outcome. She carried a highly decorated spear, the spear of a Wind Rider that had seen battle and taken tokens from each one. And not just her spear, her bone helmet that rested at ease on her belt was painted and adorned to signify her status.

Tassa waited until she had her student's full attention. "Glad to see you're finally awake, Yaya," Tassa said.

Kiyadeh wanted to correct her teacher for the mistake, but the childhood name had stuck ever since she nervously, and accidently, blurted it out on their first meeting. Besides, a display of displeasure would have ended in extra chores.

Kiyadeh straightened herself, "Forgive me, Tassa. I have no good reason."

"Is there ever a good one?"

The left side of Kiyadeh's mouth curled.

"Don't worry. I let you sleep in."

"Thank you, Tassa."

"Do you know why?"

"No, Tassa, I do not."

"Because it's a special day. Your special day. You see, you're done."

"Yes, Tassa…Wh, what?"

"There isn't more I can teach you. After eight years, you're as good as you're going to get."

"Oh," Kiyadeh sounded surprised. "Does that mean I'm going home?"

"Yes, you're going home. I mean, if you don't want to go back home there are plenty of things I can find for you to do here," Tassa said, amazed at Kiyadeh's lack of excitement.

"No, that's not it. This is all unexpected." Kiyadeh's lips parted in disbelief.

She let her gaze fall and equally surprised herself when she finally noticed the woman standing next to her teacher. The cloaked woman hid under her hood, her almost metallic looking red hair still very noticeable in the shadows, and smiled brightly. Her skin was a few shades darker than Kiyadeh's and had an enticing blue hue. The areas of her chin and cheeks were trimmed with larger, angular scales. Kiyadeh found it odd as to why a Manyari would train scales in such a manner, and it brought memories of the wisewoman back home, but she let her returned curiosity slide so as not to be rude.

Kiyadeh pulled her spear from the boards of the front decking of the lodge and bowed "Thank you. Thank you!"

"Don't thank me just yet. You have one more thing you need to do," Tassa said ominously. "And you can get rid of that old spear. We probably should have given you a new one a while ago."

The girl next to Tassa smirked and looked impressed with Kiyadeh that she had obtained so much with subpar equipment.

"Like you said, I have to work with what life gives me," Kiyadeh answered expertly.

"So you have been listening." Tassa raised her chin with a happy curl to her lips.

"I obviously wouldn't have gotten this far if I hadn't."

"Now, that IS a good point."

Kiyadeh winced, waiting for her teacher to add something more. "And?"

"And what?"

"I thought you were—"

"Going to point out your faults instead of your merits?"

"Well, no, not that."

"It may have taken you a moon longer to learn how to land, but you had to get it just right. And sure, sometimes you needed to be saved after those wild jumps of yours, but that's because you got into places we didn't think possible. And your insistence on taking shortcuts did find us some better paths, even if it usually ended with us searching the whole of the valley for you."

"Yeah, I remember." Kiyadeh deflated and her shoulders shrunk in.

The strange girl worked to contain her smile, unsuccessfully.

Tassa grinned astoundedly. "I threw everything I could at you, and you always, ALWAYS, found ways through it. Sometimes better than I could have ever taught you. I have never seen anyone with quite so much determination, resilience, and ingenuity as you."

Kiyadeh looked up in surprise.

"You may not have been the best student or followed my lessons while learning, but by the gods, you became the best I've ever had the privilege to teach."

Tassa gave a rare bow and warm smile that Kiyadeh was sure she'd never witnessed. The whole of her body lifted up, and her ears shot outward at happy attention.

"Th, thank you. That's why you made it so difficult for me? Why you kept me here so much longer than the others?"

"Kind of… it gets lonely out here. Mostly, I just didn't want to take care of the lodge by myself, so keeping you here until new trainees arrived seemed good for both of us. They should be arriving in a few days."

Kiyadeh might have scowled, but she was too pleased by the earlier praise.

Tassa turned to the girl beside her, who Kiyadeh realized now was holding two packages, one longer, and the other small and round. "This is Noriendi. She is the new Inyari for the Orahai, and you've been tasked to take her back with you on your return home."

Noriendi bowed. "I look forward to our journey together," she said warmly.

She grabbed the old spear from Kiyadeh and exchanged it for the longer wrapped package. Kiyadeh's eyes widened as she worked out what should lay hidden inside. She bobbed her head between looking at the package and her teacher, seeking the go-ahead to open it.

Tassa imparted an open-hand gesture, and Kiyadeh wasted no time pulling loose the ties and unwrapping the shroud.

Inside was a long, decorated spear, the length of it a head or two taller than Kiyadeh. At the attack end of the long metal shaft was a large, three-bladed broadhead with a yarik stone held inside. The other end was capped with a dagger blade. The middle section was wrapped with a leather strap for comfort, and right above and below were compartments that stored additional yarik stones for rapid exchanges. The spear felt perfectly balanced regardless of where Kiyadeh held it and incredibly lightweight despite its length. The metal was cool, not cold, to the touch and it seemed to cling to her palms where she gripped.

"You are a Wind Rider and you deserve the weapon of one," Tassa bestowed.

"This is incredible!" Kiyadeh said, elated.

"It is, but you still have to work for it."

A feeling of great expectations enveloped Kiyadeh.

"And as a gift for my protectorate, we have something else for you," Noriendi offered.

Tassa helped her uncover the second, smaller package. Inside was a highly decorated bone helmet.

"It was one of our greatfather's," Noriendi added, honorably handing it to Kiyadeh, who quickly fit it onto her head. Noriendi helped with the straps under her chin and pulled them secure. She lifted the front section of the helmet which acted as a visor. "It suits you."

"I don't know what to say," Kiyadeh said, taken aback by both the gift and sudden praise.

"You know how to thank me. Put those skills to good use and get Noriendi safely back to your home," Tassa instructed.

"I am eager for my first trip into the outside world," Noriendi said. "I have no doubt I am in good company."

Kiyadeh straightened her posture in one last show of respect. She gave an affirming nod, one to her teacher and another with a smile to Noriendi.

Afterward, Kiyadeh amassed what little belongings she had, fit the rest of her gear on properly, and secured satchels to her body. She presented herself for a final inspection.

Tassa patted her affirmatively. "Like I taught you. Good." Then she gave Kiyadeh an unexpected hug.

Kiyadeh looked into the distance with a stupor that made Noriendi laugh. Tassa released her and patted her again.

"Be careful out there, Yaya. Nevold will eat you up. It has a way of surprising you, and you have to be ready. Especially if you are going to take care of our dear Noriendi here."

Kiyadeh bowed confidently before Tassa sent the two companions on their way. She waved to them one final time before they disappeared from Tassa's sight.

"That's quite the send off," Noriendi said.

"Yeah..." Kiyadeh said, perplexed.

Once completely out of sight and ear range of Tassa, Noriendi asked, "Is Yaya your real name?"

Kiyadeh sighed heavily.

The trek up the edge of the high crater walls was the first of many obstacles and terrain they would traverse, but they did so with relative ease. Reaching the top, they were amazed at the beautiful sight of the forest and mountains that they could see for kilometers. They shared the view for a moment before starting the long journey back to Orahai.

Nine Days Later

The two travelers had cleared their first nights' worth of their long journey, veiled to anyone or anything that might find interest in them. Their journey had been quick and they would soon reach the Shelf Mountains. Not really mountains, but immensely tall plateaus and bluffs named for how they looked as if something had sheared off the top half of a mountain.

Noriendi had removed her hood while they traced the Stone Bend River to the mountain. Her level of comfort rose the longer she spent time with Kiyadeh and it was only after the second night that she decided to reveal her full face. Inyari truly were a beautiful mix of Man and Valkys. The outline of Noriendi's face was covered in hard scales, all the way to her horns, which draped past the back of her neck. They moved freely, as Kiyadeh's did, but her scales had a natural wave to them, even when resting. Her ears were also longer, but didn't have any of the hair that lined a Manyari's. Kiyadeh could only guess how the rest of Noriendi's body might differ.

The rhythm of their steps kept their conversation marching forward, though they didn't seem to have any problem finding topics.

Their almost constant dialogue and shared flask of a vibrantly green liquid called Shardroot filled the gaps between large sections of the same forest and rivers.

"You named your old weapon?" Noriendi asked.

"Yes. It's perfectly normal!" Kiyadeh defended.

"Is it?"

"Yes… I don't know. It just made me care for it more. It's silly, I know."

"Yes, but also adorable."

"I feel like you're making a joke." Kiyadeh scowled.

"Not at all." Noriendi didn't hide her smile. "What did you name it?"

Kiyadeh hesitated, and then said, "Good Point."

Noriendi looked at her perplexed. "Is that to remind you to use the pointy end?"

"No, it's something Tassa would say to me. A lot."

"Guessing never in a good way?"

"No." Kiyadeh managed a smile. "After hearing it all the time, I just wanted it to be positive."

"Is that what you're going to call *this* spear?" Noriendi motioned to the spear holstered on Kiyadeh's back.

"Good Point? No, I don't think I will name it anything."

"That's too bad, you could have named it some menacing, to strike fear," she joked.

"If you think of one, let me know."

They both had a laugh but changed the subject as if they already had another planned. Kiyadeh began to admire Noriendi's silver hair and how it shifted between different colors of whatever was around. She grabbed strands of it and let it flow through her hands. It took a bit before it completely ran through her fingers because of the length and felt enjoyably silky as it did.

"Your hair is beautiful."

"Thank you," Noriendi beamed.

"If you don't mind me asking, what makes Inyari special? Other than the hair of course."

"It makes most Manyari jealous, I know." Noriendi cracked a knowing smile. "What my hair really does is give me the power to see ghosts," she mocked eeriness.

Kiyadeh pursed the side of her mouth, and Noriendi laughed at the face.

"We get the color because we are nearer to the original union." Noriendi continued.

"Original Union?"

"Did they not teach you about that?" Noriendi wanted to retract her words, not sure if she had said too much.

"I don't think I've ever gotten the chance. Tassa was only concerned with teaching me to fight, and I was really young when I left home."

Noriendi's tone changed, "Oh…Well I am this way because I am closer to the original pairings of Valkys and Man. It's also why my scales are like this," she brushed her cheek scales, "but being an Inyari is more like a title. We ARE Manyari, we've just been chosen to live with the Ykahri in their village of Awahi. We learn from them and are sent to communities to pass information and knowledge. Sometimes we choose to stay at the places we are sent."

"Ykahri? Our Valkys ancestors? I didn't know they were still alive."

"Oh yes, very much alive and well."

"I've only ever heard stories, and they never felt like anything more. I've heard even less about the half of us that is supposedly Man, still out there living normal lives. It all feels unreal. I feel like they must have forgotten about us too. We're just stories…"

"Even if they have forgotten, we are still here living out the legacy they started, and most importantly, we haven't forgotten," Noriendi said triumphantly.

Kiyadeh took a moment to feel better about the idea, working through the feeling that she carried the history of two peoples inside her.

"Do you think there is any place where Man and Valkys live together?"

"Not in Awahi," Noriendi said disappointedly. "If there is a place where that is still happening, I don't know of it, but wouldn't that be a beautiful thing?"

"You think it could happen again?" Kiyadeh asked doubtfully.

"You do not?"

"Maybe, but it would take a lot of effort on both parts."

"Why do you say that?"

"From what I've heard, the Children of Man aren't welcoming of anyone who isn't their own, or the Valkys," Kiyadeh hesitated, remembering something, "I've seen firsthand what drives them. They are too wild to be reasoned with." She let the information wash over Noriendi. "I can't see them finding common understanding."

"We wouldn't be here if that were true." Noriendi stopped. "You shouldn't doubt anyone's ability to change."

"It's not that…"

"If they can't see their way to compromise, we have to help them. We might be the only ones who can. We are children of both, and yet, of neither. The world always seems to forget where it came from."

Kiyadeh retreated with embarrassment, but Noriendi didn't let her stay there. She grabbed Kiyadeh's hand, holding it tightly as she brought it to her face for Kiyadeh to focus.

"I want nothing more than to rebuild those unions. I would do whatever I could to make that happen, and I know you could do the same."

"Yeah," Kiyadeh took her other hand and overlapped it on Noriendi's. "You're making me start to think we could."

Noriendi bashfully smiled. "You are kind."

They took a long glance at each other before releasing their hands. They continued their walk with reinvigorated steps.

"How long did it take you to reach the lodge from your home? Awahi?"

"Not long," Noriendi answered shortly but without animus.

"So where is Awahi?" Kiyadeh probed.

Noriendi purses her lips and unconsciously looked up for a single blink. "I can't say."

"Oh."

"It's not that I don't want to tell you, but it's important that I keep it a secret. It's my duty."

"I understand," Kiyadeh muttered.

"I know you do. With the few tribes left we want to keep them safe, and there are even fewer Ykahri and only the one village. If Awahi was ever found, it could be unfortunate for everyone. Though I don't think that would ever happen."

"It would be incredible to see, I'm sure." Kiyadeh looked at the trees around her. "I've only seen about two places in my life, and they both were forests. I would leap at the opportunity to see something different."

"Maybe one day, I can take you there. When things are better."

"I'd like that," Kiyadeh dreamt aloud.

"You've been asking a lot of questions. It's my turn.' Noriendi pondered for the briefest of moments. "Why don't you tell me about your male."

"Ke?"

"*Kay*? That's an oddly short name. Did you not like him?"

Kiyadeh chuckled. "No, that's just what I call him. His name is Kemahni."

"A pet name? That sounds like a serious relationship," Noriendi said, playfully bumping into her, latching her arm around hers. She moved her face closer. "Please, tell me more."

Kiyadeh rolled her eyes, looking away, but enjoyed the feeling of their arms intertwined. "No, we were just," she hesitated, "good friends, you know?"

"I don't know, that's why I asked."

"I don't know what I can say about him, he's... a boy. They're all pretty much the same, aren't they?"

Noriendi let go of Kiyadeh's arm. "Are we all the same?" Noriendi said, slightly defensive.

"Well, no, but—"

"I have so much to teach you."

Kiyadeh frowned at the idea that she needed to be educated.

"Yaya, the male soul is as uniquely vibrant and as important as ours. Maybe even more so, since they are so rare. You shouldn't treat him lesser."

"I know that. I don't," Kiyadeh fumbled for words. "He IS very special to me. I'm pretty sure we will have First Union."

"Oh yeah? Does he know that?" She smirked.

"Well, no, but it makes sense."

"Because you were good friends?"

"Yup, the best," Kiyadeh said, not believing her own words.

Noriendi relaxed back into a happy trot. "I know it's not your fault you haven't seen many males, but that's why they are always a blessing when they arrive. Hopefully, I can help the Orahai with that problem." Noriendi tapped Kiyadeh on her unsuspecting nose. She continued walking and Kiyadeh was quick to follow. "Your tribe is lucky," Noriendi continued. "Most rarely get two Inyari in one place, even if one of us is older and may pass in the near future. There aren't a lot of us to spread throughout the tribes."

Kiyadeh remembered her Inyari, who'd seemed ancient at the time when she left home, and wondered if she could still be alive.

"How many Inyari are there?" Kiyadeh asked.

"Total? I don't know, but I grew up with eleven other sisters and I was the first of us to venture out. I had a few options where I could go so that gives me an idea. Most places I've never heard of and were in far off locations that didn't sound pleasant, but let me tell you, I'm glad I chose Orahai. I heard it was beautiful."

"It is, if you like forests." Kiyadeh smirked.

Kiyadeh instantly recounted old memories she had stored and tried to form an entire picture of the village in her head. The images weren't clear, but the feelings that returned were warm and comforting.

"If we keep this pace, I think we can be there before the next moon changes." Kiyadeh estimated.

"Let's get moving! We can camp on top of the Shelf if we make good time," Noriendi said, charging forward. "I'll even tell you a ghost story!"

Kiyadeh shook her head and jogged to keep pace. The two headed down river, along the base of the Shelf Mountains, and slowly traversed upward to the flat summit.

The sky shared the setting reds of the sun with the dark rising blues of night and stars. Opposite the sun, the moon was rising with the tip of its prismatic sea beginning to show. Noriendi stopped the moment she noticed the change in sky and quickly found the large celestial body. She moved to the edge of the bluff and lowered her head, and brought a flat, open hand to her chest in line with the moon's sea.

Kiyadeh had busied herself, finishing setting up a communal food plate in the center of their camp, still in her armor with her spear strapped to her back. She rummaged through their provisions and happily found a bottle of wine. More curiously, she found a corked bottle with a green liquid, where within floated a yarik shard wrapped in roots.

Kiyadeh stood excitedly and turned to ask, "Is this *Shardroot*?"

Noriendi, lost in prayer, said nothing as she communed with the approaching night.

"Noriendi?" she asked as she approached. "You alright?"

The quiet girl finished mouthing the last of her words and lifted her head.

"Perfectly. Just thankful for the day, and asking for a safe night."

"Does that work?"

"More than it doesn't." Noriendi tilted a curious head. "Do you not speak with the gods?"

"Not sure I believe much of that to be honest."

"No? Did something happen?"

"Not really. I don't know. I guess I've never really believed if I'm honest. I went through the rituals, said my prayers, but when I got on my own, I stopped."

Noriendi stared inquisitively, not wanting to interrupt. It made Kiyadeh wonder what she thought of the faithless, and it made her slightly embarrassed.

"I mean, I have deep respect for those who do believe. I think it's a beautiful thing, faith, even if I struggle with it."

"I don't expect everyone's view of this life to be the same. The journey to find faith and one's own truths is one we take alone and nothing is wrong as long as you look to better yourself and those around you. I believe in those who watch us from above, and that they left this world for us to be its caretakers."

Kiyadeh's eyes were alight with wonder and amazed at her conviction. She slowly followed Noriendi's gaze to the moon above with its crystal sea.

"I guess the moon does look like an eye, doesn't it?"

Noriendi laughed. "It kind of does." She paused to take a look at Kiyadeh. "I do know for sure that even if the gods are not real, the connection we have to this land, its creatures, and each other is real." Noriendi picked up Kiyadeh's hand and held it. "And we affect that flow by the smallest actions."

Kiyadeh blushed and her miniscule face scales shifted, reflecting a different color along her cheeks. She placed her other hand below Noriendi's to cradle it and smiled affectionately. Noriendi offered the same smile in return and eventually they sat together, admiring the moon and its stars in quiet stillness, hands still touching.

"I think we were meant to meet," Noriendi said.

"Me too," Kiyadeh agreed.

Noriendi finally noticed the bottle of Shardroot as the evening began to grow long.

"Careful with that, it's strong stuff if you've never had it before." Noriendi grinned.

"I haven't. May I try?"

"Of course! I may have taken three more flasks than I was supposed to." Noriendi smiled even more mischievously.

Before Kiyadeh could uncork the flask, the sound of the bottle of wine being knocked to the floor rang in their alerted ears. They removed focus from each other and slowly turned their heads to the center of camp.

Neither reacted to the creatures that blocked the sun's dying light and cast long shadows over them. Their black feathery bodies quivered slightly as they slowly lifted their arms to reveal large wingspans. They began to eat their food, prompting Kiyadeh to swing her spear around and pointed it ferociously.

The Valkys hopped defensively in the air, holding themselves aloft on cushions of yarik wind with a single flap of their wings. After calming themselves and taking the time to examine Kiyadeh's spear, they suddenly became exponentially more interested in the two Manyari. They noisily chirped between each other and landed.

"What are they?" Kiyadeh asked.

"Sukwa," Noriendi added.

"Why are there Valkys here?"

"I don't know, but there is no need to be alarmed."

Noriendi pushed Kiyadeh's arm down, felt her resistance, but eventually lowered her spear. Tensions lowered, and a head Sukwa reached out for the weapon. Kiyadeh rotated the blade to slap its claw away with the broad, flat side. The group protested and moved about but the offending Sukwa maintained its composure.

"Kiyadeh!"

"They want my spear. They're not going to get it!"

The Sukwa flinched and spread their wings again in disapproval. Noriendi hushed everyone to not let the conflict become more volatile. The Sukwa settled and became like statues when their leader spread its wings and cawed once loudly. It stepped back, and without taking its eyes off of the Manyari, retrieved the shiniest object it could find hidden in a pouch under its arm. It held out a polished silver plate and offered it in exchange.

"Give them something else, so maybe they will leave," Kiyadeh urged.

Noriendi agreed, and made no quick motions when she reached into the pouch lying next to her. She chose a yarik stone at random, and offered it with palms up and head slightly bowed.

The Sukwa moved cautiously, their heads tilted at an angle to keep one eye on the stone and the other on the spear-wielding Manyari. Kiyadeh raised her spear, and the Sukwa jumped again in defense.

"It's okay, they're not here to hurt us," Noriendi assured.

Kiyadeh listened, "If you say so," but refused to lower her weapon.

Noriendi felt a long, lead feather touch her arm before the taloned hand snatched the stone from her. The Sukwa quickly returned to its flock and they all clamored to see the stone, some attempting to take it for themselves.

"Grab your things," Kiyadeh said in quiet haste.

The two worked to not draw unwanted attention to their departure, retrieving their satchels and leaving the rest of their camp. Kiyadeh strapped her helmet to her waist belt, not having time to properly fit it. Neither looked behind them as they began to walk backwards, missing a protruding root that caught Kiyadeh's foot. She ungraciously fell, and her spear was a poor cushion when she hit the ground.

The clang echoed loudly when she hit the rocky surface and vibrated the cool metal on her back. Noriendi rushed to offer a helping hand, but when Kiyadeh reached for it, they were pushed apart by an unexpected torrent of yarik.

Noriendi was thrown through the air, caught by an awaiting duo of Sukwa. Noriendi struggled futilely, as was Kiyadeh's attempt to fight the four that landed atop her. Their clawed talons latched to each of her arms and legs, and in unison, they channeled yarik to alter the atmosphere directly around her. The pressure of the air above her increased, and the weight on her lungs made it hard to breathe. Each labored breath became harder, as a vacuum was forming to steal her air.

"Yaya!" Noriendi cries while the Valkys struggle to keep her contained.

"Noriendi!" Kiyadeh yelled between gasping breaths.

An opportunistic Sukwa reached for Kiyadeh's spear, decreasing his channeling of energy. A pocket of air opened, enough for her to turn her head and breathe. It surprised the greedy Sukwa, and Kiyadeh freed her hand. She swatted away its talons, and without much thought, reached behind her head and activated her spear.

The head of her weapon pulled apart into three sections, spinning clockwise, held in orbit by the stone that spun in opposing direction. The spear released its stored energy in a single furious burst, ejecting the Sukwa, and sending Kiyadeh skidding across the Shelf. Sparks arced from beneath her in every direction, and she could feel heat building. She quickly brought her hands to her forearms, placing the index finger of each hand to the stone on the top of her gauntlets. A quick slide down activated them, and she let her hands fall to the side.

Her fingers dipped into the rocky surface as if it was loose, pliable dirt. Her speed slowed, as she dug her right hand deep into the ground, pivoting on it and applying great stress along her arm. It lasted only until she turned on her side and was able to retrieve her spear, activating it and firing a burst of wind to counteract her swing.

She stood to see that the dry vegetation had ignited and a fire had already begun to spread. In little time, the Shelf was alight with swaying flames and billowing smoke, and from a distance the plateau looked like a mountain, complete with fire as its cap.

Kiyadeh grabbed at her shaky arm that held onto the spear, pushing away the pain, and reaffirmed her grip. She latched the spear to the clamps on her gauntlets made to help brace and distribute the stress along her arm. She knelt down while watching the Sukwa regroup. Miraculously, her helmet had stayed attached to her belt, and she calmly fit it to her head, pulling down the bone visor with great intent.

She readied herself as the four Sukwa converge with extended arms and open, clawed talons. She only needed one thrust of her legs to start her running charge, coming to full speed with her spear pointed straight ahead. As the distance closed, she pulled the spear back and summoned yarik air from within. With a final stride, she lunged forward, lancing the lead Sukwa in the stomach without sacrificing any speed.

Kiyadeh zoomed past the others that collided in a flurry of feathers. They clawed angrily at each other, squawking in obvious disapproval, before chasing their escaping prey.

Upon hitting the Shelf, Kiyadeh expelled a yarik wind that dislodged the unfortunate creature at the end of her spear, and sent herself into the final arc that would bring her to her Inyari.

Kiyadeh grinned for a split moment upon seeing Noriendi valiantly holding her ground. Noriendi had managed enough of an escape to retrieve her yarik ladened daggers but was using them only in the most defensive ways.

Noriendi cut through empty air, sending whips of water from her daggers. It was enough to keep her assailants away, but when they became more desperate and aggressive, she changed her tactics. She reversed her grip on the left dagger and slipped her pinky across the yarik stone in the hilt. The next jet of water she released froze the moment it came into contact with a Valkys. It weighed them down and they fell heavily to the ground.

Noriendi heard the whistle of another coming at her, turned with daggers crossed in defense, but was relieved when she saw that it was Kiyadeh.

Noriendi's face suddenly changed as she screamed something. Kiyadeh squinted in an attempt to read her lips, unable to hear over her speed. Noriendi's voice finally reached her, but not soon enough to warn her as she was caught mid-air by an unnoticed Sukwa.

It gripped hard around Kiyadeh's torso, pushing deep into her leather armor. Kiyadeh yelped, grabbing the talons of the Valkys and trying to pry away their grip, losing hold on her spear as she struggled to alleviate the pain. The entwined pair spun in a freefall, fighting for the top position, as the spear continued without its owner.

Noriendi checked her still frozen Sukwa before calculating the spear's trajectory. Its course would bring it over the steep slope. She shuffled backwards, leapt, and caught the spear with a firm grip, but without enough weight to counter its momentum. She landed at the very edge of the slope, slowly tipping over. With a quick touch to the stone in the shaft, the head of the spear propelled her back onto the cliff with its remaining yarik and stuck the spear into the ground to hold her footing.

Noriendi's rest was momentary as she noticed Kiyadeh still in conflict, coming ever closer to impacting the Shelf. Noriendi was quick to retrieve an *earth stone* from her waist pouch and drew a new line across it. She expelled the still useful stone from her dagger and secured the new stone with a twist. With little time to aim, she darted the dagger to near where she hoped Kiyadeh would land. The dagger sliced through the air, cutting into the rocky surface until only the hilt was exposed. The dagger vibrated and the ground swelled in successive sections, curving upward in a ramp of smooth rock.

Kiyadeh finally won her aerial wrestle, placing the battered Sukwa beneath her. A split second before hitting the ramp, she held tightly to two clumps of feathers. They impacted and bounced harshly. Kiyadeh maintained her grip, and the feathers stayed attached. The second contact with the ramp had them sliding down the stone's artificially slick surface. A line of feathers trailed them, and before coming to a complete stop, Kiyadeh hopped from the body of the Sukwa without much care.

She rushed to Noriendi, past the frozen-in-place flock, and away from the fire that was encroaching on all of them. She found her spear waiting for her but struggled to retrieve it, having to use two hands.

"Are you okay?" Noriendi asked.

"Nothing I can't handle."

"This night isn't turning out how I expected."

Kiyadeh chuckled at the dry levity.

The fire and smoke reached their edge of the Shelf. The ice-trapped Valkys panicked loudly as the flames approached. They thrashed and struggled to free themselves, the heat attacking their delicate plumage but also helping to melt the ice. It creaked and fractured until each was able to break their icy bonds.

The Sukwa left behind by Kiyadeh's flashy exit, joined their freed others, and shrieked loudly. The pack reaffirmed their pernicious intent and formed a new circle of aggression.

"What do we do?" Kiyadeh plainly asked, spear ready.

Noriendi looked carefully at each of the slowly creeping Sukwa, old scars outlining their marred past of abuse. She looked at Kiyadeh's spear covered in blood, and back to the fresh wounds that would later become lasting reminders for the avian-like Valkys. Noriendi worried their actions would do more to solidify their resentment of the world for days and moons to come. She felt herself become cold, and deactivated her weapons as she lowered them.

"What are you doing?!" Kiyadeh asked rapidly.

"We can't hurt them any more," Noriendi desperately stated.

"It's them or us."

"They're not the enemy."

"Noriendi, I've seen what Valkys can do! They are not going to let us leave here!"

The whole of Noriendi's body slouched. "They're trying to survive. We all are."

Kiyadeh's panic showed clearly on her face. "Then if you want us to survive we better do something."

Kiyadeh reasserted her position, jabbing to keep the Sukaw at bay, but Noriendi calming pushed down Kiyadeh's spear. Kiyadeh stepped back in disapproval, her foot pushing pebbles off the edge of the Shelf. She quickly glanced at them as they fell down the steep grade.

"If we aren't going to fight, then we need to leave. If we jump, we could make it."

"I can't."

"I can! I can carry us both."

"No, I can't go with you."

Kiyadeh scoffed, "Fine. Then WE fight!"

"No, Yaya," Noriendi said with a calm voice and a calmer look.

"Why all of a sudden...why are you doing this?!"

Hidden in Noriendi's hand a glow of yarik energy illuminated and flowed. Kiyadeh saw and felt the power of yarik she'd never experienced. It pulled her attention, kept it despite the eager band of approaching Valkys, or the dangerously encroaching fire that closed in around them.

"What's happening?"

"We have to do better. The world needs us to do better. All of us."

A pure, rough-cut gem rose from her hand, vibrant with lavender colors, spinning increasingly faster. The area around the stone warped and gravity pulled toward it.

"Noriendi, this doesn't make any sense."

"It'll be okay."

Noriendi offered a solemn smile. It gave Kiyadeh some peace before the yarik crystal expanded its energy in a geometric dome outwards. Kiyadeh's eyes reflected the changing tones of color before she was lifted by the outer boundaries of the dome off the top of the Shelf.

She thought she could still see inside the dome momentarily, and then a dozen new locales flashed into her mind. Vertigo took her as there was no sense of up or down, and her equilibrium shifted all about.

Her last image was of Noriendi vanishing as Kiyadeh continued to fall and a haze engulfed her. The next sensation she felt was a sudden slamming into an unknown mossy ground that knocked the wind out of her and rendered her unconscious.

Kiyadeh awoke a few hours later, lying on a forest floor, the morning sun almost to noon. Relatively unhurt, she rose to sitting, which she found not to be prudent as she felt dizzy. She waved the disorientation and searched her surroundings, unaware of how much time had passed or her whereabouts. One by one, she recognized the sounds of the forest, until she heard a river. She looked up, past the trees to confirm she was still in view of the Shelf, though they were a day away.

She felt awed by the distance and how she had been thrown so far. Noriendi's power was astounding, to a degree she hadn't seen or heard. That Kiyadeh hadn't suffered any additional major injury save for bruised muscles also amazed her. If she had been thrown that great of distance safely, her knowledge of how powerful Inyari were was significantly lacking. She was humbled by her ignorance but felt more alone than she ever had.

She took in a long breath, relaxed her shoulders, and breathed out. Every unanswered question was refused but she was unwilling to dwell on the unknown. She made a quick inventory of her spear, its remaining energy and spare stones, her pouches of items and armor. With every item accounted for, she made haste for the river to follow its path back to the mountains.

The trek was thankfully uneventful and when she reached the flat summit again, she was met with more questions. There was no sign of Noriendi or the Valkys that had previously shared the Shelf. The signs of fire were all around, burnt bushes and grass, but the vegetation had grown back a weeks' worth or more.

Calling the name of her missing Inyari failed to produce results and after wearing her voice, Kiyadeh laid in the new grass and watched the night sky return again.

CHAPTER 5
GUARDIANS

"Understand, you must love him more than yourself."
- Chieftess Ejah

Half of the Green Moon, Year 376 AA
26th autumn of the Orahai

Seven Steps Forest

"Kemahni!" Ashava's obviously annoyed shout shrieked between the trees, carried by a fury not easily quelled.

He looked back only when he heard his name vibrate inside his body from the timber of her voice.

Oh...she's really angry today, Kemahni thought happily.

As Kemahni had come into adolescence, his hard scales were much more robust and covered a larger portion of his chest and shoulder. His sleek outline was chiseled by his well-defined physique and was a bit more muscular compared to his sisters. As with older Manyari, he had garnered patches of larger scales over time in places where he would come into contact with the world or where it was needed to protect him. It normally took years for scales to react and enlarge themselves, but Kemahni had already grown his fair share.

Everyday his strength grew, and so did his prowess for evading capture. He bounded through his forest playground, his sanctuary where each path was perfectly memorized, and where he had chosen to evade his Guardian Ashava. He knew every rock and every stone. Every root that jutted out and the distance between trees. He could even judge the rigidity of the branches by their diameter.

He built up speed and leaped over a rock to enjoy the air for that split second when he was weightless. When it came time to land, he didn't appear to prepare for it, letting himself collapse into a roll, and immediately returned onto his feet.

"Kemahni!" his Guardian called once more.

He peered over his shoulder again to judge her location, his horns shifting in the wind, and ears wildly scanning. He returned his gaze forward, smiled, and ran faster. The generous lead he had helped to keep his worry off the rattling yarik stones in his pouch. He thought he had concealed his most recent heist, but she had come so soon after, he wondered if she knew. It would explain her fury if she'd confirmed the theft. He knew painfully well that he wasn't allowed to touch them and the punishment if he did, but he had trouble listening those days, especially when he didn't understand the reasons why males were prohibited from doing so much.

Why the rule against using yarik, he wasn't sure, for he hadn't found a way of accessing the power from stones, despite countless attempts. It might have not been a warning, but more of a truth, that he did not possess the power at all, as his sisters did. Maybe he was too young or there was a trick to it. Maybe he was just like Ashava, though he still didn't comprehend why she couldn't use yarik either.

"Kemahni...," the demand for his reveal came again, though a bit more subdued.

Trying to sound calm? At least she's trying something different, he thought, and immediately doubted the sincerity. He could still hear that bit of screeching hidden in her voice.

Every time they would take on their roles of predator and prey, he honed his abilities. He looked forward to it, despite how much it pained him that they did not connect any longer. It at least made for less dull days. It was almost like they were still playing games. Ashava, however, was not playing. His increasing ability to escape aggravated her to no end, and she'd refuse to admit she couldn't keep up with the changes or that she was failing to keep him in check.

Ashava nervously massaged the hard scales on the back of her hands. The amount and size of the scales made her hands look like armored gauntlets. Leather wrapped around and in between her scales protected the softer underside of her forearms. It was not only her hands that had groomed hard scales, but her shoulders were also dense and honed to points, as well as her feet. Her horns fanned flat against her head, wider than most and jagged. Despite a rough exterior, she had developed into the perfect match between alluring beauty and the fierce strength of a proven fighter. She had become the definition of a warrior goddess.

Unfortunately, any radiance that might have been was not at all present while she hunted for Kemahni. Her face contorted strangely, and her nostrils flared. An unconscious twitch in her ears worsened the longer she went without finding him, and she could barely focus her hearing on anything.

Tahdwi was at her side while they searched together, unhurried through the forest. They both suddenly stopped at the wild sounds in front of them. Tahdwi listened closer to pinpoint the noise, while Ashava slipped her hand down the handle of her axes and released the buckles. She gripped the simple, scarred and unadorned weapons. That part of the woods still made Ashava anxious, and she hadn't completely steeled herself against those memories, but refused to show fear and pressed on.

"Just come out already. I don't want to spend all day chasing you!" Ashava blurted.

Still keen to evade her, Kemahni knew he'd eventually have to give up and return to her care, but he'd push her tolerance to the limit, if only for fun.

He grinned at the thought of her *ugly face* shouting as he skidded to a stop and whipped around the large face of a boulder, the same boulder he had hid under years ago. Though he could have sworn the boulder had previously been kilometers away, on the other side of the wards. Somehow, it had shifted to this location without any signs that someone had moved it. Or maybe he was remembering wrong and the forest had grown past it. He still claimed it as his own and enjoyed it as a waymarker.

He rapidly cleared brush around its base and blissfully rummaged through his hideaway, where he pulled out a hidden satchel. Inside were dozens of other stolen yarik stones and shards, most of them looking dull and spent. He grabbed into his rough, dirtied trousers that were cut off at his knees, down into a small pouch. When he pulled his hand out, he had a fist full of other stones that still had a bit of yarik energy pulsing in them.

The energy in the stones quickly seeped away as if a leak was letting the yarik escape. He watched disappointingly, accepted them as defective, and added them to the hidden satchel. He pulled the strings tight again, pushed it back underneath the rock, and secured his pouch in his trousers.

"Kemahni!" Ashava's yell sounded uncomfortably close.

Game's not over yet, he thought, quickly covering his hideaway, rolling backwards and onto his feet. He disappeared into the forest, and a few moments later, Ashava and Tahdwi stood in the exact spot he had vacated.

"I don't like how often he's doing this," Ashava grumbled under her breath. "He knows how to get past the wards and that's a real problem."

"What is?" Tahdwi asked, half listening as she was distracted by a flower at her feet.

Ashava turned to Tahdwi, restating angrily, "Somehow he's getting past the wards without setting them off or us knowing about it."

A thought sprung into Ashava's head: *Did he turn off the wards back then?*

"Oh, that is a problem. You said it's been happening for a while. We should probably tell someone," Tahdwi said nonchalantly.

"I can't."

"You can't?"

Ashava sighed heavily. "I can't tell anyone that he can get past the wards without us knowing. Everything he does is still my responsibility and he needs to stay happy."

"Happy?" Tahdwi asked as if she misheard.

Ashava shook her head, "I'm not going to let everyone have another reason to call me a failure by finding out I can't control him."

"No one thinks you're a failure."

"If only that was true." Ashava changed the subject before Tahdwi could counter again. "Don't worry about it. Just help me find him," she asked through mildly clenched teeth.

Tahdwi saved that conversation for later and noticed footprints and trampled moss close to Kemahni's hidden stash. "He was just here."

"Why doesn't he listen!?" Ashava asked the world.

"It's what happens when two people are alike."

Ashave craned her neck slowly in disapproval. "Him and me? You can't be serious."

"Both of you are lost in the world and neither one wants to admit it… or ask for help," Tahdwi said with a careful smile. "Don't you worry, it won't be this way forever. We'll all get through this," Tahdwi finished soothingly.

"Oh, I'm not worried, because I'm not gonna let him see his next birthmoon."

Tahdwi moved into her friend's peripheral, trying to calm Ashava's storm and the anger she could almost feel rising off her.

With an infectious smile, she said, "Remember, there are fewer moons as Guardian in front of you than behind. You've lasted ten summers, the next few should be easy. You won't have to be a Guardian forever."

"You know, I don't even care anymore," Ashava said, displeased with everything, including Tahdwi's mild disbelief. She slid past her, calling, "Kemahni, I HOPE SOMETHING EATS YOU!"

Tahdwi was taken aback by Ashava's outburst. She touched one of her earrings and rubbed it between her fingers gently. The roughly cut gem glowed slightly and wind sang past her hair. She grabbed Ashava lovingly by the face to look deeply into the troubled girl's eyes.

"Well, that would be no good for anyone, would it?" Tahdwi paused. "Then you wouldn't be able to keep your promise to me." Her words sang melodically, and immediately Ashava's face calmed a bit. "It'll be okay."

"You're right," Ashava said with reluctant defeat, "let's just go find him."

Tahdwi read Ashava's face for the return to calm, smiled, and then pointed in the direction she was sure Kemahni had gone. They traveled closely, holding hands as they went deeper into the forest.

Kemahni surveyed the path ahead and knew that a main trail through the less dense part of the forest was approaching. It was how most Manyari chose to return home, and it had crossed his mind to use it and end the chase early today. It wouldn't lessen the tired lecture about following the rules but he would have loved to not have that talk altogether. Luckily, one of his other growing skills was to feign sincerity when he apologized and reassure them it would not happen again. It worked mostly, for no one truly wanted to chastise him too harshly. He was the Son of Orahai, and staying in his good graces was usually beneficial for wanting tribeswomen.

But that concern was for a later time, for his favorite leaping point was fast approaching and required his utmost attention. A large stone, about his height, that had been there since he started his escapades beyond the wards, was his favorite object in the entire forest. He liked the way it looked like a face, and how, when he jumped onto it, it made him feel like he was conquering a giant. The *giant's head* helped him gather the height needed to clear the main trail in a single bound. He enjoyed the challenge and wouldn't miss the opportunity today, no matter how close he was to capture.

Who said Wind Riders are the only ones who can fly, he thought.

In one smooth motion, he hopped on top of the rock, firmly planted both feet, and launched into the air. *Perfectly executed,* his body told him. He'd definitely make it all the way across the path, not that it would have been his first time.

In the last few months, he'd cleared the gap a dozen times, but today he could feel his blood pump faster, his muscles pushing extra hard, and it sent him sailing gracefully in an arc. It gave him that rare feeling of knowing he couldn't have done better if he tried.

But his jump wasn't the problem.

While in his perfect jump, he was suddenly met with a Manyari girl standing in the middle of the trail. Not Ashava or Tahdwi. It was someone he didn't immediately recognize but couldn't dismiss as unfamiliar. She must have heard his ruckus and, out of concern, had her spear drawn. When she saw the soaring boy, she could only offer a weirdly surprised look.

Kemahni locked curious eyes with her in mid-flight and reciprocated the look of utter surprise. A spark of remembrance came to him and buzzed about in his brain.

Where have I seen you before? he wondered.

Her markings were so recognizable to him. It was like she was from a lost dream that suddenly resurfaced. He was amazed by her colorful distressed warrior's tunic and the leather layered armor with open areas for mobility. Most noticeably though, was the large spear she wielded that looked new at first glance, with it's highly polished metal, but noticeably scratched the longer one would look.

Kiyadeh had found her way home.

She lowered her spear. "Ke?"

A split second later, he was tumbling through the bushes on the other side of the trail. He felt embarrassed, the kind of embarrassment that would sting every time you remembered it and would never disappear as there were witnesses.

Kiyadeh shook her head in astonishment. "Hey, are you alright?!"

"Ugh," he cried softly.

She looked down the end of his path of destruction to find him, but the flora was thick and she didn't see him.

"Kemahni!" Ashava's yell came again, louder and closer.

She stopped searching, stood, and turned toward the sound. Her face remained calm, but she squinted in remembrance.

"Damn it." Kemahni's muffled exasperation came from within a large fern right before he bolted out and headed away from the girl and his inbound Guardian.

"Wait a second. Stop!" Kiyadeh stumbled over both her words and steps. Within seconds, he was gone and she had lost track of him.

She looked at her once injured arm and rotated her shoulder a few times to test her mobility. Satisfied, she pulled down the visor of her bone helmet and peered through the holes with excitement, waving her hand purposefully above the triangle blade and its neatly shaped stone in the center. The head transformed, blades orbiting each other while brightly glowing whips of wind flowed all along the shaft of the spear.

Expertly, she crouched down and placed her right hand on the ground and the stone placed in her bracer glowed as it began to shift the ground beneath her. She tightened her legs and readied herself properly. The ground trembled beneath her, and when the wind increased to a furious point around her, she pulled her hand off the ground.

A straight cylinder of rock shot up beneath her and propelled her upwards as she stabbed her spear into the air. Her spear cut a vortex of wind through the trees above, into a wide arch over the canopy, soaring in Kemahni's direction. Moments later, the stone cylinder collapsed into a pile of dirt.

Kiyadeh loved the moments of perfect equilibrium when one was neither floating skyward or being pulled back to the earth. She wanted to enjoy the feeling and nothing else, but knew she couldn't waste the apex of her jump and looked for Kemahni through the forest canopy.

Fortunately for her, he only searched behind and not up for pursuers.

She began her descent and judged his direction against her own trajectory. With a small burst of wind from her spear, she corrected course to place herself far enough in front of him to be out of view. After the last burst, she started to fall with an accomplished smile.

Another quick swipe of her hand over the blade made it spin again and summoned a large amount of yarik wind at the tip. She spun her spear forward and under her left arm, grabbed further up the shaft, and focused all the wind at a point in front of her. The closer she came to the ground, the more turbulent the wind became, and a meter before she impacted, she slowed as the wind cushioned her like a pillow. Her spear dug into the ground and gently lowered her the last few centimeters.

Before the plumes of dust had yet to settle, the hurried footsteps of Kemahni hit her ears.

What? How'd he...he wasn't going THAT fast, she'd thought, hoping she'd have more time.

The loudening steps made her rush to hide behind a tree in an awkward shuffle. She listened secretly to his approach, her ears wildly trying to place his location. It sounded as if he was changing his direction randomly.

Did he see me? She wondered disappointingly, less certain of her choice of landing spot.

She directed her ears as far out from behind the tree and swore he was still on a direct path to her. She hugged her back against the tree, rapidly tied a rope to the end of her spear, and reactivated the crystal. The yarik spun the spear blurringly quick, and with half a second of aiming, she effortlessly javelined the spear. It drilled itself into a tree across from her, and she gave a quick tug to confirm the spear and rope line were secure. She gave it slack and let it lay inconspicuously on the ground, squatting in anticipation, and with each approaching step, her body tightened like a spring.

Kemahni appeared from the brush, running at his full speed, completely unaware of her trap.

Patiently she waited, *Almost. Almost*, she thought, judging his final steps towards her. *Now!*

Her body jolted into action, pulling hard on the rope. Kemahni had but a blink to react, hardly enough time to even process what was happening, as the rope cracked hard against his chest. It knocked the wind out of him, but didn't stop his momentum from sending him sprawling wildly ahead, over the rope, and landing head first into the dirt.

Kiyadeh popped her head out. "Oh," she said as she caught the end of his crash.

She rushed over and stood shamefully above him, pulling her visor up to survey the damage.

"I'm sorry, I didn't think you'd…" There was little more than a groan from his curled up, contorted position. "Hey, Ke, are you okay?"

That time, there was no response.

She groaned as well and bent down to turn him over. His dead weight was an unwelcome surprise. *How hard did you crash?* She gave him a quick inspection and dusting off.

"Great," she said sarcastically to herself.

It wasn't hard for her to add another failure to her list since, in her mind, harming a male was only slightly worse than arriving home without her Inyari travel companion.

Her mind went to a dark place, seeing herself carrying his limp body back to the village, and saying nonchalantly, '*Sorry.*'

She focused on his calm face and felt sorry for him, placing a soft hand on his face. A bit of life returned to Kemahni as he shifted below her.

"Ke, hey, come back to me!" She shook him once gently.

He still didn't give a proper response.

"C'mon, you're okay. You didn't tumble that hard."

He slowly regained consciousness and opened his eyes to the beautiful sight of a halo surrounding the girl above him.

"Ke…," the soft voice beckoned him. Not Ashava, but something close, something very familiar that brought him back to younger days. "Talk to me," she said.

Someone is worried about me? he wondered. "Tahdwi?" he asked aloud.

"No, Ke," she sounded displeased.

"Kemahni!" Ashava suddenly screeched from nowhere.

Fear stabbed into a deep, primal part of his mind and revived him in a furious panic. He slid away from underneath the girl, unconcerned with his pain or identifying who she was. He quickly stumbled to the tree where the spear was implanted and used it as a step. He awkwardly grasped the trunk with both his arms and legs, shimmying up in a desperate attempt to hide. Kiyadeh, slightly annoyed at his mistreatment of her spear, let him escape, unable to react to the absurd spectacle.

From up in the tree, Kemahni wearily demanded, "Don't say anything. Don't tell them I'm up here."

"What? No. Come down before you get us trouble." She cracked a half smile. "More trouble. Your Guardians are already looking for you."

"Pleeeaaase?" he pleaded sincerely. She thought about it but, before she could answer him, he callously added, "or I'll tell them you attacked me."

"Attacked you?!" She angrily ripped her spear from the tree. It made Kemahni climb up one branch higher, like a scared animal. "I hardly call that attacking you. I was stopping you from running away." She circled her spear around her waist and walked backwards away from the tree, staring up at him. "This is the last time I'm going to ask... Come down, or I'm going to jump up there and bring you down."

"That's not even asking."

"Then you better just come down." Neither one moved from their standoff. After a while, she shook her head. "Fine, I'm coming up."

Just as she was about to activate her spear and launch into the tree after him, Ashava and Tahdwi appeared from the tall bushes behind her. Ashava had taken a deep breath and cupped her hands around her mouth to call out again, but stopped herself when she saw the girl standing there with her weapon drawn. Kiyadeh returned Ashava's stunned look and was moved slightly by her arrival.

Kemahni eyed them curiously from his tree, watching their interaction and waiting to learn his fate.

Ashava let the air release from her lungs and lowered her hands. "Kiyadeh. You're home."

Kiyadeh holstered her weapon. "Yes, sister, I'm home."

CHAPTER 6
SISTERS

"They say we're related. Sometimes, I wonder."
- Yarin Takks

There was no denying the relation between the two girls. Those same iridescent eyes, striking face that came to a soft point, and the strong, yet elegant, bodies they'd been graced with. Yet, there were differences. Most obvious was the height, drastic to the point that Kiyadeh had to tilt her head down to make eye contact with her sister.

Ashava hadn't seen Kiyadeh in quite some time, and was less than happy with having to look up, considering Kiyadeh was younger. In Ashava's mind, the older sister should be the first in all things, always leagues ahead of any sibling that followed. The idea felt like a lie when she looked at her sister now, who stood as much as a formidable warrior as her, but even more so with the ability of yarik.

Kemahni amused himself at how he had somehow missed the obvious resemblance. From what little he knew of their relationship, their body language wrote tomes of familiarity, but not of affection. Familiar enemies.

Ashava slowly stood straight, stretching out a few more centimeters without looking awkward, and placed a hand on her hip with the other on the axe strapped to her thigh.

Kiyadeh wasn't intimidated, and countered by digging her spear into the ground and leaned against it slightly. Then she waited. Waited for Ashava to say something. A *hello*. Something befitting of a returning family. Anything. But the silence grew and nothing was said.

Tahdwi endured the pause for as long as she could, poorly containing her joy as she ambushed Kiyadeh with a hug.

"Kiyadeh!" Tahdwi cheered.

"It is her," Kemahni whispered from up in the tree, than fearfully covered his mouth.

Kiyadeh braced herself, but quickly fell into a long, heartfelt embrace with Tahdwi.

"Welcome home," Tahdwi said, muffled in Kiyadeh's shoulder.

"Thanks, Tahdwi." She wanted to add that it was *good to be home*, but lying to the light-hearted girl wasn't in her.

Tahdwi's smile had a way of convincing people to feel as she did, to want to tell her one's woes. No matter what someone said, it wouldn't faze her, and if at all possible, she would do what she could to make it better.

Kiyadeh watched Ashava over Tahdwi's shoulder, as she turned away from watching the exchange. *She's still angry at the world*, Kiyadeh thought. They released each other, but not before exchanging one more happy glance.

Kiyadeh waited again for acknowledgement from her sister, but the silence became unreasonably lengthy, and she wasn't about to spend all day staring at her sister under the hot sun.

"It's good to see you, Ashava," Kiyadeh said.

"I'm sure Mother will be happy you're home," Ashava commented.

"And you're not?"

"I was sure you'd be crying your way back home after a few weeks, seeing as you didn't want to go in the first place."

I remember that, Kemahni thought, as he recalled how she'd wanted him to go along with her.

"This is a funny way to welcome your sister back that you haven't seen in, what," Kiyadeh looked up to count the number, "six years?"

"Seven, but I don't have the time to listen to your stories. I'm busy," Ashava said disinterestedly as she continued looking around for Kemahni.

"Too busy for your sister?"

Tahdwi quickly interjected to ease her own anxiety, "Forgive us, Kiyadeh, we've been running around all day looking for another Manyari. He's been difficult to find," Tahdwi said sheepishly.

"He?"

"Yeah," Tahdwi replied ashamed, and suddenly laughed nervously, rubbing her earring. "We're just playing a game, ya know? And losing apparently." She laughed again, with Ashava looking wide-eyed at Tahdwi's slip.

A coy smile grew on Kiyadeh's lips, "Tell me this isn't a regular thing, Ashava. Losing our boy is pretty serious, don't you think?"

Without holding back her contracted face, she bit her lip and smiled through angry teeth. "All that training and your fancy weapon must make you think you're tough, talking to me like that. But don't think that just because of all this," she motioned with a fluttering hand, "that you're a better fighter than me. I'd take you in second." Ashava relaxed her tone. "But I really don't have time to set you straight," she finished and, turning her back on Kiyadeh once more, headed away, sweeping her eyes around the clearing.

Kiyadeh wanted to applaud Ashava's acting. "Well, I'll try not to worry about it too much," she spilled sarcasm, "since you are his Guardian. I'll just let you worry about losing Kemahni."

Ashava stopped looking about and calmed herself. "I pray to the gods that you at least aren't dumb enough to be hiding him from me. He isn't your personal little toy anymore, Kiyadeh. You two got away with acting like spoiled children because you were young, but we aren't playing games anymore."

"I thought that was exactly what you were doing."

Ashava pursed her lips in anger. "Just to let you know, if I get in trouble for this, so will you. I know you know something because you always made that same stupid face when you were trying to hide something."

The smile slowly left Kiyadeh's face. "I hope you find him," she returned flatly and pulled her spear from the ground.

The derision made her forget about the elusive boy in the tree, and all she wanted to do was get away.

Ashava watched Kiyadeh begin to leave and suddenly found a smile. "Hey," she called out, "aren't you traveling a little light?"

The power was pulled right from Kiyadeh's stride.

"Where's the Inyari?" Ashava grinned as Kiyadeh froze in place. "You know what, forget I said anything. Enjoy that talk with Mother. Come on, Tahdwi," Ashava barked, grabbing Tahdwi's hand and pulling her along.

"We're going?" Tahdwi whimpered. She gave an awkward, hasty wave goodbye to Kiyadeh as she was carelessly dragged away. "Wi— winds carry you, Kiyadeh!" she blessed, and before long, the two vanished back into the forest.

She felt uneasy about it all. Her return should have been a heralding event, but she knew it was a walk of the disgraced like her sister had accurately surmised. Kiyadeh's family should have been there to console her, but that hope had died as soon as the conversation began.

Their bickering used to be more or less harmless, playful even, but there wasn't that hint of joviality in Ashava's voice anymore. Kiyadeh had bore witness as a child to the events that made Ashava who she was today, but Kiyadeh never expected her to be so scornful. Had she not been sent away almost immediately thereafter, she might have helped Ashava, but she hardly recognized her now. All she saw was a stranger.

Kiyadeh mused at the short-lived reunion with Kemahni, as it distracted her from the harsh truth of her last few weeks. She wished to have his carefree life, with only the responsibility of a child. She envied him and would have been content to chase him forever through the Seven Steps and forget what was happening in the rest of the world. But dreams were dreams, and the sound of Kemahni deftly landing on the ground suddenly reminded her what had led to this place.

She cringed at the idea of him watching the whole conversation unfold, judging both of them.

What he must think, she wondered.

"That was close," he said with a relieved sigh, bouncing around, spry as ever.

Maybe nothing, she guessed from his reaction. "You're welcome, Ke."

"Ke..."

"You don't remember me, do you?"

"I do. Yaya."

Kiyadeh laughed. "You know you were the only one that used to call me that..." Until Tassa. And Noriendi. "Do you still have trouble saying my name?"

"No...," he said bashfully.

"Just call me Kiyadeh, okay?"

"Sure."

They both let the uneasiness fill the air.

"Why'd you act like you didn't remember just now?" Kiyadeh asked.

"It's not that I didn't remember, it's just...I was surprised. No one calls me Ke anymore," he trailed off. "Not even Ashava." He quickly changed the subject. "I suppose I should thank you."

"It'd be nice."

"Well...thank you for not telling them were I was," Kemahni said cheerfully.

Kiyadeh smiled slyly, devising a new plan of returning with him. If she could bring the 'Son of Orahai' home safely, it could be a way to dull the edge of the harsh news she would have to break to her mother, and at the very least show that she could keep one person safe in her care.

It would make quite an entrance. I'd be a HERO...until I wasn't. While she mulled over her plan, Kemahni looked curiously at her with almost submissive eyes. She read his face, and then a random thought came to her. *His life with Ashava couldn't have been easy. I can't imagine what it must be like for him to have her as a Guardian after that day. I still can't believe they let her.*

She closed her eyes for a moment and took a deep breath. "Relax. I won't say anything."

"Good," he said, as if he hadn't been afraid at all. "So, um, I guess... welcome home."

The smile once again returned to Kiyadeh's face, and she was shocked how desperately she needed kindness. Coming from him made it special for a reason she couldn't immediately understand. "Thank you."

Kemahni soon returned to acting as if everything was normal, though he did look a bit anxious now. "I guess I owe you," he said unwittingly.

"Yeah you do," she replied, lowering her gaze. "When I ask for my payment, you'll know. All you have to do is say yes."

"Oh...kay..." he said, wary of her look. It was predatorial and it scared him. He decided now would be the best time to leave, but he'd only taken a few steps when he felt the shaft of her spear tap him on his shoulder. "What? I wasn't gonna run!" he lied.

She lowered herself down the shaft of the spear until her face was a centimeter from his. She smiled with confidence, and a long, unsettling moment passed.

"Then we have a deal," she said. After a final deep look into his eyes, she casually stood and holstered her weapon. "Let's go," she beckoned, confident he would follow.

Kiyadeh walked victoriously away, with the idea of a prize that would make anyone in the village insanely jealous. All she had to do was stick close and make sure he fulfilled his end of the bargain.

Meanwhile, Kemahni had a sinking feeling that churned his stomach in ways he'd never felt before. He had just acquired another female to watch over him and critique his every action. Another bit of freedom was forfeited, and yet he was somehow okay that it was her.

That it was Kiyadeh.

CHAPTER 7
RELIEF

"Everything is equal...some are just better for the situation."
- Stonecrafter Xoma

Later that evening

Orahai Outskirts

Kiyadeh gave Kemahni a wide breath as she led him back into the village. Rain clouds in the distance looked full and ready to pour. The road and the fields that surround Orahai were relatively vacant, and the few Manyari that remained were finishing up random chores, not noticing the Son of Orahai's return with someone other than his Guardian. Most didn't know when Kiyadeh would be arriving home, and she wondered if anyone would remember her after the long absence. She didn't expect an excitable crowd of people to greet her, but it would have been greatly appreciated.

In the dimming light of day, she could still make out the shapes and forms of the village, a silhouette she remembered well that hadn't changed much, if at all. It made her feel as if she hadn't been away, and she soon felt the safety that only came from being home.

She unknowingly smiled, and Kemahni caught a glimpse of it while she was distracted.

As he twisted his torso more, he began to walk in a strange, almost sideways shuffle. The more he turned, the more exaggerated his steps were, but he wanted to make sure he was seeing her face correctly.

"What?" she questioned when she noticed him staring and walking crooked.

"Nothing," he quickly answered. He locked his head forward, at attention, and walked straight again.

She ignored his obvious deflection and went back to admiring the village that grew bigger with each step. The road had gradually started to fill with other villagers, returning for the day, baskets in hand and provisions to last them another few nights. Kiyadeh didn't notice the bubble that seemed to surround Kemahni and her, but he did immediately. It was their form of respect, where he would be given the right of way, but never too far as to not be noticed. It was as if he was plagued by something beautiful. Something everyone wanted to see, but no one wanted to get near.

They took the opportunity to acknowledge him with a proper hello and compliments, but at best, it was a poor attempt at courtesy and didn't help the feelings that most of them only did it out of obligation. He hated how different it made him feel but adapted to their platitudes, refusing to worry about the things he couldn't change.

Kiyadeh had moved closer when she finally noticed the perimeter of other villagers sharing the road, making sure it was known that they were a traveling pair. By the time they had reached the edge of town, she was but a large step from Kemahni and had to place a hand out to brace herself on his back when he came to an abrupt stop.

"Why'd you stop?" she asked.

She hadn't heard or seen the duo of Wind Riders descend near Chieftess Ejah, who shielded her eyes from their landing, but Kemahni had seen the line of important people waiting for his return and remorsefully looked away.

Chieftess Ejah, Kemahni's mother Saleal, and Ashava, made a small circle around the guards for information.

"We haven't found him," one of the Wind Riders immediately said, lifting her visor.

"He'll be back anytime now," Ashava predicted.

"You shouldn't be so calm about this," Ejah voiced, on the edge of upset. "If anything has happened—" Ejah cut her sentence short and gently parted her people. "She is home," the Chieftess said slowly.

Ashava scowled in disapproval of her mother's reserved joy. Saleal simply held her hand out, and without question, Kemahni went to her. She swooped him under her arm and held him close, but not before giving him the 'disappointed mother' look. He held her tight as an apology. The other family would have their own discord.

"You're a bad liar," Ashava said.

Ejah, missing Ashava's words, approached her daughter. She welcomed her safe return but slowly grimaced.

"You're alone." Ejah questioned, waiting to be corrected.

"She didn't make it?" Kiyadeh confirmed with a sorrowful nod and averted her eyes.

The beginnings of rain pattered the ground. A worker finishing in the fields, ran back quickly to activate the yarik boulder to receive the rains.

"I am glad that you are home safe. Come, we'll all speak further, indoors." Ejah said calmly and turned to lead the group back to her hut.

Her mother's welcome wasn't much warmer than Ashava's, and still not the reception Kiyadeh wanted. She didn't resent the response, she knew Ejah was Chieftess first and mother second, and was ready to accept the consequences of her actions.

Ashava emphasized being the last to turn her back to Kiyadeh and strode away seemingly satisfied. Kiyadeh didn't notice Kemahni being pulled away by his mother next, and stood frozen for a moment.

Kiyadeh's mind floated back to the time when she had a companion at her side. A silvery-haired girl who she'd rewrite time to spend one more day with.

Chieftess's Hut

A chill of evening air seeped in through the laced woven divisions in the animal hide walls. The cold and rain was taking its chance to steal warmth from the room. Ejah fought back by reaching into one of the metal clawed holders that haloed the main supports, and traced new and different lines over those that already glowed radiantly on the yarik stones.

Her fingers started at the base where there was no fire and pulled upwards. The thick, red stone wasn't hot at all, and the fire moved out of the path of her finger while she worked. When finished, the flame grew higher and wider at the peak of the stone. It cracked and popped, not unlike wood when it suddenly released trace amounts of water as trapped steam, looking similar to earth cracking under pressure. The random sounds added a nice atmosphere to the almost pure silence in the room.

Ejah, at very least, wanted to make the environment as comfortable as possible before she had to address any important questions.

She returned to her seat made of wicker stalks and leather cured hides, where she rested near one of the larger yarik stones that ebbed pulses of heat. She composed herself and grimly surveyed everyone's sitting arrangement; how they polarized themselves, cardinal to the other.

Kemahni and his mother sat directly in line with Ejah, as she wet her lips in anticipation to speak. Kemahni leaned against his mother for support but only got a mild response as he pushed into her since she was distractedly waiting for the Chieftess to break the silence.

Ejah's daughters sat as far apart as they could; Ashava, to the left and closest to their mother, with Kiyadeh opposite and close to the wall. Kiyadeh hadn't looked at Ashava the entire time she was in the hut, unwilling to give her the satisfaction of meeting another self-aggrandizing smile. Kiyadeh focused on her mother as well.

Kemahni had no real grasp of what was happening, anxious from the tension and lack of speaking. He prayed that he would not be the main topic or used to start any arguments. He wasn't a stranger to mild discipline but knew the more severe punishments were saved for others that failed to uphold the tribe's ways.

"Kiyadeh," Ejah spoke after breaking her long stare into the fire.

"Yes, Mother?" Kiyadeh answered, sitting up in attention.

"What happened to the Inyari?"

Kiyadeh nodded and said, "Noriendi," wanting them to know her name, and looked sorrowfully into her mother's eyes. "She's gone. I... failed to protect her."

Ashava scoffed, and her mother glanced at her harshly, informing her that her input was not necessary.

"What happened?" Ejah asked.

"Valkys. Sukwa. We were on top of the Shelf when they attacked us."

"Sukwa? Have they really come that far?"

"They seemed desperate but wouldn't take anything we offered. They tried to take my spear."

"Hmm...I've never known them to bother with any stones, let alone have a want or need for them. I wouldn't doubt they were pushed out of their homes and were looking for any type of resource."

"Pushed out, by who? Other Valkys?"

"More likely Man is expanding their territories again," she reluctantly admitted.

Kiyadeh's words fell low. "All I know is there was more than we could handle and... she sent me away. She saved me, somehow. When I returned to look for her, she was gone. I am sorry."

"Sorry? That's all you have to say?" Ashava interjected again.

"Ashava," Ejah's motherly tone rose.

"She doesn't seem that affected by the loss, I mean. She doesn't even have a scratch on her. Did you even try to save her?" Ashava sniped.

Kiyadeh stood up, grabbed her spear near her and jabbed it into the ground with the scratched surface facing her sister. Ashava was slightly surprised by the damage of her weapon, but only showed it momentarily.

"You weren't there, and you don't get to tell me that I wasn't affected!?" Kiyadeh snapped. "I did everything I could, everything I was trained to do, and yes, I know I failed her. I will never see her again, and I have to live with that guilt."

"Yeah, but it's everyone else who suffers. Our Wisewoman isn't going to last forever and soon we'll have none."

"You think I don't know that?!"

Ejah and Saleal looked to each other knowingly, while Kemahni shied away from the argument.

"You still think you're so damn special. You probably even think that you were something to the Inyari?" Ashava laughed at the undeniable truth when it silenced Kiyadeh. It took a moment for Kiyadeh to remember how to hold a normal, untelling face. "See I knew it, it's true," Ashava concluded.

"You don't know anything," Kiyadeh dismissed.

"I know you could have done more," Ashava asserted.

"Ashava! Enough!" Ejah yelled.

The heat of the room rose noticeably with the yarik *stones* glowing faintly brighter. It effectively quieted the room.

Kemahni tried not to stare at the power Ejah seemed to give off, swearing that he could actually see it flowing from her in pulses. It was not the first time he had thought he'd seen energies lifting off a Manyari, just the first time it was so overtly obvious to him. He looked around at the others but no one else saw what he had.

Saleal stayed calm, but squeezed on Kemahni's shoulder.

Kiyadeh stood purposefully and faced her sister. "Who exactly are you angry at here? Because I have done nothing to you. You act as if I did something to you. If I did then please do tell me. Tell me what would make you happy, sister? Because if I have done anything wrong, know that I am NOT afraid to pay for it. I gladly accept anything as punishment...but I'll tell you what I won't do. I won't let my own sister speak to me as if I'm some kind of stranger!"

"Kiyadeh, calm yourself. Sit down," Ejah sincerely asked.

Kiyadeh did not sit but tried to otherwise listen to her mother, closing her eyes and controlling her breathing. When she opened them again, she gave a quick glance to Kemahni, who felt his time soon approaching.

Kiyadeh turned to Ejah. "Mother, I am sorry. I can't tell you how it hurts me that I have failed everyone. I will not fight any punishment, and I promise you I'll find a way to make amends." Kiyadeh looked anxiously to Kemahni again, letting her eyes rise cautiously to the Great Mother, priming for her next words, "And maybe I can do that now."

"I can't wait to hear how," Ashava jeered.

"Kemahni has asked me to join him in *First Union*," Kiyadeh said, intently looking to him for his required confirmation.

Ashava's mouth gaped at the unbelievable idea, while Kemahni looked utterly confused, attempting to understand what was being asked of him.

"What? No. How does he even know? It's too early for him to decide," Saleal insisted.

Ejah tilted a contradictory head, slowly peering at Kiyadeh. "It's not a secret, and there is not really an age when he's supposed to choose. The Wisewoman usually has a hand in this, but again, nothing is carved in stone."

Saleal maintained a disagreeing face.

"Now may be as good a time as any to let him know."

Saleal turned Kemahni to face her. "Kemahni. Do you know what it means to choose someone for First Union? Are you choosing to bond with Kiyadeh first?"

Kemahni looked alarmed, unable to break his gaze with Kiyadeh even as her intensity became too much. Her eyes informed him that it was time to fulfill their agreement, and the words to speak were slowly building, when Ashava interjected.

"You ungrateful *boy*, how dare you! I've kept you safe all your life, so you would choose Tahdwi—" She blushed as she cut her words short. "You can't just give it away like that after everything I've done for you! You tell her no!"

"I, I…" Kemahni stammered.

"He doesn't owe you anything, Ashava," Kiyadeh said.

"How'd you do it?" Ashava bit as she fumed.

"Do what?"

"How'd you force him into it? This is why you were hiding him earlier, wasn't it?"

"I didn't force anyone. We are friends. We were before I left and still are. That's why he chose me."

"Barely. All you did was chase him around constantly. You should be forbidden from bonding with him at all for letting our Inyari die, because you obviously can't protect a life." Ashava waited for her mother to side with her request, but Ejah was faced away, having given up trying to calm the sisters. "Mother?"

"Ashava, this world has become a very, VERY unforgiving place. We should all be glad that your sister was able to make it home safely. She might not have come back at all."

"No, you can't use that excuse! You have to punish her!" Ashava said in disbelief.

"I will do what is necessary, not as you would like. Don't forget who you are talking to, Daughter. Kiyadeh *will* have a debt to repay, but one that I will choose."

Ashava slammed her hand and foot, making the ground shake, and stood in protest. "This is wrong, and you know it. You gave me much worse, this whole village did! And now you want to act like what she did wasn't as bad?" Ashava scrambled through her memories. "You welcome her back as if she never left. Don't think I've never noticed—you've always treated her better, loved her more. She's always been the better daughter! Not like me, the unwanted, bastard of a child," she swallowed. "The useless one."

Ejah parted her mouth, raising a calming hand to her, but Ashava waved off the request.

"No. I don't want to hear it. I don't want to hear whatever excuses you have for her, or any of the lies you're about to tell me." She caught Kemahni's almost scared stare and remembered the timid child he used to be. She lingered on the thought until it became unbearable and turned to leave. "Forget it. I don't care."

"Ashava, don't walk away," Ejah ordered, but the anger kept Ashava moving. "It was your choice as Guardian to take all the responsibility for caring for the boy. Rewards, and all the risk... We gave you a second chance and she will get the same."

"Second chance?" Ashava erupted. "No. I can't...I won't do this anymore. I'm done being treated this way." Ashava gestured with her head to Kiyadeh. "You can have him," she said with finality and walked out the door and into the growing rain.

"What?!" Kiyadeh frowned.

"Ashava, come back!" Kemahni jumped before anyone else could and made for the door.

His cry hurt fiercely when it hit Ashava's heart, forcing tears to her eyes. *These are the last ones, Kemahni,* she pledged to herself.

"Son, leave her be," Ejah said.

The calmness of her voice surprised and bothered Kemahni. "But she's—"

"She'll be okay."

It was a comment that everyone accepted. Everyone except Kemahni. It was the second time in his life he felt he had let Ashava down, and when he tried to call the vanishing girl back, he couldn't find the courage to speak.

Ejah gave into the weight of things and sat without fighting gravity. "By our gods, I'm not even sure why we still hold onto half these rituals. They just complicate things, but I certainly am not going to be the one to start breaking traditions. But sometimes..."

Saleal released her child from her protection and went to the side of her hurting friend.

Ejah felt the hand of comfort. "I'm fine. We have been through much worse. I know we will make it through this too." She hoped, and then looked to the boy. "As long as we have you, things will be fine."

Kemahni recoiled from the value she put on him.

Ejah stood with the help of Saleal and went to place a hand upon Kemahni's shoulder. "What is it that you want, Son? The choice is still yours, and we will support you, whatever you decide."

His choice could mend years of pain or break a newly made promise, and the whirlwind of outcomes made any decision seem impossible. He cared about his people and found some happiness in helping his tribe, but he didn't understand the value of the decision he was being asked to make.

Ejah looked at the boy and thought of the unfortunate life he would lead. About how everywhere her people managed to find a foothold in the world, there was uncertainty and a battle to survive, not just in life, but in keeping people together.

"Kemahni?" Ejah said to grab his focus.

"I, uh…" The hesitation made Kiyadeh's ears perk.

With all eyes on him, he took a deep breath and prepared himself.

"Whatever is best for the tribe, I will do it," Kemahni affirmed.

The lowest point of the day had finally settled into the quietness of night. Kiyadeh finally got the chance to remove her pieces of leather armour. It wasn't that she felt overly safe, or relaxed, but she had to take some weight off herself, if only physically. Kemahni and his mother had retired for the night and it was only one daughter and her mother who remained, since the other wasn't expected to return.

Ejah helped Kiyadeh out of the laced leather cuirass. "I'm glad you're home," she said as she pulled the armor over Kiyadeh's head.

Kiyadeh managed a small, "Yeah, me too," and moved onto unlacing her boots.

"You look well. And strong. I heard you jumped farther than Trainer Tassa after your first year."

"I did. I don't think she ever let me forget it."

"I knew you had the talent." Ejah said, and secretly thought Kiyadeh must have gotten the share of yarik ability that Ashava did not.

Kiyadeh half smiled. "She made all the training harder for me afterwards because of it."

"Well, it didn't stop you, I see."

"No, I guess not." A wind blew through the leather draping the front door and made her think of her sister. "What happened to Ashava? When did she get this bad?"

"Life has been..." Ejah paused to choose her next words, "difficult for her. It hasn't been easy for her after she chose to still be Kemahni's Guardian. The girl tries. Everyday. I know she's trying to atone for her mistake, but I don't think the tribes's collective forgiveness would be enough."

"So I've seen." Kiyadeh pulled off her first boot. "Is Ashava going to be okay?"

"Ashava is certainly being tested, but if I know her, she'll make it through this. And she has Tahdwi." Ejah placed Kiyadeh's equipment neatly next to the bed, and helped her remove her other boot.

"Tahdwi's still with her?"

"Yes, and believe me, I am grateful for it. That girl has a well of love I've never seen, and I think she wants to protect Ashava...from herself sometimes. Tahdwi's never left her side, especially after the Valkys attack when we almost lost Kemahni."

"Tahdwi is something else," Kiyadeh trailed off, splaying her toes and shifting the scales on top of her feet.

Ejah admired the rough and enlarged scales of her daughter and smiled lightly. "I'm going to offer you the duty of Guardian."

Kiyadeh couldn't decide if she should be shocked or honored by the notion.

"It's because I know you will protect Kemahni with everything you have, and maybe he will actually listen to you. You also know what to expect, and that it won't be easy, but I believe you are capable."

"I'm...happy you believe in me, but I'm not sure I should be trusted with another's life."

"Do you believe you can do it?"

"Yes, but—" Kiyadeh responded easily.

"Do you *want* to do it?"

Kiyadeh thought for a moment. "I do, I just don't know if I should." Her mother flattened her expression, and Kiyadeh assured, "If you order me to, I would do my best."

"I am not ordering, I only ask, and I know you will try your best if you do," Ejah said, and paused for a while. It put Kiyadeh on alert for a more serious question to come. Ejah asked in a lower tone, "The Inyari girl—"

"Mother, please, don't tell me it was okay."

"I won't. Losing any life is never okay, but I know you did everything you could to save her."

Kiyadeh swung her head to the side. "I didn't have the chance. She saved me."

"You can't let this weigh too heavily on you. It does no good."

"How can't I? I didn't do enough to protect her," Kiyadeh stopped and held the words in her mind, *she was important to me.* Her eyes welled up with obvious tears, and she turned her head to force them back with a long blink. "This is why I am not sure if I can be *his* Guardian. I don't know if I'm ready for that responsibility again."

"I have no doubt you'd be a great protector for him."

Kiyadeh laughed once in disbelief. "How can you be so sure?"

"A mother knows."

Kiyadeh was defeated and unsatisfied with the answer. "I just want to rest."

Ejah read her daughter's face and nodded once. "Okay. You've had a long journey, and we'll have time to talk more in the morning."

Kiyadeh agreed and went off to prepare her bed.

"Kiyadeh?"

"Yes?"

"How did she save you?"

Kiyadeh's embarrassment returned as she slowly rummaged through a pouch on her waist. In her hand was a purple yarik stone. A long knowing stare froze Ejah as she looked at it.

"Keep it safe," Ejah advised. "Let it be a reminder."

"Yes, Mother." Kiyadeh said no more and vanished around the partition.

Ejah instinctually wanted to help her daughter lay down to sleep, but the years had transformed her once child into an adolescent warrior. Though she missed those days of upbringing, she was proud of who her daughter had become and the future that they might lead together.

Kiyadeh threw herself onto the bed without undressing fully. In the moments before she fell into slumber she felt a connection with Noriendi, and for the first time since they were apart, Kiyadeh dreamt throughout the night and only of her.

CHAPTER 8
FREEDOM

"Keep the past. It's one of your greatest weapons."
- The Wisewoman of Shonta

Waxing Full Red Moon, Year 379 AA
27th Spring of the Orahai

The past two years had come and gone, bringing the Son of Orahai into his sixteenth summer, though one could say he was much older by the muscle and scale growth.

His long hair was down over his shoulders, a difference from the usual mane of hair he would have wrapped and bound with leather straps atop his head. His red hair was done in similar braids to his mother, but with a more artful flair. His horns were more obvious with his hairstyle, and looked larger than needed, but not too big as to be cumbersome. They always seemed in a hurry to grow before anything else on his body, and he couldn't catch up fast enough.

Kemahni had been looking skyward while he awaited to be gathered. In the haze of the midday, the moon and its crystal sea could be seen slightly. The edges of its gray surface faded into the blue and set the shimmering chromatic crystals as the prominent feature above, second only to the sun opposite it in the sky. He wasn't concerned with the moon he had seen thousands of times, instead keeping his gaze up in preparation of his Guardian's return. He didn't like how silently she tended to arrive, or how she was perfecting that skill. Distracted, he missed a trio of girls traveling leisurely on their way to work the fields.

One would rarely see those girls apart, and that day was no different. Chae, the more mature and tallest of the three led the way as the two behind her were talking about things she was too old to care about. Stell, a dancer and singer with the sleek body to match, bounced her way down the path to a tune in her head while she conversed. Then there was Tobia, who held Stell's hand in order to keep her from straying off the path or into other things. Tobia was the self-designated heavy lifter of the three, with her strongly shaped arms from not just the muscle but hard scales that flanked the outline of her body.

All at once they spotted Kemahni, seemingly lost in an absent-minded daze, and stopped abruptly. They looked curiously at each other before scanning the area for any onlookers and, more importantly, his Guardian. All three smiled in unison and took to their opportunistic approach.

"Son of Orahai, you are all alone. Where is your Guardian?" Chae asked.

"She was called home by Chieftess," he replied after a mild startle at their arrival. "She will be back soon. I was told to wait here."

The trio slowly encircled him without causing alarm. Tobia ran her hands over his horns and petted the ends of his furred ears. Kemahni shook and recoiled from her, bumping into Chae, who had bent down to meet him. She slowly crossed her arms over his chest like the embrace of a serpentine predator.

"The bonding is coming soon. Are you excited?" Chae softly asked.

"I guess, yeah," he said flatly.

"Sounds like it's going to be fun," said Stell.

"We are definitely looking forward to it." Tobia smiled.

"Are you preparing alright?" asked Stell.

"For what?" Kemahni wondered.

"The bonding of course," Tobia said.

"Do you suppose no one set him up right? Has no one told you about what happens during the bonding?" Chae proposed, still holding him.

"How irresponsible of the Great Mother," Tobia feigned disappointment, holding his chin.

Kemahni broke free, annoyed by their forwardness.

"She... I know what will happen," he lied.

The three girls look at each other unbelieving.

"It's easy. It shouldn't take long," Kemahni guessed.

"What would be the fun of that if it was over quickly?" Stell amusedly questioned.

"I heard the longer you bond, the better chance for another male," Tobia added.

"And we should do what's best for the tribe, don't you think?" Chae suggested.

Kemahni became increasingly confused, his face revealing a lack of understanding.

"We're only here to help," Chae continued.

"There's a few things that we can teach you before the day so you know what to do," Tobia interjected.

"That way, you won't do something wrong during First Union," Stell said.

"And if you happen to change your mind about the order to receive, we can help you with that too," Chae offered.

At that point, Kemahni had been spinning in circles trying to listen to what each one said. It was physically and mentally disorientating, and he was unsure how to respond. Chae eventually stopped his rotation to face her. His eyes jumbled about trying to maintain eye contact with her.

"We just want you to make the best choice," she said. "For you and the tribe."

"And not what's best for you, right?" Kiyadeh suddenly announced, having walked back to meet Kemahni, saving her yarik for what would have been a short jump.

All three girls did their best to hide surprise, failing miserably as they backed away. They formed a line on the other side of Kemahni, placing him between them and his returned Guardian.

"Only the gods really know what's best," Chae insisted.

"I didn't think a Wind Rider would be afraid of a little competition." Tobia unconsciously rubbed her large, center scale. "If anything, we were only trying to do everyone a favor."

"And how's that?" Kiydaeh asked.

"No one *really* wants to be first. Don't you think it will be better after he knows what to do? I think the girls after us would be thankful really," Stell remarked.

Kemahni soon found that, although the conversation was about him, no one cared to include him in it. Kiyadeh sauntered up to the three girls, resorting to her signature show of power through planting her spear and resting against it.

"You all are assuming that after me he'll want to continue," Kiyadeh boasted. "He gets to decide when he's good and done, and you'll all just have to sit and wait."

"You shouldn't feel so special being First," Stell glibbed.

Kiyadeh chuckled. "Why not? You all would. And to be honest, I'm not worried. He already made his decision to choose me, and none of you are going to change it." She ended with a smirk.

"That's not very becoming of a Guardian, is it now?" Chae rhetorically asked.

"My job is to protect him, not your feelings."

"We'll all have our chance," Chae said as she straightened proudly.

"Stop talking about me like I'm not here!" Kemahni finally fumed.

Everyone went stark silent for a long while, whether from embarrassment or shock, or in Kemahni's case, anger. The sounds of nature filled the still air. Kiyadeh moved in cautiously to console him, placing her hand on the outside of his fists. He relaxed slightly, but didn't release the tight clench.

"Ke, I didn't mean—I'm sorry."

The three girls took the opportunity to escape, backing away quietly toward their original destination. Kiyadeh's ears flicked at the sounds of their departure, irritated as they whispered quietly and inconsiderately, barely muffling their laughter. Kiyadeh became torn between confronting the girls and continuing to console Kemahni for her misstep, eventually choosing to do neither when she saw the Great Mother with a wooden branch she used as a staff and a basket heading her way.

Saleal's staff was held tightly to her back with crossing leather straps. It was ordinary enough, a well-chosen piece of wood, straight as nature could make. It was wrapped with thin leather at two points where one would have a good balanced grip on it. At the very top was a self-sustained orb of water that held its shape with the power of a yarik stone at its core. Within the watery boundaries was a school of bewildered fish; small and perfect for bait.

Upon reaching Kemahni and Kiyadeh, and noticing the obvious situation with her son, Saleal lodged her staff securely in the ground. "Mahi, are you okay?" Saleal asked as she followed his gaze to the leaving tribeswomen.

"Yes, everything's fine," he answered quickly and started to walk away.

"Mahi, shouldn't you wait for Kiyadeh?"

Kemahni refused to answer, but waited out of learned habit to listen to his mother and Guardian. Saleal peered at Kiyadeh, who was still showing signs of embarrassment.

"Mahi, please wait there." She curiously approached Kiyadeh to ask, "What happened?"

"Some of the girls were talking to him about…the bonding. They were trying to convince him to change his mind on First Union. I got defensive, but mostly, he didn't care much for the way we were talking about him as if he wasn't there," Kiyadeh admitted.

"I see."

"It's difficult when I feel like I have to defend myself against my own sisters."

"I understand that."

Saleal looked back to her son again.

"Can I ask you?" Kiyadeh waited a beat for the Great Mother to nod. "Does he know what and how the bonding day will unfold?"

"He knows a bit, but I've been slow to reveal all the details to him." Saleal internally scolded herself and took a breath. "Let me take him for the afternoon. Some time away will hopefully help and allow me to get this all sorted. Meet us later." Saleal gestured with a nod to the area before the river.

Kiyadeh nodded appreciatively. "Okay. That's probably for the best. And I'm sorry."

"No need. We'll all get through this and it'll be okay."

Kiyadeh let out a slow trickle of staggered breaths.

"This falls on me. Him and I were always meant to have this conversation, and I've been putting it off for quite a while. It appears now is the time," Saleal said with a hand on Kiyadeh's shoulder. "We'll talk more later."

Saleal left Kiyadeh to catch up with her son, and spoke lovingly with him. He looked back at Kiyadeh, who had her head lowered in defeat. When she rose to meet his gaze, they shared a look, one he could not hold. Saleal handed the woven basket to Kemahni and ushered him toward the river.

When the two were out of sight, Kiyadeh looked to the sky as Kemahni had done, to the moon that had watched the encounter.

"This better all be part of your plan."

Cascade River

"Mahi, come," Kemahni's mother said as they reached the banks of the river that curved through their lands. "Let's sit," she then asked and patted him on the shoulder. "It's okay."

"I don't want to go fishing," Kemahni objected, and waited anxiously, head flicking to sounds around him. "I didn't want to come back here." He stopped to think of Ashava.

"I know, I know, but you don't have to worry. You're safe with me," his mother said, nervously scratching a discolored scale on the inside of her arm. "No one will bother us here."

Kemahni dipped lower in the grass, flattened his horns, and hid his ears. He controlled his scales to minimize the shine they might reflect, and subconsciously touched the larger patches of scales on his body to make himself feel safer. Saleal did the same, and he often wondered if he had learned the tick from her, or if it was just something Manyari did.

"It'll be good for you to get away for a while," she tried again to reassure him.

"Why here?" He shook his head.

"It's the best place for Flat Skippers. I promise you, nothing will hurt you, not as long as I'm here," she said, though she wasn't overly convincing as she looked around.

Saleal sat without much of a fuss, like a fisher eager to catch. She cleared a spot for him as well and waited until he was comfortable enough to find his way to her side. He did after a while, resigned to sit in the sand.

She dug the staff of imprisoned fish between them, and without being asked, Kemahni routinely pulled out a bundle of twine rope and started to separate the individual lengths. She smiled and thanked him, before reaching deep into her satchel. She pulled out yarik stone shards, taller than they were wide, with a few basic lines carved into them that she inspected. The fact that they were smaller didn't stop the stone from catching the light and bending it in a way that always enticed Kemahni's curiosity. He looked at it with a half glance, not wanting to seem too interested.

Saleal requested a strand of rope from Kemahni, which she used to construct a cradle of looped knots at one end. She gave the line a quick tug and secured the shard tightly inside. A quick rub of the shard coaxed it to activate. Previously unseen lines of energy began to glow faintly, and she touched the tip of the shard to the very edge of the orb of water on the staff. She blocked one of the lines of energy, holding her thumb there. It rippled the orb from the point it made contact, all the way to the exact opposite pole and back again. The waves stopped when they met at a center point, and when she pulled the shard slowly away, it extracted its own miniature globe of water, along with a single confused fish.

Kemahni continued to practice his stoic, non-reaction, though Saleal plainly noticed his restraint and half smiled. She tethered the completed lure and took it to the edge of the bank. With an effortless flick of her hand, she sent the bait, and its watery hold, into the river. The shard's globe blended seamlessly, vanishing and becoming indistinguishable from the water.

"Did you want to talk about what happened earlier?" Saleal asked.

"No, I...no."

"You know you can talk to me about anything."

"I know."

A long time passed with no tug or bite on the line, but neither one seemed to care. Kemahni stared at the baited fish in the river. His mother traced his view and back again, then finally to the globe of fish on her staff, who couldn't contemplate their fate.

"Kemahni," she said, and his ears popped out of hiding. "Life... Life is interesting. As much as I like to think I know, I've never really figured it out. Even now, there are things that are new to me, just like all the new that is happening for you. There are so many things that come our way whether we are ready for them or not, and a lot of times there are no quick answers. If you ever feel lost, or don't know what to do, that's normal. And it's okay. Finding answers to questions is part of being alive, part of living in this world. We all have to find our own truth, and I have no doubt you'll find yours."

"What will I find?"

"Anything you're willing to put the effort to discover. Nevold is a big place, and there are things that I don't even know."

"Like what?" he doubted.

"Mostly big questions: Why are we here? How the world can be so beautiful and so cruel at the same time. How to be a good mother." *Why I brought you into this life*, she didn't say.

He turned to her, watched while she was lost staring into the slow moving river. "I don't know what you mean?"

"Maybe not now," she agreed kindly. "You will someday."

Her lips parted a couple more times as if she wanted to continue but nothing escaped. When something caught on her lure, she did nothing to reel it in and eventually the line stopped tugging and became slack.

"There is one thing I do know well," Saleal eventually said. "Even if we stand still and choose not to move, the world will go on without us, whether we care to be part of it or not." Saleal looked seriously at him. "The most we can do sometimes is just try, keep moving, and hope for the best."

Kemahni shifted to look at her fully before she continued.

"There is a lot of life we don't get to choose; how we are born, and usually how we leave this world. I know that it might not feel like you have a choice in anything, but how you react to the things not in your control is always a choice."

A soft sadness came to her voice. "There are a lot of things that are going to start happening once the moon shifts. I'll do my best to prepare you for it, but it is up to you to act. When the time comes, you have to make the decisions, because no one else can."

"Yeah," he feigned maturity. "Will it hurt?"

"The bonding? No. Quite the opposite. What you will share with everyone will make you feel like nothing else can. You will be closer to people than you have ever been before."

"Closer?"

"Yes. The bond you make," she faltered, "it's...hard trying to describe it."

"That's okay. We don't have to talk about it."

"No, you should know exactly what's going to happen."

He didn't object, and Saleal started off in as detailed a description as she could remember from her own experience. It had been years since her bonding, and it took her a moment to collect the thoughts.

Kemahni took her words as something akin to a fairytale. The magic and prestige that went along with it didn't seem to fit anything he knew, but at the same time, it didn't frighten him. It was the way she painted each part as a beautiful experience, and went into deep detail about how the act would be initiated. How his lack of knowledge would never hinder him. How each of the girls would help him along and, when unsure, he needed merely to trust his instincts.

She tried to describe how he would share his body, soul, and his yarik essence with others, but found it a hard task to accomplish, having trouble choosing words to portray what could only really be experienced. Saleal referred to the pleasure of it, and to not be afraid. She ended by letting him know that no one accepted the responsibility of wanting to become a mother lightly. Everyone did so with the knowledge that it would change their lives, for better and for worse, and it was all for the sake of the tribe.

During the entirety of the story, Kemahni said nothing. There wasn't much he could contribute since it was more of a lesson than a dialogue. And despite all her best effort, she knew she'd leave things out, unintentionally or otherwise. When she finished, he returned to looking at the sand in front of him and processed what she had said.

"Everyone?" Kemahni asked.

"No, only those who are ready and willing. It's also why having to pick your *First* is important."

A while passed with Kemahni silent, thinking of Kiyadeh and then inevitably, Ashava.

"Is Ashava...Will I be bonding with her?"

"No." Saleal sounded surprised.

"Oh."

"Did you want to?"

"If she wanted to."

Saleal was somber for a noticeable moment. "I'm not sure what she would want, but no one's ever told you…"

"What?"

"Those who cannot use yarik cannot bear children."

He wanted to ask why, but that final revelation didn't eclipse the new information he was still piecing together about the coming day. His blank gaze made him look catatonic and his mother watched him closely for any reaction.

"Are you okay?" his mother asked, and he nodded slowly. "Was there anything else you might want to know?"

"What happens when it's all over?"

Saleal thought for a moment. "You get to rest."

He nodded once more and reached for another strand of rope to give her. Straight-armed, he presented it to her without looking.

"And then, will I stop being treated different? Can you take me to the outside?"

Saleal paused. "We can worry about that later. Let's get through the next moon first, alright?"

She took the strand from him, immediately placing it beside her. She slid across the sand to seat herself closer to him and hugged him across the shoulder.

"Everything will be just fine. I promise," Saleal said as only she could.

He pushed his head into her chest, grabbing her around her waist, and listened to her heartbeat. The river and her heart became the only sound, and they stayed at its shore for however long it took the world to feel right again.

Everything will be okay, she told herself as she teared up, thinking of the future.

Saleal finished cleaning up their spot and grabbed the basket. It made the calming sounds of shifting waters as she opened it. She inspected the fish inside, each in their own individual globe of water; water that didn't leak out of the woven basket regardless of how hard it was pressed against the walls. She hefted it over her shoulder and pulled her staff from the ground.

"Mahi, are you ready?" she asked, but got no reply.

He hadn't heard her, being a short jog down the river's bend, standing on the low branch of a tree. He was staring listlessly at something in the direction of the village.

The momentary worry faded when she saw him in the tree. They had been finished for a while, and she could tell he was ready to leave by how easily he was distracted by someone in the distance.

"Mahi," she more loudly called for his attention.

"Uh huh," he half responded, still staring.

"What are you looking at?"

"A spirit…"

Saleal was never sure she believed in an afterlife but loved the way he tried to describe it when he sometimes saw supposed spirits in a way she would understand. It sounded like daydreams and she cherished his view of what she couldn't see herself. She knew that he would never be more free than when he let himself escape in his mind. It was a good reminder to let herself enjoy her time with him as she was constantly aware that it all could be taken without warning. She refused to let the ideas sour her thoughts and continued admiring him.

Kemahni's eyes squinted and focused far into the distance, past the slots between tall grass as he shuffled back and forth on the tips of his toes to get a better look. Saleal smiled at his impatience.

"You can start heading back, but don't travel too far ahead," she said when she reached the trunk of the tree he was in. Kemahni broke his concentration only long enough to give the first semi-smile he had all day. "I'll be right behind you." Saleal smiled with a half-furrowed brow.

"Okay," he said and swung down from the tree to speed off in a hurry.

Saleal watched until her son disappeared into the grass, a moment that lasted long enough for Kiyadeh to arrive unnoticed at Saleal's side.

Kiyadeh cleared her throat to pardon herself. "...how'd it go?"

Saleal's heart jumped internally, but she showed no outward signs of it. She turned calmly to Kemahni's Guardian. "He isn't angry any more."

"That's good. I'm glad to hear."

"He is strong. He'll be ready when the time comes," Saleal said in an attempt to convince both of them.

"And you?"

"Have to be. I'm the Great Mother," Saleal joked.

"Even so, I can't imagine how this is weighing on you. I feel like the following moon will be most difficult."

"I'm preparing the best I can," Saleal said, hiding her feelings. "Tell me about your preparations. How are they fairing?"

"Well, I suppose. This whole affair arrived sooner than I thought it would."

"It did," Saleal agreed with an increasing sorrow.

"It's exciting, I'm scared, sad, plus a bunch of other feelings I'm not sure I can even describe."

"Good, feel them all. They will help you as you take this important step. I'm glad you will be there with him."

"Yeah, me too," she said humbly. Kiyadeh took a deep look at the trees beyond the Cascade River that had yet to recover completely. "I haven't been back here since..."

"That day. I don't blame you," Saleal finished.

"Ashava never talked about it, not that she would with me. I know she went through a lot that day, and I wish she would. I wanted to help her, back then, but she got angry every time I asked. So I stopped asking. I understand that she wanted to move on and probably forget, but I don't think she ever really dealt with any of the pain."

Saleal let her speak uninterrupted and watched as she crossed to the other side of the river, atop a few stones peeking out of the water. She stopped at a two and a half meter tall young sapling that had sprouted amongst the downed and trampled trunks of once vibrant trees. The ones that still stood had healed but retained deep scars across their trunks, and the area around them was uneven from deep pockets of pushed down soil. One could almost see the footprints that were once there. The trees in front of them had made a "V" corridor, far beyond their view.

Saleal joined her, compelled to touch the tree. "Where we forget, the world never does. "

Babbling of liquid voices came together to make a low rumble in agreement of her statement. She glanced back to see if her son was still in view, but there was no sign of him.

Kiyadeh was fixated on the gouging imprint of a Valkys paw that had healed on the trunk of a tree. She remembered the river and forest as being bigger, but she was smaller then. Life was bigger, grander when there was still wonder to the world without worry.

"You know, I almost didn't become a Wind Rider because I was so afraid after that, but when Tassa took me up for the first time… my whole perspective changed."

"How so?"

"Being above the trees, away from it all, it was like nothing could touch me. I was free. I wasn't scared after that. I was like—"

The shadow of a *daring bird* zipped between them and Saleal looked up. "A bird," she said, amazed.

"Yes, actually," she said matter-of-factly, missing the bird Saleal was referencing.

"And not just one," Saleal said as a flock followed the lead bird.

"Oh wow."

They flew in formation, but not in a coordinated way. They were a mass of birds making unnecessary movements but always in the relatively same direction. Once in a while one would stall and fall toward the ground. The others would chase after the falling bird, and before any of them would hit the ground, they would spread their wings and grab the wind.

The performance lasted for a moment longer before they disappeared back over the canopy, into the forest.

"They came back!" Saleal said joyfully, "I wasn't sure they ever would."

"I envy them," Kiyadah said. "I think I only now realized that, fairly soon, I won't see much of the outside world."

"But they live simple lives, where you can always be much more."

"More than a mother?"

The word mother struck Saleal, and she paused. Kiyadeh, like her, was making a choice to be a mother, but given the choice again, she wasn't confident she'd choose the same.

"You don't have to be a mother," Saleal said.

Kiyadeh arched her brows, staring at nothing. "Tell that to Chieftess."

"Kiyadeh..." Saleal said with concern, "you know your value isn't limited to that. We will have plenty of children coming to this village."

"I know, but this is something I have to do. I need to add instead of take away. I want to protect something." Kiyadeh looked down at her feet.

"And you will and you have," Saleal told her and embraced a reluctant daughter.

Kiyadeh felt undeserving of the confidence in her, but eventually accepted the love and let herself sink into the Great Mother's arms. She wiped away a happy tear, and stayed long enough to not feel awkward but enough to feel a bit more whole.

"I'm going to go get Kemahni. Thanks for talking with me."

Saleal gave a short nod and, with a helpful pat, Kiyadeh went on her way to find the Son of Orahai.

CHAPTER 9
SEEING

"Seeing what is, isn't just looking with your eyes."
- Mar'chea, the Blind Fisher

Orahai Village

"It's less than a moon away," Tahdwi said, "You won't have many chances left."

Ashava sat and thought of the truth in her friend's words, letting her eyes track across the room without focusing on anything particular.

"You say that, and you may be right, but what difference does that make now?" Ashava asked to be convinced.

Tahdwi sat next to her and wrapped her arm around Ashava's shoulder, letting their heads fall together.

"I would like to think a lot. For both of you. I've been trying to help you understand that nothing is final. I want to believe you can find a little solace in all this."

"I just...after all this time, what am I supposed to say? Forgive me? I'm sorry?"

"Why not?"

"Because I don't think it will do anything. Because I don't think he'd care. No one else has. Tahdwi, you're the only one that gave me any forgiveness."

"You're sweet, but I never gave you that."

Ashava rolled her head away from Tahdwi's but was pulled back by a caring hand.

"I gave you love and love is always my answer to the world."

"Yeah, but it's easy for you, and I don't know if it's in me to face it the way you do. With that unnatural optimism."

An appreciative smile slid across Tahdwi's face. "So I've been told. But right now, don't try to have any view other than your own. Embrace the unique life you live, and find what leads you."

"Like love?"

"It's not a bad place to start, because it's always there. Try to reclaim love for him. You did once, and though it has changed, it never really goes away."

Ashava didn't outwardly agree but turned her head into Tahdwi's neck as if hiding from the emotions.

"I know it's exhausting letting the past determine just how you feel about the now, but you can change that," Tahdwi reassured.

"Even you couldn't change the way people think of me, and I know you've tried."

"People are stubborn," Tahdwi teased with a smile, "but with a little effort, you can make a start. It will take some time, but I believe you can do it."

"I've tried."

Tahdwi breathed a moment and pulled Ashava from hiding.

"Have you?"

Ashava didn't answer.

"I think it's time for you to face it all and let go of all those feelings you've been holding, the ones that are stopping you from healing."

Ashava remained slumped in thought.

"In less than a year there will be new beginnings, for the children and for you. You just have to decide where you want to be then, by doing something now, while you have the chance."

Ashava straightened her back and stared out the door, and for an instant, remembered walking with Kemahni as they planned another adventure. Her focus eventually returned to Tahdwi and she faced her with a grateful smile.

"You would have made a good Wisewoman."

Tahdwi cracked a knowing smile. "I don't need the title, or the responsibility."

Ashava stood with a renewed purpose but hesitated to exit. "Thank you," she said without turning.

"Mhmm," Tahdwi acknowledged, "I'm here if you need anything."

Asahva nodded in understanding, and left her friend who was far better than she was.

Orahai Outskirts

Kemahni finished his short jaunt from the river, into the tall, wild grass fields. He ran and ran, his pace never slowing, and never losing track on his objective. On his approach, he hunkered down cautiously, so as to not scare the spirit away. The more he watched, and the closer he got, the better the clarity of the spirit became. It was glowing and round, like a small sun that he swore even felt warm. He crept closer, eventually coming out of hiding, angrily parting the grass in front of him.

"You! Go away. Go away before you bring something else bad here," Kemahni defensively swatted at the spirit.

"Best of day, Son of Orahai," an elderly voice broke into the conversation.

"What?!" Kemahni's voice rattled. He turned to see the Wisewoman had appeared, seemingly out of nowhere, to involve herself in another matter of village daily life. He gave her the courtesy of his full attention, putting aside the affronting spirit. "Best of day... Wisewoman." He lowered his head in a half bow.

"I believe you will find kindness works better," she mentioned.

He looked back to the spirit that was beginning to take a different form. That of a slender, more feminine shape.

"For what?" Kemahni shied away.

"The spirits," she then said obviously, with a toothy grin. "Like the one there."

Kemahni stared blankly, doubting they shared anything unique other than being Manyari. He looked curiously at the spirit next to him, watching it fully form and kneel down to examine him.

The Wisewoman shuffled towards the spirit with the help of her staff, "Spirits are here to help us find our way, but sometimes," she reached out a hand, exactly where the spirit was floating, "we can also help them on theirs."

The spirit reverted to an orb and began to spiral away, disappearing in a flash of light back to where it came from.

Could I have sent the other spirit away too?

Until that moment, Kemahni had felt patronized by the Wisewoman, but understood that she believed and possibly saw as he did.

"Is that really what happens to us," Kemahni reservedly asked, "when we pass? None of the ones I've seen looked like Manyari."

"It might be that you did not recognize them. When we escape these bodies, we become free. We do not need to hold the shape of what we once were. We become the thing we always were. Souls. Life. Energy, pure and simple." He bobbed his head slightly, in appeasing agreement. "And if you listen close, the spirits can speak, pass their knowledge onto you."

"Like what?" he immediately regretted asking.

"Life is a circle. It is always changing from one thing to the next, now and forever, Gods willing." The Wisewoman placed a hand on his shoulder and braced herself on him instead of her staff. "Your life too, is about to change. You get to bring life to this tribe like no one else can."

"Yes…" he appeased, knowing uncomfortably well, hoping to end the conversation quicker.

"I know you do. You're such a bright, beautiful child. Our children will truly be blessed."

Kemahni knew a *thank you* was in order, but he felt compelled to save it.

"I look forward to our future," the Wisewoman finished happily. With one last tighter squeeze, she released him and went back to bracing herself on her staff once again. "Be well, Son of Orahai."

Away she went, in her typical gating fashion, with the chime of her staff to keep the rhythm of her steps. Each lessening chime eased his anxiety, and when her sound was gone, he laid down in the grass. Immediately his body became heavy, and he let go of the weight of the world, falling into his own reality.

After what felt like a lengthy slumber, he returned back to his senses and the body he'd always known. He began to move his arms and legs as if fitting himself back into his body, and when he fully awoke, he found himself staring into the eyes of his Guardian, Kiyadeh.

Her eyes tracked back and forth over his face. She said something, but a tone in his ears deadened the sounds. His horns had extended their full length straight from his head, and his ears pointed to the side relaxed, making two protruding v-shaped ornaments on his head. He let his head fall heavy to the side and saw the grass had laid down with him, in a perfect circle, the same diameter as the tallest part of him.

With nothing to say, time rushed past them, so much and so quickly that the grass's imperceivable reach for the high sun could be seen.

She pulled his head by the side to look at her. "Ke, are you with us?" she asked, trying to read his expression.

"Yaya."

She scoffed, "Ke…you know I don't—"

"Yeah, I know. Sorry, Kiyadeh."

"It's fine."

Her response sounded almost apologetic, thinking that it might be the last time she would hear her childhood name.

"Sometimes when I can't find you or you disappear, I think the worst," Kiyadeh continued.

"Like what?"

"I don't know, like..."

"Like I ran away?"

Kemahni said it as if he knew what she was thinking, to which Kiyadeh's face immediately soured.

"Why would I run? Where would I go?" He looked to the wards just beyond the river. "I told you I've been past the wards many times—"

"And you still haven't told me how."

"I only stopped doing it because you asked me to. You said it worried you."

"'Cause it did."

"I wish everyone wasn't so worried. I can handle myself. I'm quick, faster than anyone here."

"I believe you. But it's my job to keep you out of danger, and I'm trying my best."

"I know," he agreed and closed his eyes. "Everything is dangerous when it comes to me. No one ever gives me a chance to prove myself, and I would prove them all wrong."

"Maybe," she smirked, "but it's not that, we just all want to protect you."

"All I want is to be normal and do the things everyone else gets to do. I want to learn to fight. I want to use yarik."

"We don't show you for your safety. Yarik can be dangerous to you and others if you don't know what you're doing."

"There's that word again, Dangerous. I've watched plenty of people use it, and it doesn't seem that difficult. You do it."

Kiyadeh frowned and gave an elongated, "Yeesss," and took a quick breath. "It took a lot of training to get where I am."

"I don't expect you to understand. The only one that really did was...Ashava."

"I'm trying to understand, I really am."

Another silence came and fed the awkwardness. Kiyadeh retracted from the topic and looked to the wards with Kemahni.

"Let's not talk about it."

Kemahni didn't disagree and it gave her little confidence to continue.

"Did, did I see the Wisewoman?" she asked, and Kemahni nodded. "Did you have a good talk with her?"

"She did most of the talking."

"Yeah, she does that. She have anything good to say?"

"No, not really. All she talks about is me."

"You know the Inyari. *Males* are their life's mission."

Kemahni eyes leveled in disagreement.

"It's a weird obsession if you ask me." She smiled, looking for a reaction, but when he failed to laugh, she grimaced. "Why don't we go back home? I'll make us some food."

He gave an apathetic, "Okay," though he was exceptionally hungry.

He stood with great effort to face the sun, eyes closed, and let the warmth envelope him for a moment. Kiyadeh started their walk back, and he unconsciously followed.

Kiyadeh worked through the short list of recipes she knew, picking a meal he'd enjoy. She slowed to meet him and satisfyingly matched his rhythm but quickly forgot her idea when she turned to confirm the selection. Kemahni had his eyes closed, moving with an oblivious walk, one she admired with its sure steps that looked as if he was turning the world.

"So, about the bonding..." Kiyadeh suddenly said.

He stopped with a heavy foot and became rigid, and a mild guilt struck her at disrupting his serenity.

"The bonding," he confirmed as if it wasn't at the front of his mind.

She maintained her excitement and added, "I'm really looking forward to it."

"Yeah…," he responded apathetically, and continued walking again.

Kiyadeh met his stride. "Do you want to talk about it?"

"Do you?"

"Kind of. I just want to know if you need any help or anything. Chieftess was very thorough in her description of the bonding and what will happen." She let her head bounce to the side with a slight smile. "She really didn't leave any details out. I couldn't help but think it sounded a lot like when we used to wrestle," she joked and looked him over. "You might put up more of a fight now." Her attempt at levity failed, as Kemahni's expression remained unchanged. "If there is anything I can help—"

"No," he interrupted, "I know what's gonna happen now. My mother…she told me," he said almost embarrassed, then quickened his pace to move out of step with her.

Kiyadeh slowed and hung her head, but eventually trotted back to Kemahni's side.

"And you're ready, right?" Kiyadeh questioned.

He halted abruptly, which Kiyadeh hadn't realized until she heard only one set of feet. She briskly turned to see him staring intensely at her.

"Can we not talk about it?"

"Don't you think we should? I just want to do it right. If something's bothering you, you know you can talk to me."

"I just want it to be over with so maybe we can all move on, and I can be free to do what I want."

Kiyadeh let her mouth open before actually speaking any words, "Ke, you are free…"

Kemahni forced a chuckle.

"Let's not make any plans just yet," she swallowed.

"What do you mean don't make plans? I've waited all these summers and I finally get my chance to start living, and you're telling me not to look forward to when this will be done?"

"No, it's not that." Kiyadeh stole his angry gaze and unexpectedly hugged him. What anger he had slipped away, whether from the shock or the enjoyment he felt from being hugged by her for the first time since he could remember. "This is all new for me too and I'm not always good with change. I wish we would just go back to being kids and didn't have to do any of this. I like the way it is now, and...there's just a part of me that is scared to lose you if you decide that you want to leave after this."

"Kiyadeh...you won't lose me," he said, surprised by his own words and laid his head into her shoulder ever so slightly. She held tighter and he could feel a long, heavy breath push her chest against his. When he broke away, embarrassed, he stared past her and blinked a few times, not sure he believed what he saw. "Ashava...."

"Ashava?"

Kiyadeh's sister and Kemahni's former Guardian waited in the most patient way she knew how, still appearing unavoidably annoyed while she had to wait.

"Getting started already?" Ashava jabbed.

"No." Kiyadeh pivoted, maintaining calm everywhere in her body except for her voice when she said, "I was comforting him, which is part of my job as a Guardian."

"Yes, I know," Ashava said dejectedly. "I've come to talk to Kemahni."

"Me?" He moved forward curiously. "About what?"

Kiyadeh wanted to inject a concern, but Ashava continued without considering her sister's possible protest.

"I want to," Ashava took an uncomfortable pause, "fix things... between us."

Kiyadeh couldn't infer her sister's intent and silently observed their conversation.

"Fix what?" Kemahni asked.

Ashava breathed a not-too-obvious sigh. "I never wanted to be on the other side of you."

"I don't know what you mean," Kemahni spaced his words.

"You and I, we haven't been...*right* for a long time."

"It's fine."

"It's really not though. To be honest, I was okay with the rest of the village not liking me. I came to terms with that a long time ago.

Honestly, I never needed their approval, but there was a time when you were all that mattered to me. I know it will never be like that again, but I enjoyed that time. I miss that."

"Why are you telling me all this now?" Kemahni asked.

"I didn't know if I will have another chance."

"Why wouldn't you have another chance?" Kemahni looked to Kiyadeh for an explanation, "What is she talking about?"

"I'd like to know too," Kiyadeh inquired.

Ashava stuttered another breath. "Look, I'm no good at this. I don't have good words to say what I mean. All I'm asking for is for there not to be," she motioned with a swift hand between the two, "whatever is keeping us apart. And so, after the moon changes..." Ashava couldn't bring herself to say the rest.

Kemahni became increasingly confused and frustrated by Ashava's withholding information and demanded to know, "What?! Kiyadeh, what is she talking about?"

Kiyadeh narrowed her eyes. "I don't know, Kemahni, and I don't know what she's trying to accomplish here." she said, placing herself between the two. "What do you plan on getting from upsetting him right now? He's got enough to worry about without you playing games. If you really care, then wait for whatever forgiveness you're looking for until after the ritual."

Ashava scoffed at the idea. "Yeah, maybe I'm looking for some forgiveness...some sort of peace, but why would that be wrong for me to want? I'm deserving of something after all I've been through."

"You shouldn't be putting it on him to suddenly make everything better for you." Kiyadeh held a breath. "I certainly don't believe you're doing this for him."

"Not just for him, everyone. Or did you forget what he's here for?"

"Ashava, stop," Kiyadeh said harshly, then gently turned to see Kemahni with an amassed confusion about him. "It'll all be okay. Let's go."

Kemahni didn't object, tired of no one speaking truths, and headed past the sisters to return to the village. Kiyadeh followed but was halted with a quick snatch of her arm by Ashava.

"This was my one chance. You couldn't let me have that, could you? I guess I'm the fool to think anyone in this tribe would treat me any different. Not even my own sister." Ashava gripped harder as her typical anger began to rise. "I'm going to tell you something, and you're not going to want to believe me when I say it, but sure as I live, I promise you, you will believe me."

Ashava's eyes bore seriousness and prepared Kiyadeh to hear her next words.

"Kemahni will not live past the bonding, and it will be yours and everyone's else fault."

"What a lie. I feel sad for you, sister." Kiyadeh tried to reclaim her arm, but didn't make a single step away, before she was pulled back.

"Look at me. Am I lying?"

Kiyadeh's anger flattened as she began to believe the smallest amount.

"I was shocked too when Mother told me. You're not supposed to know, no one is, but I want you to know so you can think about it when you're with him, draining his life away."

"Ashava, let go of me," Kiyadeh demanded with a stern calmness, "I don't need to hear any more."

"Mother told me when I was Guardian. I'm guessing she thought the information wouldn't affect me, since I couldn't have a child. It worked. Made me focus on the one thing I could do. Protect him for the rest of you." Ashava took a solemn moment. "But none of that matters now because he will die still hating me."

Kiyadeh growled after having her fill of lies and tore her hand from Ashava's grip, ripping skin and scales away. "Chieftess will hear about this."

"No, she won't."

Kiyadeh chuckled. "Why, are you going to *try* and stop me?"

"I don't have to. Take my *sisterly* advice. If they know you know, they wouldn't let you bond at all. It...taints the ritual and almost assures you or the rest of the tribe won't have children. Or so I've come to understand."

Kiyadeh stood aghast, not wanting to believe, but unable to ignore her sister. She broke free of the fear holding her, and moved quickly to catch up to Kemahni.

A pained smile cut across Ashava's face that slowly faded as she watched Kiyadeh attempt to console Kemahni, expertly concealing the worry Ashava knew she had to be grappling. Suddenly, lingering memories resurfaced as Ashava imagined herself where Kiyadeh stood, with a much younger Kemahni. If she would have allowed it, tears would have easily escaped her, but she stayed true to the promise she gave herself and forced away any possibility of emotions, painful or otherwise.

The flock of daring birds returned, swarming above Ashava. Her head felt heavy as she peered skyward and closed her eyes, hoping her world would be changed when she opened them again.

"I'm sorry, Tahdwi. I tried."

One month later

The tables had been set for the *Feast of Bonding*, each one filled with more Manyari than could comfortably fit. At the middle seat of the head table sat the Chieftess, with her two daughters to the right, the Great Mother and the Wisewoman on the left, and Kemahni right beside, sitting on a constructed chair-like alter that was higher and more extravagant than everyone else's.

As he looked about, he saw more and different sisters than he had seen before. He had not been told of any visiting tribes or wandering Manyari having come to the village, but he was certain there were more. Or was it that he'd never seen the whole of the tribe all in one place, at one time? Regardless, seeing so many was overwhelming and especially difficult when each of the girls had been polished with styled hair, white dresses he was seeing for the first time, and with wreaths of flowering vines around their necks.

Pairs of mothers and daughters would approach the table whereas the daughter bowed slightly while keeping direct eye contact with him, taking a flower with it's stem coiled around a yarik shard from their own wreath, and slowly adding that beauty and color to his offering wreath that lay on the table before him.

The mother of the prospective daughter would next present an offering to the Great Mother, with a standard, 'We thank you' being the praise given to both. The platitude almost always caused Kemahni to retract a little, and he found himself reaching for his mother's hand throughout most of the event, the tightness of his grip becoming painful that she had to switch positions of their hands every time someone new would come to the table. Ever since the encounter with Ashava, he couldn't rid himself of the feeling there was something wrong about the occasion and he was not privileged to the secret. He saw it on everyone's face and the way they spoke to him, but there was no way to know, and certainly nowhere to hide.

Kiyadeh, who sat on the other side of Chieftess, had her own wreath and gifts she was receiving for having been chosen for *First Union*. The blessing of 'Best union' was said to her with a to-be-expected bit of jealousy, that she detected the first time someone said it. No one wanted to offend, and Manyari are nothing but graceful when defeated, even in a competition such as this. The offerings were the prize for the victor, and once the festivities got into full revelry, any feelings of jealousy would be dulled by food and wine, for they all knew they would get their chance.

Kiyadeh had her own bit of reservedness and discomfort from the attention, distracted by her sister's words she didn't want to believe. She took a few opportunities to look down the table at Kemahni, but only exchanged a glance once. She smiled appreciatively, raised a glass in a gesture that asked, *Good?* He raised his glass, half smiled and smelt the fermented grapes. It opened his nostrils and filled his nose with a pleasant odor, and he behaved as if he was familiar with the drink. He took a sip. He did not enjoy it. When she finished her drink, she saw him staring down at his barely touched food. When she went back to her wine, she found the taste bitter, and put the glass down. She didn't drink for the rest of the night.

Kemahni never found his appetite, barely taking bites of his favorite foods, recognizing the fish he had once caught with his mother. He ate only when he thought no one was paying obvious attention to him, a nearly impossible task as everyone was eager to serve him, never letting his plate be empty.

Saleal watched her son's slow withdrawl into himself. He barely acknowledged the girls when they came to greet him, Saleal having to do the duty of thanking them when Kemahni did not. It was only when Saleal would touch him on his face or head, that he returned for a moment and was able to give her a smile that he was okay, one that she wasn't sure she readily believed. As much as they all said it was a night for him, it was not, and it took a draining toll on him.

As the moon began to rise above the tree line, and meals were finished, Ejah rose, to which the sisters of Orahai immediately fell quiet.

"There is nothing greater than the sight of all of you," the Chieftess addressed. "This night is for all those present, and all the ones who aren't. For those who gave, and those who will give, for tomorrow night, we renew our vow to each other. To continue in this world, and let no one but ourselves choose if we belong, to fight any who would push against us! To that I say, we are Manyari and we are still here!"

Cheers peppered through her words, each yell digging deeper into Kemahni, and each glance of expectation cutting at his soul. As to salt the wound, Ejah shifted her focus to Kemahni.

"Kemahni. Our shining light. Our tree that is about to bear fruit. You unite us all so that we can be better than we were."

Ejah bowed and placed a hand on his head. Everyone followed her lead, creating chains of people linked by hands on one another until everyone had their heads lowered in silent prayer, all facing Kemahni.

He kept his eyes open, sweeping over the litany of people spread across his vision, until he ended upon his mother. Her hand on his shoulder felt heaviest of all and incredibly cold. Chieftess Ejah's touch felt detached and unreal, and amidst all the people, Kemahni felt alone. The hush that took over the village was eerie and Kemahni couldn't stop the silence from ringing in his ears. His mother squeezed his shoulder to remind him she was there, but it felt as if she was reaching out over an eternity.

As he looked about, small orbs of light began to appear to him, one after another, until the dark fields and trees beyond mimicked the stars above. Their presence brought a peace to him, but for reasons he didn't know. A few found their way to him, almost enticing him to follow. He suddenly felt compelled to stand, to follow the spirit wherever it seemed to want him to go. When he tried to move, nothing happened. The orbs continued to move away, and Kemahni was finally able to move his arm to reach for the orb.

Please take me with you, he silently spoke to the spirit. *I don't want to do this. I can't. I'm not ready.*

The spirit paused and slowly returned to him. It rested gently in his open palm. He closed his fingers around it and, when he did, it showed him a lifetime worth of images, none of which were completely clear. After a while, the only thing he was left with were emotions, not all he could be sure were his.

A need to escape came to him in successive waves, until it was all he felt. It focused his mind enough to grab hold of a single vision, a vision of himself floating above large tracts of crystals that stretched as far as he could see in both directions. Kemahni wouldn't believe what he saw was anything but another tormenting false reality coming to him when he was most vulnerable. As if to punish his skepticism, he was suddenly pulled away from the gifted vision, falling parallel with the crystals, into a blinding light.

When his vision returned to the village, everyone was still in the same place. The spirit that gave him the vision slipped out of his hand and wisped away, along with all the others far in the distance.

Again he tried to move, tried to follow, but seeing the ocean of people paralyzed him into inaction, as well as the years of forced dedication to his tribe. Any want to fight the finality of his situation did not give him strength. He simply closed his eyes in submission and listened to the horrible sound of silence.

While everyone kept their eyes closed in solemn prayer and thankfulness, Kiyadeh peeked one eye open and saw the tear that Kemahni didn't want anyone to notice. His face contoured and willed it away with a growing anger. She forced herself to close her eyes and save herself from the image, but she saw his pain even more clearly when it was the only thing her mind could see.

The bitter peace ended when the Chieftess lifted her hand, and the Wisewoman rang her staff three times. The Chieftess helped Kemahni to his feet, and the Wisewoman did the same for Saleal.

"Son of Orahai, and all of you, rest well tonight. Tomorrow, our day will be full," Ejah instructed, exciting the congregation to cheer loudly in response.

Together, the two leaders ushered Mother and son to walk down the center of all the rows of sisters, each showering them with a white powder before bowing respectfully.

The voices compounded and grew to a deafening roar until it was all anyone could hear, but the sound didn't reach Kemahni. Nothing did. He let his legs carry him forward without thought.

His eyes closed to protect him from the clouds of white dust and shut out the sights of the world. And, as Kemahni headed into his last night, he met the weight of purpose and its crushing reality that he finally had to face.

CHAPTER 10
ESCAPE

"Working to find purpose is living life."
- Shardroot Brewer, Pelan

    There was a moment, right before the moon set, when Kemahni had finally managed to fall into a deep enough sleep to dream. It was glorious to him. Serene views of fields and lightly billowing clouds took over everything. He felt peace one only gets during those times right between asleep and awake. A jumble of memories and random thoughts came to him that shifted to his mother for a while; the immortalized woman who *saved* her people by bringing him into the world.
    Once she materialized completely, he opened all the doors inside his heart and let her love wash over him. The longer they were together, the safer he felt, but as dreams do, it slowly came to an end, losing form and leaving him with only feelings. His sleep was no longer his last bastion and sanctuary as he was jolted awake to the sound of clanging instruments and singing villagers. It was an uproarious

jubilee that stung his ears and made his vision blurry as he tried to block the chaos that was storming outside his home. The day had just started and already a worry and anxiety dug deep into him, deeper moment by moment.

His battle for sleep the night before had him fighting against his own mind as it raced through the uncertainty that was *the Ritual*. It was all he could fill his head with; all that was allowed to enter since he resigned to it. As detailed as his mother's description had been, the feelings and concepts he was supposed to understand were things he'd never felt or experienced before, and no one could really instruct him how he was supposed to make it through the day.

Had he pleaded for an alternative to the ritual, he knew he would have been met with patronizing pity. *Your fear will go away once it starts. You will know what to do when the time comes. You are doing a great thing. This is for everyone.*

When the next morning crept upon Kemahni like slow breaths, he adjusted to it like any other, but it was without its usual welcome. No bird songs were sung nor had the sun yet to peak above the forest to fill their home. Finally awake, he listened to the sound of the crowd of people coming nearer. *Nowhere to go now.*

He didn't greet anyone in the procession of people as they started to pour in. He was reserved to lay there as long as they would let him. The first to enter was Kiyadeh, complete in battlegear with spear in hand, fulfilling her duty as Guardian.

When she spotted him not moving, she worried but was relieved when his chest rose from a longer breath. She shook the feeling and, having forgotten her immediate duty, hurried to spread the doorway open. Kiyadeh lowered her head respectfully to the Wisewoman and Saleal as they entered ceremoniously.

Kemahni's mother knelt down behind him and placed a hand underneath his head.

"Up, up, Mahi," she said gently.

On any other day, he would have joyously arisen to her voice, but her call stabbed both of them, knowing it would be a difficult day. She dug her hand completely under him and felt heaviness in her arms as she pulled him upright. The dead weight and lacking resistance would set the tone for the rest of the day.

Saleal hefted Kemahni's wreath, full of flowers and stones, struggling to lift it and keep Kemahni from falling back over. She hated something about having to struggle to hold the weight of both, but garnered the strength to resist gravity, and awkwardly placed the wreath over him like an offering to the statue of a god. He didn't move for a long pause, but she followed traditional procedure and backed away respectfully, simultaneously admiring and distasting the way he appeared. Before either were ready, the Wisewoman broke into chants, waving her ritual staff of hanging yarik stones and crystals in random directions. During timed breaks in her chants, the Wisewoman grabbed handfuls of a white powder hidden in her sleeve and showered Kemahni with it.

Saleal knew to hold her breath, unlike her son who coughed. The Wisewoman was keen to approach him from all avenues and diligently coated him with the powder that clung like ash.

The room became increasingly hazy, but Saleal was able to see a white, milky puddle form in his cupped hands, watching her son's tears slip off his face and mix with the powder. He hadn't seen his mother's concern through his blurred vision but knew it well when she broke decorum and pulled him into her lap. The Wisewoman stopped abruptly, overtly perturbed by Saleal's sudden interruption of the ritual.

"It'll be okay," Saleal promised.

"Please don't make me do it. I don't want to do it," he said, fighting the years of conditioning. It was a fight he was losing, along with the strength to maintain any facade other than fear.

"It won't be much longer. Just be strong for a little while," Saleal said, holding back tears of her own, feeling wrong for giving him such a kind lie.

Kiyadeh couldn't help stealing curious glances when she heard him sniffle, regardless of explicit instructions not to view the christening. She lowered her gaze whenever she was in the Wisewoman's line of sight. Kiyadeh's successive glance froze images in her mind of Kemahni worsening, up until he did not react at all. It was then that Kiyadeh stopped watching and held her guard post.

The Wisewoman grew impatient and continued the ritual without concern. It went on longer than either Kemahni or Saleal expected, and painfully longer than Kiyadeh wanted, until mother and son were completely covered in white powder and the healing leaves of the forest. When the Wisewoman was satisfied she had fulfilled her duty, she left the way she came. She burst into chants and song, with a strength not seen in a woman of her age, and announced to the village that the boy was ready and today would be the most glorious of days.

Many of the other Manyari who had been waiting outside joined in the chant and, soon, it became a chorus of eager recipients. It echoed throughout the village, one voice starting another, and new voices kept the old chants going.

Kiyadeh had still been holding the doorway parted after the Wisewoman left, watching Saleal caress Kemahni and rock him lightly. She waited for them to gather the will to exit, promising herself that despite the flood of mixed emotions—guilt, compassion, worry, and eagerness—it was still her duty to make sure they fulfilled theirs. She waited as patiently as she could.

Saleal could tell that Kiyadeh lingered by how the light was still pouring full into the room with a Manyari-shaped silhouette in it.

"He needs…to get ready," Kiyadeh said, confirming her presence.

"I know, but he's going to need a moment." Saleal informed her. She brushed off some of the white powder. "And so will I," she said with a meager smile.

Kiyadeh understood, happily giving them the space and time they wanted, and let the door close softly. Outside, she maintained her guard, watching the crowd and chaos of people morph into a jubilant display.

Saleal spoke to her son once they were alone. "I'm proud of you, Mahi. I know you will make it through today, because you are strong. And remember, I am always here and I will always love you."

Kemahni did not know how to take her words. To him, it felt as if she had given up, as if she was giving him her last, departing words before she handed him over. It did somehow make a small but important part of him feel better. Her words could always ease his pain, and when he gathered the strength to show his face, there was a sadness hidden behind his renewed conviction, a look that made her whole body cold.

I will pay for this the rest of my life, she knew.

She buried the thought behind her face and mind; behind the fluctuating beat of her heart. She did everything she could to give him the strength he would need to go on. As they looked at each other for a long time, their connection grew deeper and stronger. He finally embraced her equally as tight, and their love rejuvenated. They drove away the bitter cold that was devouring them and finally found the joy and courage to face the day.

She gave him one more squeeze and released him from her hold, turning quickly to retrieve his ceremonial clothing, and to prevent him from seeing the tears she failed to keep. Kemahni rose slowly to his feet, in better spirits, not resisting while she dressed him. He'd never looked so graceful before, never worn something so brightly colored, and it amazed her how the outfit completely transformed him. It visually marked the milestone in his life, leaving his old self behind, and announcing the new him to the world.

"You look good." She smiled.

"Thank you." He nodded bravely.

"Ready?"

As his mother waited for him to answer, a spirit snuck inside from the rear of the hut. It bobbed once and phased back through the animal skinned wall. Kemahni blinked, bringing his attention back to his mother.

"Yes, I…can I be by myself for just a bit? Is that okay?" he asked quietly.

"Of course," she agreed and handed him the cloak he would wear to hide as he traveled from place to place, though everyone knew who would be under the cloak. She gave him one more loving look and then walked out the door to wait outside with Kiyadeh, but when she stepped into the light it was the elder sister, Ashava, who waited.

"Ashava?" Saleal questioned.

"Where's Kemahni?" Ashava asked.

"He's just finishing getting ready. Where's Kiyadeh?"

"She went to get blessed for *First Union*," Ashava said without any detectable hint of animosity. "I'm keeping guard until she gets back."

"That isn't necessary. I will see that he gets to where he needs to be."

"My sister said the same thing, but it's not my choice. I want to be here as much as you or probably anyone else wants me to be, but I listen when the Chieftess orders me to do something."

"Well, let your mother know he will be there shortly, and that *I* will bring him," she instructed Ashava.

Ashava didn't argue. Instead, she sat down in the shade of a tree across from the hut and calmly waited. They stared at each other from across the footpath, neither one outwardly upset.

Ashava didn't budge as spans of time stretched, longer than what should have taken Kemahni to finish getting ready, though she hadn't really noticed. The festival was a prime distraction, as she watched the people weave their way through the village, dancing and singing.

Saleal noticed her son's lateness and became worried. She postponed her stalemate with Ashava to check on him. Immediately upon entering, her worry solidified when she noticed that the hut had been opened in the back, the stitches untied in a haphazard fashion.

"Mahi..." She swallowed.

Her heart sank and stomach tightened. For the first time, his disappearance gave her real concern. In the same instant, she felt relieved.

Let him go, she wildly contemplated. *He'd be better off... free. Go. Don't let anyone find you*, but the dream was cut short by the reality that *he'd never survive the night. Not alone. The world would swallow him, but what was worse? Dying there...*

Or dying here?

The Great Mother slowly headed for the exit at the back of the hut, but before she could reach the opening, there was an odd rustling of fabric. She paused and pleaded to the gods for Kemahni's return, with the little part of faith she had left.

It was Kiyadeh, not Kemahni, who curiously poked her head inside. Kiyadeh stopped in place, her white dress looking odd with her spear in hand. The dress was rather simple in form and design, but something about the way she wore it made it more graceful. Delicate even while wielding her weapon. She lost her balance, bracing on her spear, when she saw Saleal staring straight at her. She acted as if she hadn't been caught, trying to quickly retreat and pretend she didn't see anything.

"Kiyadeh!" Saleal said, as she dashed to grab the young Manyari.

Kiyadeh froze when snatched and began to spout apologies. "I'm sorry, I thought, uh—"

Saleal quieted Kiyadeh's nervous ramblings with two fingers on the girl's lips. "Calm down. You're not in trouble," she assured. "I need you to go find Kemahni."

"Where is he?" Kiyadeh asked but remembered the opening in the back of the hut and Saleal's calculated panic. "He ran?" she asked, worried that it might be true.

"I don't know, but we need to find him. I'll take care of things here while you go look," Saleal ordered.

"Okay." Kiyadeh easily acknowledged. "But why me? Shouldn't you go?"

"I can't. It wouldn't look right if both of us suddenly disappeared, and I trust you to keep him safe."

"Of course, Great Mother."

"And keep this between us. Don't tell anyone."

Kiyadeh paused at the sudden responsibility. "Great Mother, I need to know something..."

"Kiyadeh, later. We have to find Kemahni."

"This is about him. Is he...to be sacrificed?"

Saleal froze at the comment, giving Kiyadeh the answer she didn't want.

"I need to know, even if it means I can't bond with him, I just want to know the truth."

Saleal's continued silence spoke sentences about what was true.

"All that you need to know is he needs you right now. You're still his Guardian. Please find him." She handed her the large ornate cloak Kemahni had left behind.

"I will do my best." Kiyadeh agreed, grabbed the cloak, and quickly exited the tent.

Saleal composed herself and turned to guard the door. She peered through the small division in the door to see if Ashava was still waiting across the way. The tree was absent of her, and Saleal ventured outside to see if she had moved elsewhere, but Ashava was nowhere in sight.

Unbeknownst to Saleal, Ashava had been hiding on the side of the hut, and saw Kiyadeh wind burst across the fields in the direction she thought Kemahni might have run off to. Instead of pursuing, she turned back toward the center of the village to recruit some help.

The celebration was continuing strong throughout, the singing and dancing kept in time by drums and stomps, creating the village's rhythmic heartbeat. Mugs of wine and mead were never less than half full. The Manyari of Orahai became more amorous and less clothed as the day went on. The whole of the experience became a single physical representation of the energy spilling out of each of the girls in the village. It passed like a force from one to the other in a frenzy of building desires. For a day that would come around so rarely, they made sure it was an uproarious occasion that would last for as long as possible. By the end, it would be nothing more than an exhausted community, filled with drunken Manyari huddled in their huts recovering, praying that any one of them would be blessed enough to have a child. And if they were very lucky, a boy.

Tahdwi was in full candor, having found herself in the center of the group of Manyari, many of them vying for her attention. She hardly noticed any of them, enjoying more the way her white dress flowed around her as she danced about, the drape of it accenting her movements. When she did give another Manyari attention, something as slight as glancing look, they'd come over to her and dust her with a familiar white powder, offering her a flowering wreath of courtship.

Each of the girls would spend countless hours preparing intricate wreathes of vines and flowers to give one another as blessings and symbol of their intent. She had been quite popular during the celebration and, to the dismay of many a suitor, returned every wreath presented with a parting kiss on the cheek before continuing to dance.

A taller girl with short but beautifully decorated horns had a determined joy that made her hard to ignore, grabbing Tahdwi's attention for longer than most. The girl glided in between two others on their separate approach to Tahdwi, spun them to face one another, and made them dance together. The couple soon became enamored, seeing something new in each other, and soon forgot about their original target. Tahdwi watched and had admittedly been impressed with the tactic of the girl as she twirled closer.

"Happy day, Deuna," Tahdwi acknowledged.

"Looks like I'm not too late," Deuna exclaimed as she spun around Tahdwi, looking for a possible hidden wreathe.

Tahdwi giggled. "I didn't know you were interested."

"Pretty sure the whole village is interested. I saw a lot of sad girls on my way over here."

Tahdwi smiled. "Oh?" She danced away. "I am still waiting for someone."

"I could be that someone."

"Maybe, but I wouldn't want to add you to my total of sad girls. Besides, aren't you missing something?"

Deuna raised an eyebrow, smirking on the same side with her mouth. She pulled from her belt a single wild flower, bright and blooming.

"Always joking, Deuna. I know you are not trying to court me with a single flower." Tahdwi laughed.

"Why not?" Deuna said definitively. "No one ever said I couldn't. Everyone just keeps trying to outdo each other, and I think they're doing it wrong."

"Are they now?" Tahdwi shimmied.

"Yup." Deuna says before she handed Tahdwi the flower. "While the others try to impress you with lots of big flowers, I know you deserve better."

"I admire your confidence," Tahdwi said, already moving to return the flower, "but this is only—"

"One flower?"

"Yes." Tahdwi graciously held the flower by its steam to return it to Deuna.

"This flower is you, Tahdwi. You are beautiful on your own. You don't need anything extra. In a field of a hundred others, you are the one that stands out the most."

Tahdwi was taken aback and stopped dancing, blushing brightly.

"I've always seen that. But I don't want to keep you." Deuna took the flower from her hand and placed it in Tahdwi's hair. "I don't want to hide you away or pretend you're mine. I want everyone to see that something as beautiful as you can be real. And if you gave me the chance, I would show the world how beautiful you are in every way."

Deuna's victory smile kept Tahdwi's words lost as she touched the flower in her hair.

"Tell me I'm wrong about any of that, and I'll go."

Tahdwi couldn't think, distracted by the feeling of her heartbeat throughout her body. It completely replaced the drums in the village and started her own syncopation. Deuna waited, and they read each other's faces.

"I..." The moment Tahdwi was about to finish, she caught a glimpse of Ashava coming her way hurriedly. "I... I have to go."

"I'd be good at helping raise a child! Think about it!" Deuna asked and sighed heavily.

Tahdwi ignored everyone else on her way to Ashava, forgoing dancing and immediately embracing her.

"Tahdwi."

"You're late," she said, a hint of relief in her voice.

"Yeah. Sorry." Ashava said, pushing Tahdwi gently away. Ashava glanced to see the flower in Tahdwi's hair, not thinking much of it. "Are you okay?" Ashava wondered aloud.

"Yes," Tahdwi offered as she embarrassingly removed the flower.

"I need your help. I'm pretty sure Kemahni is trying to run away. We need to bring him back before he gets too far, and I need you to help me track him."

"Are you sure?" Tahdwi said with mild shock.

Ashava nodded. "It's just the kind of thing he would try today. His mother was hiding the fact he did, and Kiyadeh is involved too."

"Of course, yes. I'll help you."

Ashava suddenly blushed and stumbled over her words, "You deserve...I'm not going to let him... I'm going to make sure you have your chance."

Tahdwi smiled and rejoiced quietly at Ashava's subtle, unspoken show of affection. She rocked on her heels and kissed Ashava lightly on the lips, long enough to enjoy the contact between them.

Ashava blushed harder in reply as her scales flared out, giving her a spiny outline. She grabbed Tahdwi slowly by the back of the neck to hold her in the kiss longer. Eventually, they separated, lingering for as long as they could.

"Let's go!" Tahdwi said as she grabbed Ashava's hand.

Together they hurried out of the village to catch the runaway Manyari.

CHAPTER 11
TOGETHER

"We are never apart when we have loved each other."
- Mother to Daughter

Orahai Outskirts

Kemahni hadn't made it very far in his escape into the fields. The white powder, mixing with his sweat, kept getting into his eyes, making it near impossible to see the spirit he was following or navigate the path.

He stopped several times to clear his vision, each time rubbing his eyes so vigorously it made his face red. All the squinting, wiping, and running built into a headache. Eventually, he slumped to the ground in a defeated mess behind a solitary tree in the field. He cursed, and tried to continue, but when he stood to brace himself on the trunk, his arm fell into the tree. It felt cool, and he excitedly stirred the pool of rain that had collected from a heavy downpour two days before. He eagerly scooped the water to wash himself of the powder and cleanse the recent and awful memories.

After the strenuous effort to cleanse himself, he couldn't find the drive or strength to dry off. The water started to cool him as it evaporated and unconscious shivers ran down him. He lumbered back into the field and flopped his body down on a cushion of grass to face the warming sun that was kind enough to not vanish behind some lazily floating clouds. He thanked the sun, or whatever controlled its trek across the sky, that it shared its rays long enough to warm and dry him.

He looked at the sun through slotted hands, wondering about its creation and if it too was a spirit of the sky. He reached out his shading hand, turning it to grasp at the sun. He widened the space between his fingers until the light was too much, and he had to close his eyes.

He rested for a while until the sharp sound of yarik wind struck his ears and brushed across him.

Yaya... at least he hoped.

He prayed whoever it was didn't see him, though he doubted he would have any kind of luck staying concealed in the less-than-tall grass. One would only have to look in his direction to spot him.

I should have kept running, Kemahni disappointedly thought.

"Ke..." Kiyadeh's familiar voice announced.

Out of all the people who could have come to retrieve him, she wasn't the worst, but he wouldn't have welcomed anyone. It oddly felt like he was playing Grave Walkers, and he hadn't chosen a good place to hide, but there was no more time for games.

A few seconds later, Kiyadeh came into view, hovering over him to block the sun, much like those uncaring clouds he worried about. He kept his eyes closed while she took a moment to assess if he was physically unharmed and then stepped away momentarily to place her spear out of sight. She carefully laid down next to him and for a long while, nothing was said as they listened to the wind. She inched secretly closer to him with her exacting movements, easing herself parallel to him, perfectly content to lay with him and face the warming sun.

As much as Kemahni told himself he didn't want her to be there, her presence had a calming effect. He wanted to look at her when she turned on her side and rested her head on the grass, but he found the sky was an escape for his thoughts and far easier to face.

"What's going on, Ke?" Kiyadeh asked.

"I don't know."

"What do you want to do?" Kiyadeh asked.

"I don't know."

"We can stay...we don't have to go back right away," she said, sure she didn't want him to return at all. "I know this isn't easy. It's scary not knowing what you're supposed to do."

"I'm not scared."

"I am," she said with a soft smile. "I told you before, I'm not good with change. I'm not even sure I want to do this anymore."

His ears lifted a bit.

"But we can't stay out here forever, and whenever you want to go back, we'll go together."

He sighed. "How can you even ask me to go back there...to all that?"

She hesitated. "I used to have a good answer, one that everyone has told you your entire life, but now I just want to know what you want," she said, and waited, wanting him to look at her and see the compassion in her face that her words were desperately lacking. He obliged, finally looking at her through the haze of his still blurry vision.

"You know what I want? I want you all to stop pretending to know what it's like to be me and let me live a normal life," he said dismissively. "I thought I was doing the right thing. It all made sense once, but these last few days... It's like everything has changed. I don't like the way my body is feeling right now. I feel detached, and I'm angry. I'm sad, and nothing feels the same. I hate the different way everyone is looking at me. It's like they don't see me anymore. I feel like a thing. Worst of all, I know everyone knows something I don't, and there's this awful secret. I know things won't go back to normal, and you..." He stopped his next thought from leaving his mouth, knowing his words could wound her without trying. He had to face away to continue speaking. "I don't know what to do and no one seems to care," he calmly added, and realized his body didn't feel cold anymore.

"I care," she said, slightly offended.

"Then stop being like everyone else and stop avoiding answering what this ritual is for. Give me a real answer about what is gonna happen after today, because no one else will. Not even Mother."

"I...really, I'm not sure."

"Alright," Kemahni took the deepest breath he had all day, "then let's not waste any more time finding out."

Without warning, he rolled over on top of Kiyadeh, straddling her tightly between his legs. It made her immediately uncomfortable, yet oddly excited, as she squirmed to get free. She stopped when he pinned her with little trouble. She had never experienced his strength first-hand, unaware of his power, and realizing that she had been right. He had been hiding, holding back before.

She laid perfectly still when he began to move closer—close enough for her to feel his warm breath on her lips and his skin touch hers as he pressed flat against her.

Kemahni felt warmness pulse in him, starting in his stomach and working its way through to the rest of his body. The sensation grew fiercer the longer he pressed his body against hers, making him want to explore her in a way previously unknown to him. More than that, it was a feeling that made him want to share something uniquely special with her. A chaotic mix that made him feel joy and anger at the same time. A feeling that seemed natural. He growled low in protest of not being in control of his emotions, and how they seemed to override everything.

He reached a slow, tracing hand down the length of her white dress, breaking a chain of vines that looped her waist as a belt. She didn't stop him as he continued down her body, passing the hem of her dress, touching her lightly twitching inner thigh. As he started to inch his hand towards the middle of her body, he watched her reaction.

"Is this what you wanted? What you and everyone else always wanted?" he spat.

"Kemahni," she said disappointedly.

She frowned when trying to deny it, but he was right. She and everyone in the tribe had always looked forward to this day, but knowing his life might come to an end to fulfill his life's worth sickened her the most. How could she or anyone else allow his breeding slavery to continue and then use their survival as an excuse to ease their guilt.

She hadn't the strength left to look him straight in the eyes and avoided his judgemental stare, not wanting to imagine the awful things he must have been thinking, especially any that were meant for her. She suddenly believed she could change the rules in that very instant, guide his fate away from the path it was on. She could be the one to save him.

But her thoughts passed through, for all her mind wanted to focus on was the enjoyment of how his wondrous body felt against hers. The way his torso pressed down when he breathed in, and how she was kept motionless from the pressure applied from his flexing muscles. Or the slow dance of his fingers that brushed her leg as they took a path to wherever they wanted. His hips pushed against hers and a warmth built inside her that was more wonderful than the sun. She had fantasized about this moment when they would bond and all the things her mother had described, though it still wasn't enough to prepare her for when it actually happened. She succumbed to being submissive as she had never done and neither one played their roles as *'the protector'* or *'the protected'* any longer.

As the moments stretched, Kiyadeh's entire view of him changed. Not simply the physical, as she had somehow missed his transformation from boy into man, but something more than that. The sun, resting behind Kemahni, creating a halo of light, and his details faded into shadows. What was left was a silhouette of a stronger, more ephemeral being. Witnessing him made her feel as if she was in the presence of something grander than herself, and she finally understood the power that was hidden inside him. A power that they coveted, and most likely feared, though she was not scared by it. Entranced, she disregarded the time that slipped by her, trying to make the moment last as long as she could.

Kemahni didn't share her experience. All, if any, enjoyable feelings felt tainted to him. Forced. Not just from him, but what he wrongly assumed were force, rehearsed actions coming from her. Disgusted by it all, Kemahni bitterly moved off of her in a rough manner before any further physical interaction happened, somewhat annoyed that she hadn't fought back. The sun he had been blocking blinded her, and she quickly turned her head and shielded her eyes.

While she rolled to her knees and hands, she heard the rustle of the grass near to her. When her vision returned, she looked up and saw Kemahni standing above her, spear in hand. Suddenly, all her good feelings were gone.

"Ke, what are you doing?"

"I'm taking your spear and I'm leaving."

"Ke…" she said dubiously.

"Don't try to stop me."

"You can't."

Kemahni gripped harder to the spear. "I can!"

Kiyadeh frowned. "No, what I'm saying is that you won't last out there. Not on your own."

"You don't know that! No one knows what I can do!"

She sighed at the argument and his lack of any training, but abruptly recalled that even with all her skill, she hadn't fared any better in the wild. She had lost a companion to a far more dire situation and couldn't bear to let him join that list of people she'd failed.

"Okay," she said plainly. "If we are going to do this, we need to head back to the village first to get supplies."

"I'm not going back there. You're just trying to trick me. You're gonna hand me over as soon as we get there."

"I'm not, and no, I won't," she said with conviction, staring him in the eyes. "We'll leave while we're supposed to be…together. They won't disturb us and it'll give us time to get away."

"So, all of sudden you want to help me? Why? Why now?"

She moved closer. "Because, whether you believe it or not, I care about you and I want to protect you. It's a promise I made to myself that I would protect you from everything and anyone. That hasn't changed. Not ever."

His shock hit him hard, and he did his best to not show her. He couldn't grip the spear tighter, but he tried, pulling it closer to his torso in fear that he might lose it at any moment. He stared for however long it took him to read her face, and finally, he relaxed, wanting her compassion.

"Give me back my spear and we can go back together. No one will know you were gone."

It took Kemahni a long while before he finally lowered the spear and let the point sway to the side and away from Kiyadeh. She stood cautiously without any aggressive, retaliatory movements.

"If this is going to work, you can't tell anyone. We have to stall the bonding until nightfall, so we can—"

"I shouldn't be surprised by any of this," Ashava scolded.

At the crest of the hill, Ashava stood calmly, flanked by Tahdwi, who was still in her white purity dress. Neither looked outwardly upset, but Ashava's tolerance was at a low.

"You were just stalling." Kemahni accused with betrayal as he turned to Kiyadeh.

"No, I didn't," Kiyadeh promised, giving the two arrivals an angry look, "I don't know how they—" As she tried to move forward to clear her name, she was faced by the point of her own blade. "Ke, I promise you," and quietly said, "I meant what I said."

"I almost believed you," he said dejectedly, chuckling, "but I knew I couldn't trust any of you." He backed away slowly holding the spear steady.

"Don't give my idiot sister any credit. We didn't need her help finding you." Tahdwi unnoticeably shied from the comment. "Besides, you always come to the same place and cross these same wards."

Kemahni looked slightly surprised, and Ashava smirked.

"I figured that out a while ago, I just never knew how you were getting through." She shrugged. "If you were smarter and chose a different route, you might have actually had a chance of escaping."

Trying to regain a misplaced confidence and handle of the situation, he readied the spear in the jump position much like Kiyadeh would.

Across the way, Tahdwi grew anxious and tried to inject her concern, but was halted by Ashava.

"Let him do it, let him learn," Ashava mocked.

His eyes leveled as he mimicked a sweeping hand over the jewel in the center of the blade. Nothing happened at first, to the surprise of none of the girls. He grunted in disapproval, tried again, tapping annoyedly on the crystal.

"Ke, stop, you can't just force it to obey. Please stop before someone gets hurt. I can fix this, my sister can't do—" Kiyadeh cut her speech when she saw yarik flow out of him in a twisting line and back into the spear's crystal.

CHAPTER 12
FIGHT

"You can't lose if you keep getting back up."
- Master Brixius

Kemahni was unprepared for the first time he'd experienced that zip of energy; that mysterious power buried deep within, locked away and never meant to be accessed. It was like a new emotion. A new sense that was open to him. The feeling burned itself into his subconscious as the prelude to yarik. It was energizing, as if his body extended past its physical limits, reaching into the unseen ethers, and channeling it back into the world through his body.

"Yarik is flowing out of him," Tahdwi amazed quietly, "into the crystals?!"

Ashava didn't contain her shock either, stunned at the revelation. "How is he doing that?"

Lines of energy, like those carved into yarik *stones*, drew themselves from his fingertips to the first knuckles. The spear shook as more of his yarik flowed into the stone. He gracefully pulled his hand away from the stone, and summoned visible streams of wind out of the spear. It began to swirl around him in an elegant dance as he slowly backed away, moving the spear between the two sisters.

Once Kiyadeh shook her amazement, she stood to protest, "Stop, Ke!"

Her voice couldn't carry over the sound of sharp winds whipping past him. They gradually grew stronger and began to unsympathetically push him around. His arrogance fled the moment he was no longer in control, the disbelief contorting his worried face. The wind's intensity grew exponentially, and he held on as tightly as he could until the spear was ripped from him. His hands immediately stung, splaying his fingers to relieve the pain left by the wild weapon that escaped his grasp.

A backlash of yarik that had nowhere to go cascaded back into him with angry retribution for not controlling the power lent to him. The pain was doubled, and he fought it long enough to glimpse the spear lodging itself into the ground a few meters away. It swayed like the tail of a fleeing prey, mocking his failure. Shortly thereafter, the spear deactivated and gave a low whistle as the wind disappeared and it finally came to a rest.

"Kemahni?!" Kiyadeh yelled, concerned.

"Why?" he questioned, assured he could have handled the power. He stomped a few steps back towards the spear when a voice locked him in place.

"LEAVE IT!" Ashava suddenly ordered. Despite the outburst, she was mildly amused. "I could say that I'm surprised that you chose today of all days, but I'm not. No more of this, Kemahni. You've caused far too much trouble, and I'm not going to let it continue."

"I'm not going back!" Kemahni inserted.

"You're such a child, and I wasn't asking," Ashava reminded him.

Kemahni looked to Kiyadeh for a brief moment, remembering her offer. Ashava chuckled at the exchanged glance.

"Ashava, go to the village. I'm bringing him back," Kiyadeh informed.

"Oh no. You don't get to give me orders," Ashava growled.

"I'm his Guardian, and he's not going with you."

"HA! Guardian...no. Not for long," Ashava said with a bouncing tone.

"What?"

"I heard what you said, WE heard what you said. You don't get to run away from your words, sister." Ashava grinned.

Kiyadeh scoffed and moved to retrieve her spear.

"I'm sure Chieftess would love to hear that you were planning to leave with him?"

Kiyadeh's blood thickened, and it became hard for her to move, almost falling forward and barely catching herself.

Ashava threw a quick glance to Kemahni. "You should have picked a better partner, because why would you trust her with your life? She doesn't have a good history of keeping people safe," Ashava reminded with a growing, sly smile. Her words began to flow with a righteous fervor, "You won't be alone in crime, sister. His mother will join you, I'm sure of it."

Tahdwi didn't hide her shock and wanted to question the veracity of that claim.

"Think whatever you want. You're wrong," Kiyadeh said.

"Neither you or his mother are very good liars. I could tell the moment each of you opened your mouths you were lying for him. And now, because of it, none of you are safe," Ashava finished, satisfyingly tilting her head at Kemahni and casually shifting her weight to one leg.

Kemahni seethed from the comments, flattening his ears defensively under his horns. A stream of several uncategorized emotions raged in him, directed in a beam that he hoped she felt.

Ashava welcomed the glare, the hate, and let it wash over her.

Tahdwi felt only his pain and calmly stepped forward. "Kemahni, please, don't fight. I promise you, if we can calm ourselves and return home together, everything will be okay," Tahdwi said convincingly.

It would have been impossible for anyone else to have said it sweeter, and from anyone else it would have sounded like a lie. Had the situation been different, Kemahni might have listened to such a sincere request, but he knew none of it was said with *his* best interests in mind.

"Everyone keeps saying it'll be okay, but everything is not okay! I'm tired of hearing it! Tired of all the secrets and everyone pretending that all of this is for me, when it's for all of you!" He dashed for the spear again and no one stopped him. He leaped horizontally, used the embedded spear as a pivot point and swung around it. He secured his feet facing them and pulled the spear out in a large arc over his head with a shower of ground debris. He leveled the spear at the two girls and waited for someone to act. The display impressed Kiyadeh, and Ashava too if she'd ever admit it, but his former Guardian simply held her smile at his brashness and felt victory approaching when she noticed his hands shaking.

"Have it your way. Tahdwi." Ashava signaled Tahdwi to come forward.

"Alright..." Tahdwi said.

When Tahdwi reluctantly stepped forward, Ashava put herself into a more aggressive posture in preparation.

Kiyadeh felt her heart race. "Stop, Ashava! He'll go back. Tahdwi, you don't have to do this."

Tahdwi closed her eyes, fighting her want to meet Kiyadeh's gaze and trying her best to block the girl's suffering pleas.

Failing to reach her, Kiyadeh begged, "Kemahni, put the spear down...please," but was ultimately ignored. "Listen to me! I'm his Guardian!" she frustratedly yelled at the others.

"You are nothing."

Some part of Kiyadeh shattered from the fear that her sister might be right, for her words had no weight to them. She could only watch as Kemahni and Ashava's visions tunneled between each other as they prepared for a fight, long since coming.

"Do it," Ashva instructed.

She rubbed her left earring and took a deep breath. A sweet song, like when she spoke, escaped her lips in a constant breath.

Kemahni's ears perked and came out from hiding beneath his tightly spiraled horns. The song was upsettingly beautiful to him. It was a serene and tranquil melody that he didn't want to hear but couldn't refuse. In between the notes of perfect pitch were hidden words that he didn't consciously hear.

> *Be heavy as stone.*
> *Calm as untouched water.*
> *Gentle as a breath of wind.*
> *And rid your heart of fire.*

Kemahni knew of the mystique that surrounded Tahdwi and her ability, but he was completely unprepared when he felt the song pass through him. He listened and couldn't help abide by its command. The whole of his body became weak, and he tried desperately to maintain his defensive posture. His anger slowly became distant and ineffective. His once focused vision blurred to near blindness, and every time the words echoed in his head, the effect compounded.

"...you can't do this...you can't make me go back," he said, "don't make me..."

He fell to the ground in a heap of a defeated boy.

Kiyadeh also grew heavy and weak, but was able to stay upright. Kiyadeh thought she knew enough to protect against Tahdwi's *singing winds*, but knowledge and experience were two very different things.

"Tahdwi, stop. Kemahni..." she cried, fighting the yarik to speak.

Ashava strode victoriously to Kemahni and towered over him. He searched with what strength he had for the spear that was once in his hands. He felt the cold metal and grasped it shakily. Kiyadeh watched with shock as he rose to unstable feet. His hand slowly crept to the crystal at the blade, only to be then stopped when he was assertively backhanded by Ashava. It sent him back to the ground with the spear flying loose.

Tahdwi stopped her song on an abrupt note. She tracked the spear through its short flight, until it disappeared in the grass. She shifted her focus to Kiyadeh who was on the verge of tears, frozen, and staring at Kemahni.

Kiyadeh slowly scanned to Ashava, who refused to acknowledge her, and when her eyes locked with Tahdwi's, hoping to find sympathy, Tahdwi remained vigilant and unemotional.

"Tahdwi, the ritual...it's going to kill him!" Kiyadeh gaspingly yelled.

A second shock rocked Tahdwi to the core. She looked to Ashava for confirmation, who was bearing her displeasure of the outed secret with clenched teeth.

"Ashava?" Tahdwi asked.

"Don't listen to her. You can't believe anything she says, not after what we heard her say before."

"You're the one who told me, Ashava!" Kiyadeh divulged. "Do you think she will forgive you after it happens?"

Tahdwi's confused grew, and she tried to search her own feelings and memories for a glimmer of truth. "Is it true?"

"Tahdwi," Ashava said flatly.

"We all knew something was wrong with this, but none of us wanted to think about it." Kiyadeh addressed Tahdwi, "I'm sorry you have to find out this way, but it needs to stop."

"You can believe whatever you'd like, but the fact remains that he's caused far too much damage to the tribe, and I'm not gonna let it continue." Ashava flipped Kemahni onto his stomach, and pressed him into the ground, harshly forcing his arms behind his back.

With the last fight in him, he struggled feebly against her, causing Ashava to reassert herself by digging a knee into his back. He whimpered at the pain.

"Ashava!" Tahdwi cried, but the words were ignored.

"Stop moving," Ashava said in mild annoyance.

"Get...off of me!" Kemahni bellowed groggily.

Ashava laid her entire weight on top of him and spoke secretly, "I tried to help you through this, make it easy for you, but you just couldn't do as you were told. Look at what your selfishness brought you. I wish I never made the mistake of thinking that caring for you would make me better."

"You can't—"

Ashava didn't let him finish as she forced his face to meet the ground. Ashava reached behind her in a summoning motion, never taking her eyes off the boy. Tahdwi sadly came forward and disappointedly gave Ashava a rope. With it, she began to bind him.

"Ashava, get off him right now!" Kiyadeh said, having recovered from the song.

Kiyadeh had retrieved her spear and was pointing it unerringly at Ashava. The bonds of a family whisked away on the wind that began to pour out of Kiyadeh's spear. Sisters were turned enemies, standing at opposite ends of an impossibly wide chasm they helped carve.

"You're not gonna fight me, so don't you point that thing at me. I'll drop you just as quickly as I did him," Ashava smirked.

"I'd like to see you try!" Kiyadeh chopped through sharp words.

"I don't think attacking me is going to help your case. How can you not see that you're going to lose everything. There's nothing you can do now that will protect you once they find out everything you've done. No *First Union*, no tribe, no nothing."

"I don't care about that," Kiyadeh said.

"Of course you do. It's the only reason any of us put up with him."

Tahdwi wanted to object, but Kiyadeh answered for her.

"I did, but I was wrong. We all are and it has to change," Kiyadeh demanded.

Kemahni managed to roll his head to see her, and stopped struggling for a moment.

"I don't know who you're trying to convince, but stop. It's pathetic and it's not going to make the punishment you deserve any less worse."

"That I deserve? Is that what you were hoping for this whole time, to see me punished?" Kiyadeh's eyes narrowed.

"I was at least willing to pay for my mistakes. You haven't once paid for any of yours. You or his mother won't even take responsibility for filling his mind with ideas that he was special. That he was above it all. For some reason you all forget we keep him here for the one thing he is useful for. You pretending he is anything else is just sad, *sister*."

Kiyadeh raised her spear a little higher. "I won't warn you again. Let him go, Ashava!"

Ashava smirked widely, and then turned her attention back to completing her knot.

The final binding tug on the knot made Kemahni feel as if his shoulders were being pulled out of their sockets. He let out a horribly, pained cry, which went ignored by Ashava as she tried to lift him to his feet. He refused to stand, either because of the pain or the bit of will he had left to fight.

"Stand," Ashava barked.

Kemahni writhed despite the pain.

"Stand!".

"ASHAVA, PUT HIM DOWN!" The *Great Mother's* ordered with authority, and Ashava momentarily froze at the command.

Saleal, still dressed formally and not fully cleansed of the white powder, marched in a direct line for Ashava and her captive son. And she wasn't alone, she had traveled with a subtly furious Ejah and her two Wind Rider guards, who appeared surprisingly uneasy at the situation.

"Now!" Saleal reinforced. The sound reverberated and unsettled the powder in a small plume around Saleal's upper body in a perfect aura.

Tahdwi wasn't without her own amazement, but the image of the Great Mother made her more anxious and worried than awestruck.

Ashava's righteous justice returned and she stood strong. "Or what?" she genuinely inquired.

"Girl, you really don't want to find out," Saleal growled while stopping just out of striking distance.

Kiyadeh looked in awe at Saleal and how the white powder lifted from her but wasn't making its fall back to the ground, staying in a static silhouette around her.

"Threats? Really? I don't know why I have to keep reminding everyone what's at stake! Why am I the only one who's not afraid to do what's best for our people?"

"Mother...!" Kemahni cried for help.

Ashava was quick to elbow him in the sternum to knock the wind out of him. "Quiet, this is all your fault," Ashava said calmly. "Do you see now what kind of child you have raised?" she shot at Saleal.

That was all Saleal could tolerate, as she balled her fists and growled through her teeth, "That's it—"

Ejah was quick to stop Saleal with a hand on the shoulder and a coarse, "Enough!" The single word stopped time, and no one moved until the Chieftess spoke again. "Ashava, bring him here. Carefully."

Ashava did as she was asked and walked past them all, one by one. She passed Tahdwi, who couldn't look at her, passed Kiyadeh, who had yet to lower her weapon, and finally Saleal. Before Ashava could move further, she felt a tightening around her arm. Saleal had grabbed her so quickly that she hadn't noticed and was convinced no one could have stopped the Great Mother if they tried. Ashava's hold on Kemahni slipped slightly and there was a momentary glimpse of fear in Ashava's eyes. Saleal squeezed her forearm as hard as she could, unable to vocalize her rage.

"I-If you want to say something, don't tell me...Tell Chieftess," Ashava looked to her mother. When Saleal looked to Ejah too, Ashava broke the hold on her with an expert twist of her body. She immediately began to bleed from the area where Saleal had grasped her, nail marks deep in her skin, but pretended as if it was inconsequential.

She fixed her grip on Kemahni and hefted him up on her shoulder. Victoriously she led the way, in a proud march, back to the village before anyone could follow.

Ejah took barely a breath to survey the damage. "Return home, all of you," she steely said, not waiting to collect her other daughter, Kiyadeh, before heading back as well.

The Wisewoman had arrived as the situation resolved, standing to the side and carefully examining Kemahni as he passed her. She narrowed her eyes upon seeing his arm hanging limp and the fresh yarik lines. Her gaze continued to the field where Saleal attended to the unmoving girl. The Wisewoman braced herself on her staff, the complete disappointment of the day gripping her. She reached up to a purple crystal on her staff and rubbed it covertly, closing her eyes.

Saleal gently pushed Kiyadeh's blade down and deactivated the stone. Kiyadeh's eyes started to water as soon as she let her weapon drop. All at once, the emotions of the moment slammed into Kiyadeh, and she resorted to crying to pass the time until the pain subsided or an answer would hopefully come to her. She felt lost and scared of what would happen to her and more importantly to Kemahni.

"I'm sorry, I tried. I didn't mean to let it...I'm sorry," Kiyadeh muttered.

Always the mother to comfort tears, Saleal pulled Kiyadeh close. "It's alright. It's alright. You did what you could." She pushed her own anger aside to ease Kiyadeh who had trickles down her face. Saleal watched disappointedly as the band of Manyari returned with her son to the village. Her quick calm reverted back to stalwart focus and she sternly proclaimed, "This was never your responsibility. It was always mine."

CHAPTER 13
REALITY

"What we work for is a life that makes sense."
\- Seventh Chieftess Mayta

Orahai Village

There was no celebration that filled the village as the evening silently rolled into dusk. The whole of the tribe waited on the sharp edge of doubt, keenly aware of what had happened. Rumors began the moment Kemahni was brought back, bound and beaten, filed through the village as if a prisoner. He was hefted upon Ashava's shoulder, refusing to walk when offered, and never admitting to any notion of wrongdoing. She would later confirm the rumors of Kemahni's desertion and embellished her *heroic* efforts to bring him back. Hardly any of it would want to be believed, yet the people could not deny what they saw. Old tales and feelings resurfaced of past males and the dire outcomes that would befall those who disobeyed.

Night fell unceremoniously, and the answers that might have calmed everyone had yet to come. It left some angry and confused, but most felt lost and afraid. The energy of the village had been sapped away and the only visible life left came from the lamps that circled the Chieftess' hut.

The oddly shaped lamps of yarik fire and wind puffed out flames in quick, random intervals, like a dwarfed mountain threatening to become a volcano but bound to the stone. Past the pulses of flames, a heat of greater matter was poised to spread out of control. Tensions had been contained until Ejah and Saleal finally had their chance to speak alone and freely. The air was thick with anticipation. Ejah kept a skillful check of her displeasure with the Son of Orahai while Saleal did the opposite and let forth her anger.

"Something needs to be done about this," Saleal ordered.

"Something will be done, but I'm not going to go around handing out punishments. Not when we are this close. We must think this carefully through and hope we can salvage his mind and put him back on the right path," Ejah said.

"You want to wait, when there is a lot we can do that doesn't require any discussion? You need do something NOW!"

Ejah halted when questioned in a tone she hardly heard since becoming Chieftess, tolerant of her long time friend.

"Why do you think so differently now? These girls are doing the exact same thing you and I did. Nothing has changed. You're letting the fact that you gave birth to him cloud your thinking. He is not solely your son, you know that."

"I don't see how that matters! Did you not see that he was in danger today?"

"We both know how Ashava can be, but I think that's a little excessive to say she was putting him in danger. If anything, Kemahni posed more of a danger to himself, and us, by his actions."

"You want to blame him?"

"Yes. All of this was his choice. He chose to run away, he is the one who used yarik, Saleal."

Saleal stammered, "I don't know how that is impossible, we made sure of that."

Ejah's eyes fell to a pouch on the table, chalked with white powder. "Unless he wasn't given the adequate Essence," came the accusation in her voice.

"Even if I were to stop, and know that I didn't, there are plenty of others who would have given him his daily amounts. You included."

Ejah judged Saleal's trustworthiness before continuing, "We are lucky he only used yarik once, because had he used too much of it... he wouldn't have enough to pass to others, and then where would we be?"

"Ashava's mistaken. Kiyadeh even said it was she who activated the spear, not him."

"I know what my other daughter claimed," Ejah said disappointedly, "but you saw the yarik lines carved into his hand. Tell me, who am I to believe?"

"Again, none of that matters, for it does not give Ashava call to treat him like she did."

"Who's to say her reaction isn't also a product of this whole fabrication of freedom we present to ourselves or the illusion of choice we give these children. No one detests the way this has become more than I, and if there were another way, I would gladly entertain it, but you know we can't force his obedience. Nor anyone else's, Man or otherwise. Bonding has to be a choice. He has to want it... or at least believe he does. I feel like we have failed greatly in this area."

"It's because he is different."

"You wanted him to be different," Ejah repeated flatly. "Saleal—"

"He is. He isn't cruel, he does care about people. He wouldn't harm them. If we could take our time with him, let him get used to the idea of bonding over seasons. Learn to repair the lines. Give him a real choice, so that he wouldn't turn out the same as his fathers. It could be possible."

"We don't know that Saleal. YOU don't know that," Ejah emphasized each word. "And time is something we just do not have."

"Tell me when he's ever acted out aggressively!"

"Today, Saleal! Today. It only takes that one time for everything to change." Ejah growled. "You changed the moment you became a mother. I changed when I started this tribe and became Chieftess. And he is changing now, into something that we won't be able to control."

"We can save him, find a way so that he doesn't have to sacrifice everything with no say in it. He deserves to be treated like family." Ejah wanted to interject but Saleal continued, "I know better than anyone what his life means and what it brings, but I'm supposed to protect him—love him, raise him. Not watch everyone else use him until there is nothing left," she ended almost in tears.

Ejah sighed heavily. "No one doubts your commitment to him or this tribe, Saleal, but this isn't about your love for him. This is about survival and the love we have for each other."

Saleal gave a doubting look.

"That love you have for him is shared by everyone. He brings joy and hope to us all, and for that we love him deeply. Without him we don't have a future, and hopefully someday we can rid ourselves of this curse that has seemed to follow all Manyari so we never have to do this again."

"Then let it start with him, let him be the first that won't be like all the others."

"We can't. Not now. If we do nothing, he becomes like the worst of them, and we can't afford to have another season without children. No one cares to think about how close we are to disappearing, so we have to focus more on the things that help us through these dark days. Ashava continues to do what she does because she loves Tahdwi. You will call her actions misplaced, but she knows that the next generation is more important than the last, just like everyone else in this village knows."

"She shouldn't be praised for what she did."

"No one's praising her," she almost chuckled. "You're right to feel the way you do. I even agree with you; there was a better way of handling all of this," Ejah conceded. "But I have to work with what has been done, not what could have been done differently. What we should all be thankful for is that we have him back safe, and that tomorrow we can move on."

"And like that, it's all swept away?!"

"You need to stop looking at everything so broadly. I'm not ignoring what has happened, and this is not an either-or choice. I feel as if I am repeating myself. I truly fear you may have forgotten your responsibility as Great Mother. You were to nurture him, raise him to understand his place in the world like only you could. Who he has become falls on you more than anyone."

"You're saying this is my fault?!" Saleal's mouth curled, showing angry teeth.

Ejah's brow arched upwards. "I'm saying this is all our fault. We should have never let it get this far."

Saleal bit on her cheek.

"Saleal, we are too few to take any chances. No one likes this life that has been forced upon us, where we trade one life for many, but this is how we survive." she said definitively.

"Survive." Saleal looked lost in the word. "If our numbers worry you, ask for more from the other tribes. Request another Inyari. Encourage our sisters to bond with each other. Ask for a male from another tribe. Anything!"

"I'm not going to knowingly suggest to our people that they risk their lives, just to carry a yarik-less and probably barren child. That puts an end to anyone's family line, and how is that beneficial? Those births sap the mother's life to survive and survival is low for both of them. You know what I went through having Ashava, and I will not ask our people to do the same. And why? Simply to save Kemahni from fulfilling the purpose he was born and raised for?"

"A choice I'll never understand."

Ejah pressed her lips together to hide her clenched teeth.

"Yarik hasn't ever brought us peace or prosperity," Saleal bit down on the words. "It had us hunted as animals by both Man and Valkys alike. And now we hide here, expecting a miracle to happen every so often. And why not ask the others to sacrifice as much as we are asking him to, unless you want to finally be honest and tell me that his life is worth less than everyone else's."

A shock took away Ejah's ability to counter.

Saleal continued, "If this is how we are going to treat each other, what's the point? We are no different than the rest of the world."

"I've never heard you speak so foolishly. We are nothing like those out there!" Ejah sounded insulted and broke her calm face. "I'm not going to let you continue as if none of us have sacrificed anything raising this child. We do. Everyday, whether you let yourself see that or not." Ejah almost cracked a smile. "You can act like you are so vastly different from Ashava, yet you both are so singularly focused on your emotions and neither care to understand anything greater than the small world you built around yourself."

Saleal looked bewildered by the casualness of her comment. "You think me understanding her will change my view of what she did?"

"Why we do things is as important as what we do." Ejah controlled her breath for a moment. "But I know that won't satisfy you, so tell me, what would you have me do to fix this? Should we lash her? Remove her horns? Exile her? What more could we do to her that would satisfy you?"

Saleal scoffs, "You wouldn't do any of those things."

"No, I wouldn't, but it certainly sounds like you want to make an example of her."

"I would take anything at this point that shows you care about him!"

"This whole tribe revolves around him, and most of our sole purpose has been to protect him and take care of him. Is that not showing we care?"

"No, because he isn't free!"

"No one is!" Ejah argued fiercely. "No one goes through this life without having to pay for their choices or freedoms. We are all indebted to something. I will not feel wrong that we choose to exhaust his life now in order to create more life, especially if it prevents him from growing into the monster we've seen so many become. I won't let this tribe suffer to absolve ourselves of guilt for keeping him contained."

A lull fell over the conversation while they gathered their thoughts. Ejah turned away from the Great Mother and took the opportunity to activate another yarik stone, before tossing it into the fire. She stared longingly into the flames that slowly reinvigorated from the new stone. The fire's light pulled forth a memory that made her long for a time when she used to play recklessly with yarik to make unnecessary fires. How it was all she could do some days while she waited for stars to appear at night. She dreamt of having no responsibility again, when she only cared about her adventures with Saleal and the deeper love they might never share again.

One for many, Ejah said quietly to the fire and anyone who might hear her whisper.

"I have to ask," Ejah said louder, still facing the fire, "did you have anything to do with his escape?"

"The fact that you ask means you think I did. Or that I could," Saleal responded sourly.

"He looked intent on leaving this time, Saleal," Ejah breathed hard. "Did you tell him?"

"Tell him? The *truth*? No. I didn't want to worry him anymore then he already was."

"Nothing? Nothing at all?"

"I didn't tell him!" she snapped.

Another silence gripped the room. Ejah began to feel uncomfortably warm standing next to the fire, and finally turned to face Saleal.

"Please, Saleal, help me understand. Why is this all of a sudden a problem in your eyes?"

"He's my son," Saleal said, as if the question was unnecessary. "He's everything to me. My life, my spirit. I can't let the most important part of me just disappear. What kind of mother am I if I don't help him grow up to be better than I am? How can anyone ask me to watch and do nothing?"

"You've done more than you know, Great Mother. You brought life to us. A chance where there was none. You gave us hope." She closed the gap and placed a hand on Saleal's face, whose ears lifted slightly. "And yes, he IS yours by blood and he will always be. He will carry your life with him, and pass it to all the children he will sire.

He'll never be gone and you will get to see him in all of your *greater children*...but he has, and always did, belong to the tribe."

"We don't have to destroy *everything* he is. Everything he'll ever be." As she said it, she felt her body grow heavy and leaned into Ejah's hand. Saleal closed her eyes to stop the tears and sank to the floor with Ejah's help.

"What if we *do* tell him everything, teach him to not be like his fathers," Saleal let the words trickle out.

"Saleal, we need not go needlessly in a circle about this." Ejah turned to look at Saleal directly. "He already is better than any we've known before. Despite today, he will make a way for many to follow and will not start a cycle of heartache for this tribe. We can continue on without any loss of extra life. He will be remembered as a great Manyari."

Another pause came.

"At least stop using the Essence. Let him do what he needs to do with a clear head and through his own means. He has to know what's going to happen to him," Saleal's idea quietly zipped out of her as she dropped her head.

The request made Ejah's horns twitch in a moment of contemplation and her heart broke for Saleal. She sat lightly beside her and placed a loving hand on the back of Saleal's head.

"If you truly love him and want his life to be worthwhile, go to him. Spend the time you have left with him. Make him understand what we have been telling him all these years, that he can do more than any unanswered prayers from silent gods has ever done. He has a purpose. His life has meaning and is worth giving."

"So that's it?" Her voice was full of held back tears. "Just...let him go?"

"He will not feel pain. He'll be happier than he ever has been." Ejah stood and moved her hand to under Saleal's chin to gently pull it up to match her gaze. "You won't go through this alone. We will find a way through this together and be better on the other side." Ejah backed away slowly, letting her fingers touch Saleal as long as they could before parting. "Remember, he is not the one who must live with our decision. Find peace for him...and for you."

Saleal didn't fight when Ejah escorted her toward the door. It filled Ejah with a horrible sense of dread the way the Great Mother creeped warily through the exit, into the cold, unforgiving reality of the world. Ejah couldn't help but feel as if she was losing more than she was ready to give. She could only hope that in time, Saleal would recover, and hopefully forgive her someday. The night slowly swallowed Saleal while Ejah watched with a steely composure.

As ghostly as Saleal had disappeared, the Wisewoman appeared from the night to confer with the Chieftess. Oddly to Ejah, she hadn't heard the Wisewoman's staff until she saw it and didn't let her know the surprise when she bowed to welcome her.

"Wisewoman, it is late. You should be resting."

"On a normal night, maybe, but we both know it is not. I can rest well when all is done. We can not let this day stop us from the great work we have done."

"Had I known such a night would come, I might have never taken the opportunity to lead. Saleal and I started this tribe together, and I have never once felt so distant from her."

"She will find her way. And as I believe, these things have a way of fixing themselves. We must always remember we do right by our people through the things we do here and now, without always seeing what is to come."

Ejah closed her eyes in a moment of thought. "I cannot take any more chances. I need to ensure nothing further hinders the ritual. I will send my guards to watch over Kemahni."

The Wisewoman frowned secretly. "If you are to restore his mind, perhaps continuing to treat him as a prisoner is not the best. This requires a softer touch from a girl who might help him recover some of his love and care, do you not think?"

Ejah took a long inhale and held it until she felt the slight pain of her body wanting to expel the air.

Down the main throughway of the village, Saleal was alone, entering the hue of the moon as a ghost of her former self. She struggled to resolve an inner battle of wanting to soothe the tightening of regret that gripped her chest, and stabs of horrid ideas that filled her head.

Then the love for her son filled her thoughts, and her steps slowly went from dead shuffle to heavier, planted footfalls. Quickly, she was at a jog. Then a wild sprint.

I will make everything right.

CHAPTER 14
LOVE

"Don't use that word lightly. It has the power to change everything."
- Matchmaker Po'tolan

    How easily a bright and beautiful home was turned into a dark cell for Kemahni. Inside, he was bound with rope around his waist and ankles, secured tightly to the center post that was the main support for the hut. He barely had space between himself and the wood to take anything but small, shallow breaths.
    He was miraculously sleeping, in an obviously uncomfortable position, a task that took the better part of the night to achieve. Sleepless nights and an overexerted body demanded he rest, whether he was willing to give in or not. His persistent battle against sleep was mostly fueled by the disappointment at losing his chance at freedom and becoming an actual prisoner of his own people.

I could... could have taken my chance out there. I am strong. Stronger than anyone thinks. And with Yaya, we could have...Why didn't you try to fight for me more if you really meant what you said? I shouldn't have listened to her. I shouldn't have listened to any of them. Kemahni said to no one, inside his dreamless sleep.

Tahdwi, who had been chosen to watch him through the night, was working in the corner of the hut, keeping herself busy preparing yarik shards. She had stopped what she was doing when she noticed Kemahni's uneasy movements and slight groan. He shivered noticeably and it took a second to realize why, finally feeling the cold on her face. She had been bundled in a layered cloak knowing how easily the nights chilled her. The *fire* stones in the hut had exhausted their heat and she rose to replace them, activating them in her hands without being harmed by the fire.

Lit dimly by the renewed light, she looked upon Kemahni with unease, bothered greatly that no one, including herself, had stopped to think that Kemahni had clothes only good for the daytime. She immediately set her things aside and removed her outermost layer to lay over him. It fell off twice, finally staying in place when she tucked it in between him and the post, all without waking him. His right hand fell from beneath the fabric and she frowned at the lines that adorned his fingertips and hand. Lines very much like those of the shards she was working with. His fingers curled slightly in her hand and she caringly cradling it lovingly in her own palm. She tucked his arm back under the blanket, found her smile again, and returned to her corner to resume her work.

As she sat again, she corralled her materials, small yarik shards, crude glass flasks, and cork tops, arranging them neatly in front of her. The shards were sizably smaller than other stones used for torches or those in the wards, more akin to those used in fishing water traps. Their creation was a difficult and tedious process. Cutting slim enough along the shards and avoiding severing the natural yarik lines to maintain the energy inside was a task that few could accomplish. It was an artistry secret within her family, having learned it from her mother and hoping that one day she could pass it to her daughter. Or son.

If and when she would have her chance.

Tahdwi selected one of the shards and rolled it in her hand. She rubbed the stone to activate the yarik within and focused her thoughts on it.

The world heals through us

The shard was enveloped in a lattice of overlapping lines, glowing green with faint power. She took the short time she had to ensure it was in the right configuration before it would activate fully, for failure at that point would render the shard useless. She made quick adjustments to noticeable flaws in the connection, carving with a crafting chisel.

Once everything looked in order, she quickly wrapped the shard with a single dried vine and dropped the it into the flask. She was ready with the cork and thumbed it into the neck of the glass container. Ghostly emerald roots and branches with leaves immediately grew from the vines as it was renewed with life from the translucent shard. A sap-like liquid, green and glowing, began to seep from the roots. Tahdwi held the flask at eye-level and watched with enjoyment as the container filled. Every time she invoked yarik's powers, she felt more connected to it, as if the world was speaking back through little sparks of energy. She never tired of it and swore she did it only for the feeling sometimes, even fantasizing about being uniquely bonded to it.

The shard stopped dispensing fluid once the flask was full. Tahdwi gave it a final, happy shake and the light refracted through the flask gave the hut a verdant glow. She looked past the flash and saw Kemahni with a green aura, sleeping more comfortably. She smiled contently, and held it for a while after the flask's glow faded and the dimness in the room returned. Soon another flask began to fill and the light shone again.

Tahdwi continued for a while until she heard a heavy throat clear from just out the door.

Why won't she go home? Tahdwi asked herself sorrowfully.

Just outside, Ashava had been standing guard, counting down the hours until dawn, not having anywhere to go, or anywhere she wanted to be. The bright monochromatic moon and its prismatic crystal *Sea of the Gods* was reaching its highest point and she stared blankly at it, not caring about its origin or purpose, admiring it as it hung almost directly above her. It was one of the only things that could give her calm after that chaotic day.

Her ears perked when she heard Tahdwi exit the hut. Reflexively she grabbed the handle of her axe but loosened it when Tahdwi stepped into the moonlight with a still filling flask.

"Ashava, why are you still here?" Tahdwi questioned plainly.

"To help," Ashava responded obviously.

"With what? There is nothing I need that requires your help. I'm fine."

"Why?"

Tahdwi hesitated to answer. "You know you're not supposed to be here anyways," she said, almost having trouble looking directly at Ashava. "You should be home. If the Chieftess finds you here, you will be in more trouble."

"I'm not worried about that. I'll be fine. She's busy arguing with the *Great Mother*. She won't know I was here unless someone tells her," Ashava said with a reluctant smile. "Right?"

"Please go home, Ashava," Tahdwi said coldly and turned around to go back inside.

"Tahdwi," Ashava said, grabbing Tahdwi's hand lightly, "I came to see you."

"I know, but I don't want to see you right now," Tahdwi's voice rattled, and she pulled her hand away.

"I know you're mad, but don't be. I did this for you."

Tahdwi craned her neck swiftly. "No. Don't say that. I would have never asked you to hurt him. I would have never asked to hear what was said."

"You weren't supposed to know."

"Was it true? Have you been keeping this from me the whole time?"

"No," Ashava said with hesitation. Tahdwi tried to pull away again. "Yes, but I had to. I couldn't let anyone know, especially you. If you knew, they wouldn't have let you bond. But that doesn't matter... everything is good now, and you're taking care of him, and no one knows you know." Ashava gestured to Tahdwi who had already turned her head to look back to the hut. "Just forgive me, so we can go back to normal."

"It doesn't work that way. Nothing is normal anymore because of what you did, and now I have to live with this knowledge too."

"You can't put this all on me," Ashava said, displeased. "This was his fault. Someone had to stop him."

Tahdwi turned swiftly again. "He only knows how to live the life we've given him...he doesn't have a choice. You have a choice. You chose to mistreat him."

"Okay! Okay...you're right, I messed up." Ashava finally conceded.

"I don't care about being right, all I wanted was for you to love him."

"What?! I...I—"

"And stop blaming him for everything bad that happened to you."

"He's not innocent. He's not a child. And it was never my responsibility to love him, I just had to make sure he did the right thing."

"And who made sure you did the right thing?"

"I've always done the right thing!" Ashava defended.

"Goodnight, Ashava," Tahdwi said sternly, pushed the flask into Ashava's chest, and walked back into the hut.

Ashava almost dropped the flask, and when the frustration rushed into her, she had to fight to not slam the glass to the ground.

"Tahdwi?" Ashava called.

After a few seconds of silent protest and angry contorted faces, Ashava begrudgingly crossed the road and fumed under the tree.

Inside the hut, Kemahni let out another unconscious whimper, loud enough for Tahdwi to hear. The blanket had fallen off and he was crying lightly in his sleep. She rushed to recover him, hoping he wouldn't wake from the cold, or from the tears that she wasn't sure how to stop. She knelt down and placed the cloak over him again.

"Kemahni," she said sorrowfully, wiping his face with a cloth.

He fought the beckoning of her voice, wanting to stay lost in that place where he was separated from his body and tucked far away in his own mind. The power of her soft voice pierced the veil. He could no longer hold onto his oblivion, and in that split second before he awoke groggy and disoriented, all the bad dreams and things that had happened to him flooded back in a sudden flash of time. Each image indistinguishable from the other, but each fighting to be felt and witnessed. It made his body tense, and Tahdwi felt the rigid reaction when she touched him.

"Kemahni, it's okay…it's me." She grabbed a bowl of water near him, "Here," and held it so he could sip. "Drink." He barely drank and she had to pull it away when the water caught in his throat.

"I can't. I…just want to sleep." He sobbed softly again.

"Oh Kemahni, I know. I'm sorry," she said, not really knowing what she was apologizing for. "It'll be alright."

She quickly placed the bowl down and positioned herself facing him, hip to hip. He reflexively retracted, stopped by the post, as she hugged him around his bound arms. She held for a long while, listening to his breath steady, feeling their warmth combine, and waiting until his tears subsided. She released the pressure of her hug to pull back enough to look at him, though he didn't lift his head. Tahdwi's gently hand rested on his face, while the other retrieved a flask of the yarik-made liquid. Tahdwi uncorked the flask and it popped with its signature sound.

"We'll make it through this."

Kemahni looked blankly at her as she raised the flask to his lips. He accepted the elixir without complaint, and the moment it touched his skin and entered his mouth, the liquid began to illuminate. She helped by closing his mouth for him, and in response, the drink shone slightly as he held it. His cheeks glowed imperceptibly green, like they were blushing the wrong color. Tahdwi leaned closer to Kemahni, placing their foreheads together, and intertwined her horns with his, something she didn't realize he had never done with anyone. The feeling of scaly material rubbing together buzzed into his head and was uniquely pleasurable.

There was a long silence that followed, during which Kemahni hadn't moved. For a moment, he looked like nothing more than a body continuing autonomously, without any semblance of a mind or soul. Nothing made him react, not the drink or her touch as she caressed him.

"Kemahni, I want you to know, I wish...I could do more for you. But I'm not strong...I try to be." She took a breath. "I let too many things just happen, and I'm too late to fix it. I don't think I can change anything, but I won't be part of the bonding tomorrow. I can't." She trailed off, unsure of whether or not what she was saying was helping. "Please just don't fight anymore. I don't want you to go through any more pain for us."

With all the love, he also felt the anguish she hid. Something he never thought her capable of with all the endearing smiles that never seemed to leave her face. When she finally pulled away, that exact smile was there to be shared with him, to ease him back to the reality he was in. He returned barely a smile of his own, but it was enough for her. She saw a bit of the liquid had fallen from his lips onto his chin and caringly wiped his face clean. Finally, she gently kissed him on his forehead.

From outside the doorway, Kiyadeh had been watching Tahdwi's display of affection for Kemahni. It made her uneasy and surprisingly jealous, but she maintained a calm voice when she called out, "Tahdwi."

The curious voice broke the moment, as Tahdwi thought she'd heard Ashava, immediately backing away from Kemahni. He slumped forward without her to brace him, still floating with warm emotions. She couldn't hide her shock or relief when she turned to see Kiyadeh and not her sister. How she'd never noticed that Kiyadeh and Ashava sounded similar, especially when she wasn't looking at them, astounded her.

"Is everything okay?" Kiyadeh asked without hesitation.

"Yes," Tahdwi quickly said.

"Okay. I thought I saw Ashava heading this way and wanted to make sure. Did you see her?"

"Yeah, but she's gone now," Tahdwi said dismissively when she finally stood, "what are you doing here?"

"I need to talk to Kemahni for a minute." Kiyadeh's eyes flicked tellingly.

"I wasn't supposed to let anyone—"

"I know," Kiyadeh said quickly, raising her hands to show she was unarmed. "I'm not here to try anything, I just need to talk to him while he's still…whole. I'm not going to get another chance." The conviction showed through Kiyadeh's eyes in the dim light. They were electric and had a wavering tremble to them. "Please. I'll be quick."

Tahdwi understood Kiyadeh's need and what little time they had. She agreed with a happy nod, stepped aside, and waved her in. Tahdwi removed herself from the hut and gave them their space.

After Tahdwi was out of sight, Kiyadeh waited a moment, eventually seeing an ear creep around the edge of the doorway to listen. She expected to be overheard, but seeing the effort Tahdwi made to be secretive was oddly pleasing, though she wasn't overly happy someone might be witness to the things she needed to say.

"Kemahni?" Kiyadeh announced herself.

"Kiyadeh, why are you here?" he asked.

"I have something I wanted to tell you," she said in a way that almost sounded like a question. After a deep, calming breath she continued, "I have no idea what it is to be you. What any of your life has been like or what having this expectation held over you must be like. I never took the time to know who YOU were. No one did. We all just thought you were the same as any other male, and that you only were worth what you could give us. It took me until today to know that we took more from you than we ever gave. And I know you gave me more than I could have ever asked for. My life with you has been better. You…helped remind me what it was like to have someone important dependent on you. Someone who needed me. You made me feel like I could do something right."

He raised his head when her voice began to tremble.

"I really cared about the Inyari I was to bring back, and when I lost her..." her mind disappeared to Noriendi, "I hated myself for failing her, and never having the chance to tell her what she meant to me. I never want to waste another chance to say what I feel. Ke, you gave me reasons to go on. To care without the fear of losing someone again. You gave me purpose, made me feel not alone. Whole." She paused thoughtfully. "I meant what I said in the field, and I know everything is a mess now... and if I tried to fight, I wouldn't stand a chance. I'm not *that* good," she joked poorly. "But know that I would."

A patter of tears hit the ground near his legs, and he watched craters form in the dirt, watched her emotions make a real, visual impact before him.

Tahdwi heard the almost imperceivable sound and peered around the corner.

"But I want to promise you this, I will lead the rest of my life making sure everyone knows who you were and the sacrifices you made, for as long as I have breath." After saying that, Kiyadeh stared openly at him waiting for him to look at her. When he finally lifted his head to follow the tears, he didn't witness the pained face he was expecting. Instead, he saw happiness in her that staved away any sadness that normally came with tears. Her whole being was free from pridefulness or self-satisfaction, full of gratitude that reached beyond her smile.

Kemahni's mouth parted before he knew what to say, trying to force out a thousand words all at once, but they stayed trapped in his chest. After a few shameful moments of nothing being said, he tightened his mouth and lowered his head again.

How he wasn't moved to respond by her sincerity bothered him greatly. Like with Tahdwi, he deeply felt her words, but as more time passed, the less effective any words would have been, and so he chose to remain silent.

Kiyadeh wasn't sure what she expected him to say, but she wanted a response. The silence left her vulnerable and she retracted slightly, trying not to let it seem like she was hurt by it. She searched the pouch on her hip to retrieve a purple yarik stone fashioned into a wood and fanged necklace.

"This is the only thing I have of Noriendi," Kiyadeh said. "I don't know why I held onto it for so long. I think I was worried I'd forget about her if I didn't have it, but I know that's not true. I don't need something to remind me. I could never forget her, or you." Her voice cracked. Without hesitation, she put it over his head, trying not to disrupt his head or horns. She half smiled with contentment, liking the way it draped across his chest.

Her smile quickly diminished and she wiped her face clear. Like Tahdwi, she embraced him awkwardly, having to hug a part of the wood post as well.

Kemahni desperately choked out her name for her to stay, but she didn't hear, preoccupied with composing herself. *Save me. Please save me,* he thought he said, but when she turned away unfazed he was sure he hadn't said anything at all. He gave up trying to speak entirely when she stood, powerless to stop her from walking to the exit.

"Goodbye," Kiyadeh said over her shoulder.

And as she had appeared suddenly in the night, she was gone and Kemahni was a little less whole.

Outside, Tahdwi was straightening her outfit and tending to her hair. She waited patiently for Kiyadeh to exit, greeting her with a happy stare. Kiyadeh arched her brow, and gave a small, thanking head bow. Tahdwi surprised her with a comforting hug.

"Tahdwi?" Kiyadeh said, baffled.

"What you said...it was beautiful."

"I never wanted to say it," Kiyadeh said quickly and pulled away from her.

"I know it was not easy." Tahdwi beamed. "I'm glad you did. It was good for both of you."

"I suppose so."

"What will you do tomorrow?"

"Not be here. I can't be part of this."

"I don't blame you," Tahdwi agreed, thinking for a moment. "Would you mind some company?"

"Sure, that'd be nice. We'll talk tomorrow. Goodnight, Tahdwi." Kiyadeh ended the conversation and abruptly walked off.

Tahdwi drew in a long, sustained breath, held it, and then sighed out her nose, watching Kiyadeh leave.

Hidden high inside the hollow hole of a tree, just beyond the wards of the village, Saleal was perched on a branch. She retrieved a bound package wrapped tightly in rawhide, one she hadn't wanted to create, or have a reason to use. The package was thrown down without much concern for its contents. It slammed the ground with the clamoring sounds of metal and various materials. She jumped down after it and frantically unwrapped the leather bindings that held it tight. Inside was a satchel that she promptly opened and rummaged through. She used the faint afterglow of a *fire shard* to light the interior, ensuring the items of importance were still there. Garb, potions, jewelry, stones, and coin. She retrieved a single, specific stone, and with a double check, she rebound the package and set it aside.

Her eyes swept to the village just in view. It looked empty to her, and made her feel cold. The longer she stared, the more regretful memories arose, and it took a forceful bit of effort to ignore them.

She headed to a boulder not too far away and affixed the yarik stone into a small cavity. She opened her hand flat against the stone, and it glowed below her palm. As she pushed the boulder, it moved effortlessly over the ground, making a largely audible sound, enough to alert any Manyari who would have been within earshot. She acted as if the sound wasn't a problem and retrieved a sling satchel wrapped in a cloak that was hidden beneath the boulder.

She felt a knot in her stomach for a split second before she opened the satchel to reveal the things that had defined her before the title of *Great Mother* was bestowed upon her.

She scrutinized the leather-woven armor, ensuring all pieces were there, then quickly began to fit them on in a remembered, precisely practiced fashion. Though it had been years, time hadn't eroded her ability to don it quickly. It took less than a few minutes to finish putting it on, and when complete, she was far more imposing, even while maintaining a defined, sleeker silhouette.

The armor covered everything from her knees to her neck, and back down to her elbows in a weave of leather that moved gracefully with her. There were openings for her hard scales, and reinforced leather panels to cover vital areas like the chest, inner legs, and the insides of her arms. Fingerless gloves kept dexterity in her hands and hard leather boots gave her added traction and protection for her feet. The headpiece was the most impressive, mimicking the large scaled and horned skulls of a Ykahri. If she had been taller and with more bulk, she could have been a passable Valkys.

Hidden beneath the armor were two pairs of daggers. A traditional, normal pair, and another inlaid with yarik stones. The second set had seen their fair use but were well maintained. She slid them into holsters across her chest with a satisfying sound and felt a little safer. She inspected the more ornate design of the other set that looked to have never been used and were still finely sharpened. It was a decorative piece, still combat ready, but very much a weapon of fashion. They lacked any form of yarik, despite the jewels they were encrusted with. She placed them into the satchel without a second glance. Once satisfied, she slung the satchel over her shoulder, pulling it tight to her chest.

She lifted the lightweight but sturdy cloak and swung it around her, letting it gently waft along her body as she tied it at the front. When the cloak came to a rest, the satchel, her daggers, and her body disappeared within its shadows.

"Gods help me do the right thing," she asked of them as she looked to the moon above.

She let the light bathe her for a moment, before pulling her hair back and pulling her hood up. As the clouds momentarily covered the moon's colorful reflection, she became part of the darkness. When the light touched the ground again, she was gone.

CHAPTER 15
BLIND

"Sure, we can see in the dark, but you can't rely on that."
- Hunter Trainer Oba

Ashava had found an abandoned, full flask of wine and had managed to finish more than half in only a few gulps. She hoped it would help her forget about her encounter with Tahdwi, but it was doing a poor job of dulling her heartache and anger. She stumbled lightly through the village, not picking any direction in particular. Soon, she caught the movement of someone else still roaming but ignored their presence.

"Are you not going to share?" a voice broke into the night.

"Wasn't planning on it," she answered before she knew to whom she was answering.

A Manyari girl, tall and with smaller scales and horns, stepped out in front of her.

"What are you doing up this late, Deuna?" Ashava asked.

"Despite all that's going on, I'm still set on having a good night. Seems like you've found your way." Deuna smiled wider and moved closer.

Ashava snorted unattractively and corrected, "I'm not having a good night."

"I can fix that," she said, grabbing the bottle from Ashava and taking a long drink, but when the flavor reached her, she grimaced fiercely. "Ugh. You're drinking this? I think it's gone bad."

Ashava shrugged and took the bottle back. She chugged a large amount of the turned wine for a few seconds. Deuna noticed on Ashava's belt the elixir Tahdwi had angrily relinquished. Deuna's eyes arched in amazement, and she quickly grabbed it.

"Hey," Ashava protested, after ripping the bottle from her lips and choking down her mouthful.

Deuna turned away, uncorked the flask, and drank of the elixir. Her mouth glowed slightly, and Ashava grasped at her to take it back. When Ashava used both of her arms in frustration to try and restrain her, Deuna pivoted on her heel and pushed her mouth passionately against Ashava's. She tried to pull away, but Deuna pursued, placing a hand on the back of Ashava's head as she pushed the elixir from herself to Ashava.

As soon as the liquid was in Ashava's mouth, it began to flow through the rest of her. The displeasure with the unwanted advance faded away as she enjoyed the sudden burst in all her senses, though most surprising was enjoying the feeling of their lips touching.

Ravenous thoughts came to Ashava, urging her to make use of her hands to glide over Deuna's slick surfaces. She moved contrary to the rough manner she normally used to interact with the world, gentler with her touch. She was attentive to how the girl reacted, never forcing her movements and letting Deuna set the pace for intimacy.

Ashava's mind swam with the potent effect and the energy shared, a sensation she had never experienced and had been saving as her first time to be with Tahdwi.

Deuna pushed herself closer, and Ashava moaned, "Tahdwi."

Deuna stopped the kiss, visibly offended, if only for a moment, but acted as if it didn't matter.

"You can do whatever you want," Deuna assured, moving in again.

Ashava opened her eyes, and her rush of affection fled when she saw Deuna in the place of what she had drunkenly thought was Tahdwi. She stopped the advance.

"You don't have to stop, I don't care if you don't love me. Let me be with you, if only once."

"No."

"She won't know."

Ashava shook her head. "Wouldn't matter if she did." She gave Deuna the rest of the flask. "It's my fault. Always is."

"Ashava, no. It's okay. I don't care."

Ashava ignored her and suddenly looked past to a flash of purple light that caught her eye and the zip of a silhouette that moved in between the huts. If it had moved any faster or more silently, she would probably have missed it, but her senses were alive with yarik coursing through her. She pushed her shame, and Deuna, aside.

"What is it?" Deuna asked.

Ashava said nothing and raced at her top speed in the direction she thought it had gone.

"Ashava!" Deuna cried as Ashava dashed from her sight.

It's heading for Tahdwi, Ashava realized mid-sprint. *No,* she re-thought.

Kemahni.

It took a fraction of a moment between there being nothing in the doorway of the prisoner hut, to suddenly a dark figure standing there, scouting the room. Tahdwi was asleep in the corner opposite a sleeping Kemahni who laid oddly on the floor, still bound to the support post. Nothing about the horribly awkward position seemed to matter to whomever stood in the doorway.

The figure turned its head slowly, moving its horns and shifting its ears to more precisely craft an image with its senses. Its eyes glistened an electric color when it accurately identified Kemahni against the post. It glanced back, nodded, but as it was about to move into the room, it stopped, its ears flicking backward.

"This is what it's come to, Great Mother? Nothing left to lose, huh?" Ashava scoffed.

Seemingly disaffected by Ashava's presence, the figure stepped away from the door and stood fully, increasing its height by a noticeable magnitude.

"Great...Mother?" Ashava's voice wavered.

Ashava backed away, surprised by the transformation that was happening before her. What had seemed like one towering figure appeared to slowly become two as a second, Greater figure emerged from the shadow of the first. Ashava's mind raced, unable to resolve the image she was receiving. Her blood pumped anxiously, angrily through her, and when she blinked to clear her vision, the Greater figure seemed to have vanished.

From the darkness behind her, a pair of muscular, clawed arms restrained her, one grasping her around her mouth, the other caging her arms. It pressed a yarik stone hidden in its hand to Ashava's chest.

> *Forget the now,*
> *For what was real,*
> *is no longer.*

Ashava answered unwillingly, and her body fell prey to the yarik. She fell unconscious upright, staying erect after the Greater figure behind her released its hold. Ashava was then guided to the tree across from the hut and laid down to rest for the time being.

The two figures shared a knowing look as the Greater commanded, "Cull the male."

The Lesser nodded, contracted its stature, and parted the door into the hut. A moment before entering the hut, the Lesser's ears perked to the sound of a dagger being launched from the shadows. With a quick wave of its hand, it created a wall of altered gravity, stopping the dagger from any further travel. The dagger vibrated with a soft, ringing hum as the Lesser turned its head, and looked deeply into the darkness.

"The Mother," the Greater proclaimed.

Answering to her name, Saleal rushed into the moonlight, looking not too dissimilar to the two creatures that had invaded her home. She didn't reach their stature but did have a similar scaled shape and the helmet that looked oddly similar to the creatures' heads. She ran on silent footsteps, cloak billowing as if propelling her along, ready with a second dagger to attack.

The Lesser, more affected by the Great Mother's sudden appearance, waited for orders, holding Saleal's dagger in the air.

"We need to subdue her," the Greater instructed.

"If we cannot?" the Lesser asked.

"Neutralize her."

"Understood."

The Lesser reversed its hand gesture, the dagger flipped slowly in air, and gravity accelerated the weapon back at Saleal. Unsurprising to them, the weapon flew with extreme accuracy at her, though neither were prepared when the dagger was dodged easily and then suddenly pulled back into Saleal's hand.

"Yarik?" the Lesser proposed.

"No," the Greater assured.

Saleal had attached a thin but durable braided metal line to her dagger and used it to control the flight of her weapon and retrieve them. The rhythm of her steps increased, and she would have soon been face to face with the Lesser had her gravity not suddenly been changed.

She couldn't find traction as her feet began to slip from no longer having a downward force. A slight nausea found her as her body attempted to understand the direction she was traveling and what was her new down. She began to fall forward, completely unable to make contact with the ground. A moment before she would have reached the Lesser, it held up its arm, controlling yarik from its clawed hands.

Saleal slowed to a stop and was laid flat by what felt like a heavy weight on both her front and back. She soon found herself floating horizontally centimeters above the ground. Trying to understand her shifted perspective, she held her body still and closed her eyes to briefly give her time to reorient, finding that she still felt pulled down toward her feet, despite facing the sky. Craning her head to see either of the approaching pair threw off her equilibrium, but she fought through the disorientation to see the assailants.

They were not Manyari, but something that spoke to the very core of what she was. It wasn't until they stood above her, and she was looking into their sunken eyes that she knew what and who they were. Valkys. Ones that shared a similar scaly exterior with iridescent scales that glistened in the twilight. Smooth, yet hulking silhouettes that curved to sharp points, in a much larger and more menacing way. The unrestricted way they moved through the world as if it bent to their actions. An ability to use yarik stones unabated. Their true name snapped to the forefront of her mind.

These Valkys were Ykhari.

Saleal couldn't rightfully process seeing her ancestral Valkys half with her own eyes. They had never once been to their village and she only knew them through the words their Wisewoman would speak, like legends of protectors from afar, but she undeniably knew what they were. It frightened her more when she pieced together the reason for them being here in her village, in front of the hut that housed Kemahni. They were there for him, to quell the male that had acted against their tribe.

The Greater Ykhari reached into its pouch to retrieve a yarik stone. He covered her mouth and slid his other hand over Saleal's chest and spoke through the stone.

What was real...

But before the Ykhari could finish the spell, Saleal flicked her daggers with the limited mobility she had in her wrist in the direction of her gravity, horizontally towards her feet. As she hoped, they fell toward the Lesser at an increasing rate, surprising it when the daggers flew past its legs. Saleal fought the pressing gravity to cross her arms in front of her chest, causing the weapon's lines to swing inward and tether around the Ykhari's legs. They bound around once and, with all the strength she could, she pulled.

Saleal's body zoomed toward the Lesser. The Greater stumbled forward in an attempt to recapture Saleal, with no success. The Lesser was ill prepared to have Saleal's full weight slam into its legs and topple it. The sudden misdirection of yarik propelled the Lesser into the air, not reacting quickly enough to stop the flow of yarik as it repulsed itself from the ground.

Despite the chaos, the entirety of the conflict had been mostly inaudible. The Ykhari's feet created no sounds, their gestures fluid, and the yarik they used hadn't conjured elements that would make noises or obviously visible energies. The Greater foresaw the oncoming danger of being revealed by this new ruckus and was quick to retrieve a purple yarik stone. With a quick action, it held the stone aloft and summoned a purple dome of energy, swallowing all three of them in a flash of expanding light.

In the tent, for a moment, Kemahni was pulled awake by the light and a flow of wind, but he fell back asleep, dismissing it as a dream.

The battle was whisked away to a field kilometers from Orahai, but still within their territory and still within the wards. The dome of purple energy reemerged and deposited the fighters onto the area with little care. Saleal continued her forward momentum, normal gravity pulling her down until she skidded across the grass.

The Greater positioned itself in direct line with the sailing Lesser, extended its arms, and used its yarik to cradle the Lesser's descent, bringing them both to the ground without a sound.

Saleal rose and looked back to see the village, still able to see its details in the pale moonlight, even at a distance. For a brief second, she almost believed she saw herself battling in an afterimage, watching herself be transported by the unfamiliar yarik energy.

She dismissed the notion and confronted the Ykhari who stood two abreast waiting undisturbed for her to compose herself.

"No need to be quiet now," Saleal proposed.

"This situation can be without dire resolution nor does it need to stain your people, *Son Bearer*. The boy will pass painlessly, and you will be allowed to forget all this as a forgotten dream. You must allow us to—"

The Lesser jetted out a reflexive hand and once again stopped a sudden attack from Saleal's dagger.

"You have a nice way of saying you are here to kill my son?!" Saleal jabbed.

"Your careless actions have added to this hardship. We cannot let this continue on its course."

"Neither can I."

The Lesser looked for more affirmation, and with a calm nod from the Greater, the Lesser began to rotate its wrist to reverse the direction of the dagger. Before it could initiate the change, the dagger sprung to life as it erupted yarik wind out the hilt end. The Lesser's horns lifted in shock, and it brought its second arm to aid the gravity wall as the dagger began to press furiously. The Lesser tried to divert the dagger away, but every attempt had the dagger correcting itself, unable to change its target.

The Greater watched the dagger try to penetrate the Lesser's defense and chose to go on the offense rather than assist. It slowly reached into its thigh pouch and retrieved a yarik stone of water. It calmly pressed it between both palms until the stone activated, and when it pulled its hands apart, the stone floated and spilled forth water.

The liquid stretched and formed several dozen long spears of ice, all hanging like icicles from its claw. They broke free with a hollow ringing, as the Greater formed a fist to gather the icicles around the water stone. With its then free hand, it concentrated on the battlefield between them.

Saleal couldn't see the effects of the yarik it casted at first, but she could feel the creation of another gravity well as it swelled and pulled at her. The gravity well reached its maximum size and strength, distorting the space around it and creating a small dark center where light was dimmed.

They must have a limited range, Saleal thought, storing the information about their yarik capabilities, but limited range didn't affect the Greater's ability to engage.

The Greater sent the water stone, with its orbiting icicles, at the gravity well. It accelerated unexpectedly and, before reaching the epicenter, the Greater opened its hand and released the icicles to travel along the outer edge of the well. They reached the apex, paused for a fraction of a second, then suddenly accelerated at a disconcerting rate. The ice released from the well at sonic speeds, melting the outer layer of ice and creating comet-like tails in their wake.

Saleal prepared an earth stone in anticipation of the attack, lodging it into the ground and summoning a solidified earth wall. The icicles impacted against the wall, most shattering like glass, others chipping large chunks of the wall, but some penetrated completely through. Luckily for Saleal, who was hunkered low against the earthen barricade, none of the icicles pierced where she hid.

She looked up from her prone position, huffing a long, harsh breath when realizing that had she been any slower she'd most likely been impaled. Her momentary respite was interrupted by the increasing feeling of a crushing weight. An invisible force slammed down on the wall and the patch of grass Saleal occupied. The ground cratered in a cascading ripple of heavy gravity and sent a cloud of dust that glowed brightly in the light of the moon.

The Greater victoriously relaxed, bringing down both of its claws it had used to increase the range and power of its yarik. It finally took the opportunity to walk over to the Lesser who still had Saleal's dagger at bay. The Greater grabbed the weapon, deactivated its yarik, and tossed the dagger aside as if rubbish. The Lesser released its tension through dropped shoulders and flattened its horns.

"Is it over, then?" the Lesser hopefully asked.

"No, we still have the male to tend to," the Greater reminded.
"Of course."

As to counter their gravely quick assumption, Saleal dissipated the cloud of dirt with her original pair of yarik-less daggers, spinning in circles from their tethers as she charged forth.

If the Ykhari could look less pleased, they would, but telling expressions from their limited facial musculature was nigh impossible. The Greater went about defending as if it was another simple task. It repeated previous tactics, this time sharing the responsibility with the Lesser who created the gravity well while the Greater used both hands to activate and control two water stones' worth of icicles.

The Greater launched the icicles with deadly purpose, the two stones traveling in a helix path as they pulled forward. Once the projectiles were about to reach the outer perimeter of the well, Saleal launched her daggers in with a sharp flick of her wrist, straight for the center of the gravity. The daggers accelerated like the icicles, but were swallowed by the center sphere of altered space. She let the length of the tethered line unspool, wrapping the ends around her gauntlets and increasing her speed to match the runaway lines.

The end of the length was soon about to be taut, despite her running at full speed, and at the moment it would have pulled harshly at her, she hopped and braced her feet forward. She landed exactly when the tether pulled, sending her rapidly across the ground. The grass smeared below her boots until eventually creating a layer slick enough to slide across the ground. Keeping her toes up so as not to catch them in any imperfections, she surfed the green with her improvised plan of attack. She couldn't be impressed with herself, as she could see the icicles reaching the outside of the well, gaining potential energy as they were prepared to accelerate at her.

The closer she came, the stronger she could feel the pull of the gravity, and she worried she wouldn't be able to escape its grasp. The icicles shot out in a spread that would have surely hit Saleal, had she not jumped and tugged at the tethers, setting herself on a trajectory above and around the gravity well. She arrowed her body, minimized her surface area as she slipped past the icicles, though not without escaping one of them slicing through her shoulder scale, cutting a deep gouge, and another that struck her in the head. It wasn't till the Greater stopped controlling the yarik stone, and Saleal's helmet landed in the field that they stopped their attack. The Lesser slowly let the gravity well fade with a dissipation of energy and a hollow droning. They proceeded to look intently for Saleal.

"Were you successful?" the Lesser asked.

"Be alert," the Great instructed.

What the Greater did not want to answer, the sound of wind did, and gave signal to Saleal's third attempted surprise attack. Searching for the sound of the dagger, the two Ykhari finally looked skyward to see Saleal's remaining yarik wind dagger rapidly approaching the Greater. Before the Lesser could react, the Greater formed its own barrier to stop the dagger, and as before, the dagger kept an unrelenting force against the wall.

Emerging from the night sky, Saleal swooped down at the duo, still in her streamlined form with blood running down her face. An odd noise from the Greater attempting to warn the Lesser barely sounded before Saleal somersaulted in the air and heel stomped onto the dagger. The added force and a pressure of the wind pierced the dagger through the Greater's barrier and into its thick, scaled chest. Saleal expertly rolled off the Greater and skidded across the grass, leaving a trail of unearthed dirt in her wake.

The Greater recovered in a groan of displeasure and, for the first time, gave a show of anger. Its scales flared, spiking its body in a defensive way. The dagger in its chest didn't appear to affect the Ykhari as it reached to retrieve another stone, only to find no pouch at its hip. Looking to the ground, it saw one sole yarik stone. Then it saw another, and another, all leading in a trail straight to Saleal.

She was already searching through it, looking for the items she knew would be most valuable to them. The purple transportation stones. To her luck, she found the special inner pouch that held them and was already taking inventory. There were five, all beautifully crafted and radiating with energy. Unable to admire them as she pulled them out, she fit four between her fingers and fanned them outward.

"Manyari, you must stop," the Lesser demanded.

The Greater hushed the Lesser with a single wave of its hand and watched intently for Saleal's next action, which was to swipe at the purple stone's yarik lines randomly. She defiantly scattered them about and they began to spring to life, each expelling their energies into expanding domes of light. When fully formed, they held inside a view of a seemingly random place in the world. Some even showed daylight and places Saleal had seen. One had another Manyari village, another a city of Man. There was one with a beautiful vista of a sunset over a mountain, and the final showed a field of stone statues that felt completely out of place. She hadn't been sure if those locations were stored in the stones or by activating them without thought she had opened connections with random places. It had been the first time she'd even seen a transportation stone, let alone operated one, and its lines and workings were foriegn to her.

The Greater counted the stones she used and roared, startling the Lesser in the process. Saleal remained unfazed until the Greater suddenly drug its claws across its inner forearm. Lines similar to those of yarik stones followed its nails as they scraped against its scaly skin. Each scale vibrated then ripped away from its forearm, trailing blood, and revealing lighter colored soft skin beneath. Zips of energy traveled back and forth between the scales and the Greater's forearm as they orbited around. Quickly, the scales glowed bright fuchsia, like they were being ignited by an intense amount of heat, and their orbit began to increase in speed.

"I wouldn't, " Saleal warned, countering the Greater's posturing. She pulled out another, final purple stone and waved it for both to see. "I think you know this is the last one, and I'm guessing you wouldn't want to be stranded here, and the people here won't be too happy knowing why you came."

The Greater stayed firm with its intent to attack.

Saleal proceeded to place a thumb on the stone's face.

"We cannot return without that stone," the Lesser explained. "We cannot explain our presence here."

"Now leave my son and this village be. If we meet again, I promise you, I won't hold back."

The Greater stopped all aggression and the scales fell to the ground. Saleal hurled the stone in the air in a wide arc. The Lesser snatched it out of the air with its yarik and pulled the stone carefully into its claws. The Greater finally attended to the dagger in its chest, pulling it out without reaction and tossed it towards Saleal as if part of an aforementioned trade.

"You are not the first to think you can control them. You will soon see the error of your mistake," the Greater prophesied.

Saleal refused to give credence to their words, waiting as patiently as she could as they prepared themself to retreat. The two Ykhari looked at each other, and without discussion, used their last teleportation stone to call forth the dome of purple. Upon reaching critical size, scenes of a dark sky above softly light clouds took form along its angular interior.

Where are they going? Saleal couldn't help but wonder.

The Lesser stepped on through without hesitations, but the Greater lingered for just a moment to burn a proper image of Saleal into its mind. The dome began to make sounds of its imminent collapse, and the Greater slunk inside. The dome wavered before it collapsed into nothing, dropping the dormant stone to the floor after having spent all its energy. The two would-be assassins disappeared into the night, gone as if they were never there.

Saleal closed her eyes and became perfectly still, controlling her breathing while she relaxed her face. After a moment's rest, she recovered all three of her lost daggers that were strewn among the field. Her yarik dagger laid near the Ykhari's removed scales, which she impulsively gathered as well, not knowing what she would do with them, but definitely knowing she'd like more time for examination. She made another quick inventory and sealed the pouch.

Before wiping the dagger of the Ykhari's blood, she noticed it glistened like it was charged with yarik that moved about inside the pools of red. A drop of her own blood dripped onto the blade, and she noticed how there were no obvious differences between them. She cleansed her face and blade of blood and replaced the spent yarik crystal inside the hilt. She moved to reclaimed her still intact helmet, gouged from the strike, and dirty from rolling on the ground. It no longer held the prestige it once did, not after knowing what the Ykharis wanted for her son. She kept it though, because despite her feelings, it was still the best armor she could have for her head, and she would need all the protection she could muster. She quickly fit the helmet back on and prepared herself for the night to come.

"Mahi, I'm coming," she said to the darkness.

She activated the daggers under her cloak, and they let forth a previously unseen wind at her feet. The wind grew in a snap, almost lifting her off the ground. She directed the *yarik* behind her to power her in the direction of the village.

CHAPTER 16
AWAKE

"The day does not choose when you rise or when you start."
- Fieldcarer Leene

Time felt paused. Nothing made sense nor was anything out of the realm of possibility. Her son was in danger even before she could enact a plan that would certainly put both of them in more. The uncertainty of what would fill the rest of the night and heightened attentiveness to everything crowded her thoughts. Then worry found her and became too much. She painfully repressed every unnecessary emotion that would have her miss any crucial detail, and let her focus rest solely on reaching her son.

The time it took from the field back to Kemahni's hut happened in a flash, having nearly exhausted half of the energy inside her daggers from the constant assist. She stopped her yarik usage before reaching the quiet village and, as she neared the hut, scouted the area with two quick glances.

Ashava was asleep under the tree across the way, still under the deep yarik spell. Saleal wouldn't take chances that she might wake the girl, making sure to avoid any unnecessary noise while taking a wide berth around to the back of the tree. Saleal expertly pounced on the girl without a sound and restrained her.

To Saleal's shock, Ashava remained completely unconscious, and no matter what she did, Ashava did not awake or react. Saleal knew full well that the Ykhari had engaged her first, having watched them walk her to the tree in the first place. She took the opportunity to move the girl into the tall grass near the tree. Saleal adjusted Ashava to lay flat on her back, placing her legs together, and with a length of her tethered line, she tied it around her ankles. She brought Ashava's right arm to her chest, but after rising, Saleal focused on an oddly shaped, discolored scale under Ashava's arm. Saleal had never noticed it before, and it bore a similar look and placement to one of Saleal's own, though she didn't have time to truly compare.

With a final check, Saleal zipped back to the hut and, once inside, she could see Tahdwi in the corner still asleep and knew she'd have to deal with her as well once she tried to unbind Kemahni. Her movement kept all quiet as she promptly moved toward her son. She removed her helmet, undid his bindings, and then grabbed Kemahni by the shoulders to gently hoist him back upright.

"Mahi," she said in a mix of sadness and anger. "Mahi."

"Mama...?" he asked bewildered as his eyes crept open.

"Yes. Are you okay?"

"No..." he said, tears suddenly filling his eyes.

Saleal held him tight, trying to shelter him from the flood of emotions that was sure to come.

Kemahni sobbed into his mother but stopped when he realized he was free of the post. He pulled away with great relief to his back and stared at his mother with full eyes and slightly lifted horns.

She reassured him with a smile and hugged him again. Her ears perked, and she whispered in a monotone, half turned away, "Get ready."

The sounds of Tahdwi stirring with waking breaths alerted Saleal, as the girl rose to check on Kemahni.

"Kemahni are...Great Mother—" Tahdwi barely said.

Saleal bolted and covered Tahdwi's mouth with one hand and used the other to brace the back of Tahdwi's head to make sure she couldn't pull away.

"Quiet," Saleal commanded.

Tahdwi nodded as much as she could while restrained.

"I don't want this to be difficult."

Tahdwi agreed with another serious nod. Saleal looked for reassurance that Tahdwi would comply, but trust was not an option.

Tahdwi kept her eyes in track with the Great Mother's and softly mumbled into her hand. Saleal looked oddly curious at the willful girl's need to speak. Again, Tahdwi said two distinct words that were mumbled behind the hand over her mouth. Saleal pulled her hand a couple centimeters away from Tahdwi's face.

"Take him," Tahdwi enunciated.

Saleal pulled her hand away completely. "What?"

"You're trying to save him, right? Take him."

"I'm not playing games."

"Nor am I, Great Mother. Please. We both know what it means if he stays here. You can do what none of us had the strength to."

Kemahni, knowing full well his intended fate, understood then the love in their proposal to free him. He knew the sacrifice would bring them both far past any point of forgiveness with the tribe, but they did so without reserve. It gave him the strength to sit up, and upon doing so, the ropes tumbled off him with ease.

The sound drew Saleal and Tahdwi's attention to Kemahni, and after a moment of realization, the girls looked at each other. Tahdwi managed the start of a convincing smile and it was enough to make the notion of believing Tahdwi and following through with an escape less daunting. She casually moved her hands to the sides of her head, and it gave Saleal cause for alarm, though she did not yet react defensively. Tahdwi removed each of her earrings in turn and offered them to Saleal. The Great Mother took the gift and afterwards, no longer questioning the girl's intent.

"Do you know how to use them?" Tahdwi asked.

"Yes," Saleal easily replied.

"Okay. Good." Tahdwi took the moment to admire both mother and son and found her full smile. "I will miss you both. I'll pray for you to live a full life," she told them in a sad tone knowing she'd never see it.

"Thank you, Tahdwi," Saleal said gratefully.

Kemahni knelt beside his mother, prompting Tahdwi to reach out a hand to touch his face. She could feel herself wanting to cry but knew there was no time to add to the torrent of emotions.

"Ready?" Saleal asked as she parted from her son.

Tahdwi nodded, and the Great Mother rolled the earrings lightly in her palm and closed her eyes. She raised them to the level of her mouth and rubbed them carefully in her hand.

Dreams call you,
And you must answer.
Sleep.

Tahdwi gave in to the words without a fight and fell limp, Saleal catching her moments before she would have gracelessly hit the ground. She laid the sleeping girl on her side and watched Kemahni's reaction. It was crucial she didn't push him too far, too quickly, and damage him further in his fragile state.

"Get the rope," Saleal gently asked, and he did so, retrieving lengths of rope previously used on him with a mild bewilderment, in need of someone to give him direction. They worked quickly to bind Tahdwi, and then laid her in a comfortable resting position. Kemahni went to the wooden post and retrieved the cloak Tahdwi had used to cover him and returned the favor.

"Mahi..." Saleal gently urged.

"Is she gonna be okay?" Kemahni asked of the silent girl.

"She'll be fine."

"Are we gonna be okay?"

Saleal frowned sympathetically and rushed over to him. She grabbed his hand and held his gaze, saying, "Everything will be, I promise, but we have to go."

Kemahni blinked blankly, then gave a slow, accepting nod.

"Okay. Stay close to me."

It was still calm outside, silent as night should be. Saleal slowly stuck her head out the doorway and took in everything with a few flicks of her eyes and ears. Kemahni felt safer by her expert surveillance, but couldn't stop his heart from racing. It skipped a beat when she suddenly gripped his hand tighter and rushed them out the door.

They ran and ran and exited through the edge of town in record time, even with having to avoid main avenues and light sources on the way. They continued to race in one unwavering direction until they reached the satchel Saleal had hidden near the edge of the forest. After a final check of its contents, she retrieved a second cloak for Kemahni and tossed him a jar of a thick, black substance. She hadn't looked when she tossed the jar, but her aim put it right into his hands.

"Rub it in your hair. Make sure you get all of it," she ordered.

The sound of the cork popping signaled his compliance. He sunk his hand into the jar, and noted how it smelled highly of dried flowers with a strong earthy odor, as well as something acetic. In the dark night, he hadn't noticed how it was staining his hands and ears, as well as anything else he touched. Saleal colored her hair with much more impatience, finishing before Kemahni had gotten halfway. She turned and helped him finish and cleaned her hands by rubbing them vigorously on the grass.

The sound of his mother fiddling with a totem ward filled Kemahni's narrowed ears, able to envision them where his eyes could not see in the clouded moonlight. He approached reservedly as she changed lines on the stone at the base of the large wooden structure.

"Be ready. When I tell you, we have to pass through. This will only work for a second," Saleal instructed.

Before she could finish her tampering, the soft ringing of the ward diminished and the glow of the yarik crystal faded. The illusionary wall rained to the ground and the forest beyond was seen plainly like a framed painting. Saleal pulled her hand away, immediately worried that she had made an error and the village would be alerted. In the side of her vision, she saw Kemahni having placed a hand on the same ward.

"Kemahni?" She lost her words.

He looked sheepishly at her and removed his hand, holding it close to his body, surprised how relieved he felt to reveal his secret. Impressed, Saleal looked at the powerless ward that was no more than a stone and wood pillar decoration now. She fiddled with the stone at the base.

"It should turn back on in a bit," he informed her.

She took barely a moment to analyze the ward. "Then we should go."

She took a deep breath and warily crossed the threshold. Nothing happened, and she quickly beckoned him to follow. Kemahni mimicked his mother's slow movements and, once safely on the other side with still no alarms raised, she grasped him by the forearms and brought his attention forward.

"Once we start running, we don't stop for any reason. None. Do you understand?" she asked with a stone face, but Kemahni didn't readily respond. "I need you to say it, Mahi, so I know you understand what I'm saying. We cannot stop," Saleal instructed.

"I understand, we don't stop running," Kemahni calmly acknowledged with a nod.

"Good." She smiled.

Saleal took the cloak and draped it over him, tying it across his neck. She gently pushed his horns flat to fit them under the hood. She took a moment to hold his face in her hand and accidentally smeared a bit of black across his cheeks.

"I love you," she reminded him.

He smiled for the first time that night and comfortingly said in return, "I know, Mama. I love you."

She hugged him tightly and smiled back. The wards began to resonate again as the stones sparked back to life, glowing in steady intervals. She nodded gratefully as the walls began to fill.

"Go, I'll be right behind you," Saleal ushered her son along.

Kemahni instantly complied and started to build speed into a jog. Saleal watched him run past, but not before having her own last, melancholy look at the village she called home as it disappeared behind the closing wall. She said her silent goodbye, feeling the rush of almost every emotion she had ever felt, along with an indescribable one she hoped was freedom.

CHAPTER 17
CHANGE

"Life is a chaotic wind that you must learn to ride."
— Wind Rider Tassa

Next Morning

    The extra time Kiyadeh afforded herself that morning felt infinite, yet still not enough to prepare herself to tell her mother, the Chieftess, that she would not participate in the bonding. It pained her heart to think that her mother would have two daughters that failed her, and at the same task, but she knew deep within that she could not be a part of his end. It took the better length of an hour to muster the courage to say any words aloud to herself and even longer to ultimately want to say them to another.
    Nothing about the morning was set, and she pondered over every little detail that may or may not happen. She wondered about who'd acquire her First Union, and if she'd still be forced into fulfilling her duty as Guardian when she wanted no part of it.

Maybe I can still run away, but it seemed a selfish thought and unfair to Kemahni to do what he couldn't. Her confidence sank again, and she decided, *I should speak with Tahdwi, before I go speak with Mother. Maybe she'll have some good insight.*

Kiyadeh collected her items for the day, fitting on a more casual top and comfortable pair of bottoms, to make the journey to find Tahdwi. A serenity was returning, and it helped move her to the door, but that peace was snatched away the moment she stepped outside. She barely dodged being stampeded by the herd of frantic people charging past. Something was obviously wrong, but she couldn't understand any of the words anyone was shouting as they ran.

What is it? Are we being attacked? Valkys? she thought as she reached for her nonexistent weapon normally on her back, immediately feeling defenseless.

It disturbed her how easily hundreds of ideas rushed to the list of possibilities, the darkest finding their way to the top. Most weren't buried too deep, not after yesterday. She quickly reduced the options why to only a few when she saw the direction people were heading. Refusing to believe she was right, she joined the flow of people in a dash toward Kemahni's hut.

Kiyadeh dodged the people in her way, as if she was dodging the worry in her mind. Distracted by the lingering thoughts, her movements began to fail her and she collided with others in her path. The crowd grew more dense the closer she came to the hut, and she had to physically move people out of her way, not caring to be nice. When she emerged at the front of the crowd, she found her answers.

"Don't touch me!" someone belted.

A disorientated Ashava stumbled to stand, tearing away the bindings in frustration, as she pushed away those trying to help her. When she finally managed to stand on her own, she barely made it a few steps before she fell to her knees, the yarik still with its lingering effects. The girls she had swatted away attempted more aid despite additional protest.

Tahdwi was brought out of the hut moments later. Ashava's gravely, grey-tinted skin tone regained some color and her horns flared, when she saw Tahdwi's barely responsive body. Rage had her fighting against the helpers once again, and it wasn't until Kiyadeh rushed to her sister's side that Ashava mildly calmed. Kiyadeh relieved the rejected helpers and bore most of her sister's weight as they both shakily stabilized themselves.

"What happened?" Kiyadeh asked.

Ashava managed a strained groan.

"Ashava, what happened? Where is he? Where is Kemahni?"

"He's GONE!" Ashava sneered coldly, resonating loudly for everyone to hear.

The words silenced all other sounds, and the ears of the Orahai Manyari sprung up in a wave. As Ashava was about to release more fury, she was drawn to her expressionless mother, who had broken through to the front of the gathering.

Ejah's long breath told of deep anger, of the worry and answers she didn't want to hear, but had to ask.

"He's gone. Someone attacked me in the night. It had to be his *mother* who took him," Ashava confirmed again.

The Wisewoman joined Ejah's side, eyeing the two affected girls, as the faintest hint of disappointment graced her. Not only because Kemahni had disappeared, but because the Ykhari she summoned had failed.

"Saleal! Where is the Great Mother?" Ejah called out, hoping someone would answer. "Find her," she commanded her two Wind Riders.

They took to the skies without concern for those around. Wind bustled about, and before the dust cleared, countless whispers began to give way to a multitude of questions, crescendoing into most of them asking, '*Why*'.

The Wisewoman placed a comforting hand on the Chieftess's back. Without warning, Ejah grabbed the Wisewoman's staff and jammed it into the ground. The ringing clamour from the staff focused the attention to her.

"Find them! Ready hunting parties of three or more, a tracker in each. Spread through the forest in every direction. Do NOT stop until you reach the end of trees. If you reach the edge and haven't received word, go farther. They have half a day's lead and we have to make up for it. Start at the wards, look for any that might have been tampered with.

And no one is to harm them. Until we have answers, we cannot condemn their actions. Go!"

No one argued and moved in prepared fashion, methodically assigning themselves into groups and rushing back to their homes.

Ashava powered through her weakness and shrugged off Kiyadeh. She picked up her axes that were placed at the base of the tree and holstered them, taking a few sharp breaths to regulate her body's rhythm.

Ejah saw her daughter's struggles and broke from issuing orders to meet her. "You're in no condition to go," she commented.

"We have to find him," Ashava said.

"And we will, but you have to rest off whatever it is she did to you."

"I'm not going to let them get away with it, what they did to me, the tribe..." She grunted in pain from exerting pressure on her bruised front. Ejah held her hand on Ashava's chest to ease the ache. Ashava forced away the pain and stood straight. "I'm going to bring him back, then all of you will have to admit you were wrong about me."

Ejah hadn't expected her daughter's scathing remark, but when she glimpsed the unwavering stare and felt her repressed pain, she knew her daughter wouldn't accept anything but approval. Ejah nodded and set Ashava on her way with a squeeze on the shoulder.

"Go with care then," Ejah concluded, and went about commanding the rest of her people.

Ashava took a moment to scan the crowd while they scurried about in preparations, intent on finding the one person that mattered to her in it all. She watched Kiyadeh tend to Tahdwi, waiting for her to finally look up and lock eyes.

Tahdwi couldn't know what Ashava was thinking, but she knew the look. It was the precursor to Ashava deciding on an action that she would pursue until finished. But this look had something else Tahdwi couldn't figure out. It had an ill omen that worried her enough that she missed the several times Kiyadeh tried to get her to respond.

"Tahdwi?!" Kiyadeh questioned for the third time.

It took another moment for Tahdwi to acknowledge, and in that time, Kiyadeh followed her gaze, but missed Ashava as she had disappeared behind the curtain of people.

"How did this happen?"

Tahdwi timidly looked away. "I don't know. I slept through it. Must have been the same yarik that was used on Ashava."

"And you didn't see anything?"

"No, I'm sorry."

Kiyadeh wasn't sure she believed her, but Tahdwi wasn't one to lie. The bustle of the people brought her back to the situation along with a bit of concern.

"We have to find him before they do," Kiyadeh said.

Tahdwi shook while standing still. "I hope they don't," she said quietly.

Kiyadeh's initial shock lasted barely a moment, for the girl mirrored her own feelings. It was what she wanted for him, but there was a disappointed part of her that she might have escaped with him.

"Okay… If we want to make sure they don't, we have to stop the others from finding him. Lead them astray. Maybe get to him first."

"You'd do that?"

"It's what you'd do, isn't it?" she ended on a happy note.

They hobbled a few shaky steps and then set themselves in motion, moving with a lofty purpose.

Three days later

Seven Steps Forest

Mother and son had run for a constant two days before Saleal finally allowed them to rest. Exhaustion replaced their normal state of being, but it hadn't slowed them. Each time they thought pain and fatigue would make them give in, an impressive tenacity kept them moving at a relentless pace, though Saleal deserved most of the credit.

She never let Kemahni falter, not at all being kind with the way she demanded him to remain steadfast. She knew the consequence if they stopped even for a moment.

Kemahni wrestled with his definition of dangerous as it became an undefined and shifting idea. It hadn't struck him fully that it no longer was a struggle against the frightening unknown of the outside world, but a real battle against people who once gave their lives to protect him. Twice, they hid from a Wind Rider who had luckily picked the right direction, and twice he felt the past slipping away from him. In those moments, he knew what it was like to give away one's past in the hopes of a better future, never knowing if it was the right choice.

He knew intimately the nature of survival. *True survival*. He knew what hunger was, but not where his next meal would come from or when it would arrive. He knew fatigue and how your muscles burned to make your body feel useless. He learned how to ignore baser instincts to live, and that with enough fear and willpower, you can do more than you thought capable.

Chills ran throughout him despite how uncomfortably warm he was. Nothing felt normal as his body was in a constant chaos of changing temperatures and emotions, all maintained by the ever-present possibility of failure, and the usual sounds of the foreign world that wanted to steal his life without a concern.

And despite his warranted feelings, his mother staved away much of his worry. Focusing on her was the only thing that could distract him and helped to keep his resilience. Her unbounding power fueled him and gave him the strength to endure all that she did. He smiled each time she checked his condition, though she never returned the smile. He didn't mind. He needed to reassure her he was capable, even if it felt untrue, especially when his muscles and joints complained furiously that they might fail. But never once did he complain.

As they moved into their third day, the moon already on its rise, Saleal's smile emerged. Unnoticeable at first, but Kemahni noticed the smallest crack in her stoicism, and it made him feel safer and a bit stronger. They had made it to a major landmark inside the Seven Steps

Forest, a giant crater lake filled by the falls that surrounded it, named the Forever Deep by those who had first happened upon the lake.

The beautiful moonlight illuminated the lake and its sheer shores that lead to waters so deep that light disappeared into it, never reaching a bottom. Straight into oblivion, if the myths were to be believed. If one was not careful, the dark waters would swallow you whole starting with your mind. For the two runaways, it was a welcomed haven.

Saleal, covered in a camouflage of mud and moss, came to rest against a tree that she pressed flat against, trying to control her rapid breathing. She was appreciative of the massive trunk as her momentum didn't seem to want or know how to stop her from moving. Kemahni, caked with dried mud, fell dramatically to his knees and laid against the cool ground. He rolled to his back, breathing hard through coughs and wheezes and stared up at his mother. Saleal looked through her tousled mane of liberated hair back at him, the sweat on her face traveling along her scales in winding paths.

Saleal swallowed with a dry mouth. "Don't stop, walk around for a bit," she said.

"What?" Kemahni asked, not understanding the words he clearly heard.

"It's not good...to just stop. Walk until your heart slows down."

"I don't think I could get up if I wanted to."

She didn't fight him, lacking the energy, and let the time pass while their bodies remembered how to regulate breathing.

After a while, Saleal cautiously asked, "How are you?"

Kemahni stared at the moon and stars without blinking. "I don't know." He took a deep breath, "I'm okay, I think."

"Good...good."

Saleal let the weight of her head pull to one side, and her gaze fell to the calm waters of the lake. She watched ripples of movements from creatures that called the waters their home. Watched the wavy, mirrored reflection of the night sky, accepting the adequate representation, not wanting to strain her neck to look up. Not long after, she peered up at the moon and its red sea, finally taking in a deep, deserving breath.

Kemahni strained to sit up. "What about you?"

It took her a while to respond. "Yes...I'm okay."

"You sure?"

"If not, I will be. I'm not as young as I wish I was, Mahi," she said with a smile. "How about, once you've rested, you find us some wood. We'll make a fire and sleep here tonight."

"Can we do that?"

"Yes." She laughed. Kemahni's face lit up as he painfully tried to stand on shaky legs. She waved him to sit. "Rest a bit longer...we have time."

We have time...

Kemahni, with scant energy regained, took to foraging and proved his excellence at finding good, dry wood. The fire Saleal started easily, despite having to resort to striking rocks together to ignite dry grass. It seemed archaic compared to simply summoning fire from a yarik stone. The people of Nevold had become overly accustomed to accessing powers stored in minerals that they often forgot the world had an order to things, a life force that flowed between everything, enforcing the rules of nature, and as some believed, controlling the flow of events.

The fire settled into a steady dance of flames. Saleal rummaged through one of her satchels and laid out her yarik stones. After a quick inventory, she pulled out a small, oddly shaped chisel. Along with it, she found two rough, unaspected stones. She scraped against its surface to create lines, all to the watchful eye of Kemahni. When she finished and dug the yarik stone into the ground, the earth around it responded. It swirled into a complete dome above the fire and solidified. She gasped lightly and rushed to twist the earth stone in the ground and carve one more line on the far side of the stone. The dome carved vents into itself and allowed the heat, light, and smoke to pass through the openings.

"Almost killed the fire," she joked plainly with a dumbfounded smile. Kemahni didn't understand the humor she was attempting, but smiled anyway.

She soon carved another stone, one that was clearer and more well defined, but lacking the amber hue of the other. She balanced it atop the dome with one finger, standing it tall, and gave it a slight spin with her other hand. It rose into the air slightly, continuing the spin and began to absorb the smoke that emanated from the stone dome below.

It was a while before either of them would relax enough to enjoy the fire. Kemahni eventually sat, still anxiously surveying their surroundings, and almost missed his mother tossing yarik stones into the fire. The stones glowed, reinvigorating themselves slowly, absorbing portions of the fire. He watched from his lounging position, propping himself up to try and learn from simply watching the phenomena.

For the first time, he felt as if all the things forbidden to him were obtainable, able to be experienced. The last two days had shown more of the *real* world to him than a lifetime of sheltered living and fables. Knowledge would no longer be hidden to him, taught by an unrestrained teacher, who was more than just a well of information. Before him stood an unstoppable Manyari warrior who could teach him all that he wanted to know. A woman who would stop at nothing, able to stand against the world and win.

He pulled his admiration away from her to watch the fire through the vents. Before Kemahni could ask about the stones, Saleal sighed.

"I'm sorry, Mahi."

"Sorry?" he asked, confused.

"Yes...for so much, I do not know where to start." She looked intently at him. "I'm sorry for not preparing you for life. For not truly protecting you. I pretended like everyone else that what we were doing to you was normal, that it was okay. It wasn't, and I'm just as much to blame for what was to happen to you."

"...but you didn't do it. You saved me, so it can't be your fault."

"It is though, because I did nothing to stop it in the first place. I followed what we were told to do to save the Manyari, and that we had the right to use you like we did. But even so, I still have trouble being upset with any of it, because each desperate and selfish choice we chose led to beautiful you."

Kemahni was eerily silent as he listened to his mother lay out her feelings, tears welling in the corner of her eyes.

"I know what I've done and what it means to turn my back on our people, but I couldn't be okay with it anymore. You had to be free, even if it might have condemned them. You being free means more to me than anything else in this world."

Kemahni looked away to think of the people they left behind and felt guilt for a moment.

Saleal's posture stiffened. "Mahi, I need you to know, they will NEVER stop looking for us. And even if by some blessing they do, life will not be easy. No one will take us in, no one will give us shelter. And we can't trust anyone but each other." Kemahni lowered his head to the fire, as she finished, "We're on our own now."

Kemahni took a few deep breaths but stayed with his head down. Saleal wondered about what ran through his head while lost in the glow of the fire, certain there was a degree of trauma to his mind, but how much, she couldn't know.

She continued, "But you are free and nothing can stop you. I will try to guide you, but no one will ever tell you how to live your life again. This is your life, and for as long as I can, I will be with you, to help you...to make up for all the times I should have fought for you. My life is for you now."

Kemahni looked at her bewildered, like he didn't know the meaning of her words or the magnitude of what she promised but gave a nod of understanding.

The ache faded from the words that were trapped inside her, no longer having to protect him from the truth. She could finally rest, and so she slowly lowered herself to the ground, half facing the fire. To her delighted surprise, Kemahni joined her, laying his head in her lap. He didn't smile, not in the normal sense, but let his whole body relax into her. Eventually he looked at her, lifting his ears. She lovingly stroked them, and he settled back into a comfortable position.

The contact was immensely enjoyable for both of them. He felt safe, believing in her intent to change his world for the better, and through his love, her sacrifice was validated. They gave each other the reward of true happiness and freedom, kept safe within the touch they shared.

In that perfect moment, they existed where nothing else did, for as long as they could.

A long while later, Saleal felt a small pain grow in her sides from holding the position. She tried to ignore it, not wanting to disturb Kemahni's quiet resting, but after a while it was too much. She shifted to pull the second set of daggers free from her belt that were jabbing her in the sides. Kemahni's eyes locked onto them as soon as they came into his view and watched her place them on the ground. The fire reflected off the blades, directly into his eyes.

"Will you teach me how to use those?" he asked.

"Yes. That, and everything else."

He pushed off her lap and showed a face of childish joy that she had almost never seen. "Everything? Even yarik?"

"In time, yes," she matched his joy.

Kemahni looked down in renewed wonder, inspecting the etched lines in his hands.

"We'll talk about that too, but for now, get some sleep. We got a lot more ground to cover tomorrow."

He laid back down and closed his eyes eagerly, doing as she asked, and quickly fell asleep. Her arm found a comfortable place on his shoulder as she enjoyed his warmth. After a moment, spirits gathered like a field of stars in the darkness around them to witness the connection shared by mother and son.

Through the void of the heavens above, laced with its own shining specks, Saleal felt something. Not a moment of calm or clarity, but a feeling that put the world on a tilt. She couldn't be sure if it was just the anxiety and fear of their current situation, because it seemed to be looming everywhere. Indescribable and beyond her perception, she let whatever it was course through her and the area around her, until she grasped just the slightest understanding of it. The instant she tried to hold onto it, the more it escaped back into the nothing it was before she knew it. It only left her with an unspoken message that *'something else is changing. Nothing will be the same'*.

EPILOGUE

The blinding white light that filled the workshop finally subsided as the alterence withdrew back inside the crystal lodged in Keagan's chest. The pain that had easily found him left, and no sounds of anguish came from neither him nor the once again motionless Tam. Blood had flowed from the wound, clinging to the underside of the crystal. It collected at the very tip and as it threatened to drip, it suddenly pulled back, gathering all the red into the edges where the crystal pierced the skin. The bloodied, foriegn object fell out of the seemingly scarred over wound and made that familiar hollow ringing against the floor.

It took a good while before either one of them moved, Keagan being the first to break the statued silhouettes they both held. He placed a quivering hand on his chest, feeling the grooves of the indent, then retrieved the quiet crystal. He held it in the moonlight, and as he examined it, the light refracted against Tam.

"Keagan," Tam's distorted voice filled his head.

"I, I heard you. I feel… your pain," he winced.

The exorbitant amount of emotion that fed into him wasn't as surprising as how it slowly began to overwrite his own, wanting him to do horrible things. Not for himself but for her, in justice of her pain. He pushed aside all his own feelings and concerns and focused solely on the new.

"I will help you. Whatever you want, I will do it for you."

"Find him. Let nothing stop you." she commanded.

"I won't."

Torchlight shined in through the window, as a townsman had come investigating the suspicious light and wail.

"Tam are you in there? Is everything okay?" asked a cautious voice.

The handle and the door creaked as it opened to the night and the man standing in the door. The man immediately saw Keagan as he stood to greet him. The man felt relieved to know his worry was caused by two adolescents, but raised a curious eyebrow.

"What are you two doing here?" the man asked, clearing his throat.

Panic grew in the boy's eyes until he relaxed from hearing Tam's voice in his head. He looked back at Tam, and nodded. The watchful man raised his lantern to better his view.

"You kids need to stop doing whatever it is and go home."

Neither child responded, causing the man to investigate further. His concern rose sharply when he saw Tam's motionless body.

"Tam, you alright?"

Keagan pivoted back around, light charged in his eyes as he grasped the crystal tightly in his hand. He traced new lines across the jeweled surface that was already healing the cracks in itself.

"Not yet, but we will be," Keagan said the moment before he slammed the crystal into the man. "We all will be."

TO BE CONTINUED...

BOOK TWO

- THE MOTHER -

M. R. Moraine has never thought of himself as a writer, just an adult with a runaway imagination. Influenced by movies and video games alike, he likes to dream big with his stories. Nevertold: The Son will be his first foray into writing with the goal of being grand in scope and able to draw in readers of all kinds. With his wife and two cats, he looks to change the world in small but noticeable ways, keeping it going with stories he hopes you will love and share.

@mistermoraine
Twitter | Twitch | TikTok | Youtube